"You're in trouble, Joe."

The moment she spoke, a wave of compassion washed over Maggie. She was simply reacting to the unfairness of the accusation, she told herself. Nothing to do with any feelings for her ex-husband.

Joe was staring at her with an intensity that had once been very familiar. "The suspect had a gun, Maggie— even though they're saying he didn't. I had no choice but to shoot."

She nodded. "I believe you."

"Then you're the only person in Plainfield who does. Even my partner thinks I succumbed to the pressure of the moment."

"You'd never do that."

He shoved his hands into his pockets. "Yeah. Well. So now I need a lawyer."

"I can give you some names."

"I need the best lawyer. Especially if the best lawyer knows me well enough to know I'd never pull a gun on an unarmed man."

Maggie squeezed her eyes shut for a moment, and then heard him say the words she'd longed to hear all through their marriage.

"I need *you*, Maggie."

Dear Reader,

The beginning of a new year—this time a new millennium—is when we take stock, reflect on the past and make plans for the future. Change—whether it's changing our jobs or our family situation or how we see the world—can be difficult and painful, but sometimes we must do it to make our dreams come true.

When Harlequin Superromance asked me to be part of its "By the Year 2000" series, I thought it would be a great opportunity to write a book exploring the inner challenges we must all face at pivotal times in our lives.

Joe Latham, my hero, is about to lose everything, including his good name. He finds a woman from his past who can share his future, but only if he is willing to change. Only if he has the courage to accept himself as flawed but honorable, and be willing to share the most secret parts of himself with the woman he loves. As a writer, exploring his character helped me understand more clearly what I most value most in my own life: my family and my friends, self-truth and a job well done.

I hope you enjoy Joe and Maggie's story. I also hope that the new millennium brings you not only love and contentment, but the courage to shake things up when your own dreams beckon.

Linda Markowiak

A COP'S
GOOD NAME
Linda
Markowiak

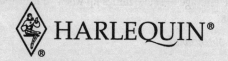

HARLEQUIN®

TORONTO • NEW YORK • LONDON
AMSTERDAM • PARIS • SYDNEY • HAMBURG
STOCKHOLM • ATHENS • TOKYO • MILAN • MADRID
PRAGUE • WARSAW • BUDAPEST • AUCKLAND

ISBN 0-373-70846-7

A COP'S GOOD NAME

A COP'S
GOOD NAME

PROLOGUE

JOE LATHAM was giving chase. The suspect was still ahead, the dark clothes he wore making him hard to pick out at this time of night. Joe sprinted, pushing himself to the limit. A few minutes ago, he and his partner had seen this guy hold up a gas station. The suspect was about twenty years old, dark, and he was wearing gang colors.

Joe's breath rasped in his throat, and he knew he'd pulled ahead of his middle-aged, slower partner. Too far. But the man had used a gun in the holdup, and Joe couldn't let him get away. The suspect rounded the corner of an old building then disappeared into an alley.

Traffic was a distant noise. This block was the beginning of gang country, and few people came here at night. There was a bar on the corner. Joe slowed for a moment and glanced around. The tavern lights were on, and there was a beer sign in blue and red lights in the window, the *B* burned out. The streets were deserted.

Hot sweat dripped from his armpits; adrenaline pumped through his body and his thighs quivered from pounding the hard pavement. But his mind was clear and focused as it always was when he was on the job. His ability to stay cool had allowed him to get out of any situation without ever firing his weapon for the past fourteen years.

Now he pulled that weapon from his shoulder holster, held it above his head in both hands. Joe edged along the building, then taking a deep breath, crouched and sprang into the alley.

Under the light of a streetlamp he saw his suspect. About twenty feet away, backed up against a Dumpster, the man was with two other young men. Gang colors all around. The Nightshade.

For a second they all stared at Joe. The suspect was breathing hard, his hand moving restlessly over his jacket. The young man's buddies were standing by, warily and with ugly purpose. The tension was silent and eerie and deadly.

"Okay," Joe said calmly, the gun pointed straight at the suspect's chest. "You two others, remember this isn't about you. No sense going to prison over a beef between me and him."

"I ain't going back there." The suspect's hand on the jacket was still moving, the voice high and strained.

"What you're going to do," Joe said slowly, "is move away from your buddies. You're going to go to that fence over there and you're going to put both hands on it."

The suspect hesitated. "I ain't going back to the joint. Not for nothin', man."

"Hook, maybe you should do what he says," one of the others said.

The other added, "No cop killing, man. We'd fry for that."

"You hear your friends, Hook? They're talking sense, pal. Good sense," Joe said. "Go on over to the fence. We'll just talk. Talk."

There was another second of utter silence.

Suddenly, someone screamed. A woman. Then the wail of a siren split the air, only a street away. Hook's hand snaked into his pocket. Joe saw the gleam of the barrel of a gun, rising.

Joe fired. Hook's legs crumpled, and he went down instantly. Joe saw Hook's gun fly out of his hand and sail high, finally landing somewhere in the litter of the alley. The two other gang members scattered like dried-up leaves in a windstorm.

Joe raced over to the suspect. Hook lay on his back. His mouth open, his eyes closed, he looked oddly vulnerable.

Joe felt his stomach give a quick heave, and he swallowed down the sudden burning in his throat. He was pretty sure Hook was dead, though he could see no wound and no blood.

Just like he'd known that Alex...

The bitter burn in his throat was worse now, like fire. His heart pounded in his chest, and suddenly his whole body was hot.

The man's hands were curled, showing the home-made tattoos—gang symbols—that marked each knuckle. Lying on the ground beside his fingertips was some kind of cheap necklace. A pendant of a skull hung from the chain, the eye sockets filled with big crystals.

Joe used his handheld radio to call an ambulance, then began methodically using the lifesaving techniques he'd been taught. He put his ear to Hook's face and listened. Hook wasn't breathing.

Of course he's not, Joe. You shot him. On one level, he knew he'd done exactly what he'd been trained for. He'd been chasing a dangerous suspect. He'd been protecting innocent people. It was what he did. It was everything he was. But on another level...

Don't think. Don't think. Count. Push. Count. *Don't think.*

He was still doing CPR when the ambulance arrived. The paramedics pulled open Hook's shirt, checked for vitals, glanced at each other and shook their heads. One put a hand on Joe's shoulder. "You can stop. He's gone."

It was official then, Joe thought, feeling his mouth tighten. His suspect was dead.

The uniformed cops were arriving, and a couple of other detectives, Joe's colleagues and friends. The alley was suddenly full of people.

"Are you okay?" Henry Muff, his partner, put a hand on his arm.

No, he wasn't okay. "Yeah," he said, "I'm okay."

"Good."

"The guy pulled a gun on me," he said, and he

heard the touch of desperation in his tone. *Tell me I had no choice.* "I had to fire."

Henry's fingers tightened on his arm. "Joe. Listen to me. Are you sure the suspect had a gun?"

"Of course. He used a gun in the holdup. And I saw the barrel, pointed straight at me. Didn't you see it?"

"I'm sorry, Joe. Look, I'd like to back you up on this but I didn't get a clear view and I didn't see what happened in the alley."

Joe looked around. "It's got to be here somewhere. It flew out of his hand. I saw it."

Henry was just looking at him.

"Come on, Henry! You know I wouldn't shoot unless I had to."

His partner's eyes were concerned. "Stuff happens quick, you know? A half a second to think, that's all you get. That necklace near his hand…if it was in his pocket… It's metal, and those crystals might gleam in the night like—"

"Look for the gun," Joe snapped. "You're my partner. Help me find this guy's gun."

Henry nodded. "Right. If you're sure there was a gun, that's enough for me." He held out his hand, and Joe shook it.

Joe's lieutenant arrived and organized the search for the gun. "Don't worry," he said to Joe. "I'm sure it was a clean shoot. It might take a while to find the damn gun is all, with so much garbage and crap everywhere."

Joe sat down on the curb to wait. He waited as police officers sifted through garbage.

They gave up at three o'clock the next afternoon. The gun wasn't in the alley. Joe studied his colleagues and knew what they were thinking: he'd lost it in the heat of the moment.

Joe looked away when the lieutenant asked him for his shield and gun. As Joe handed over the gun, he thought, *Fourteen years. Fourteen years as a good cop, right down the drain.* When he held his shield in his palm, he remembered the pride he'd felt when he'd earned his first badge. When he'd been a uniformed officer. The pride that had been all he'd had left after Alex had died....

The lieutenant spoke softly, "It's just a suspension, Joe. It isn't over yet. There'll be a thorough investigation."

"Yeah. Right." He had little faith in the kind of "investigations" Internal Affairs conducted. He knew the police force was under pressure to regulate itself more strictly. I.A. wouldn't hesitate to use him as a scapegoat.

One thing was for sure—he was going to need a lawyer. The best lawyer he could find.

CHAPTER ONE

"WE NEED MONEY, Maggie. Maybe if you'd offer to take a little less than the jury awarded at the trial, you could get the other side to drop the appeal, and we and our client could get paid a little sooner—"

"No way." Maggie Hannan pushed her chair back abruptly but kept her eyes on her friend and partner, Angela St. John.

"But we got our client at least fifty thousand more than she bargained for...." Angela's voice trailed off. Angela was thirty-nine, six years older than Maggie. She had short blond hair and a pointed chin, a sharp contrast to Maggie's dark hair and strong features. But Angela's air of youth and innocence belied her toughness. As a single mother and a criminal lawyer with a growing practice, Angela had learned to be tough. She was also practical, realistic and had managed to keep her sense of humor.

But today Angela's concern about money was serious.

Maggie was equally serious. "Karen Hartman deserves the money and she needs every penny of that judgment."

Too frustrated to sit still any longer, Maggie

jumped up and went over to the window. Pausing at the cheap wood-veneer-over-fiberboard credenza, she poured herself a cup of coffee.

In the next moment, she put down her mug and looked out the window. Her office was in the low-rent district. The window was old, the glass panes were smudged. Under an early-September sun, decaying black and brown rooftops stretched out as far as the eye could see. The river was only a thin line in the distance.

Once Maggie had had a perfect, tinted glass view of that river. When she'd made senior associate in her former law firm—the most prestigious in Plainfield, Ohio—she'd earned an office with a huge, new window.

She'd take smudges any day.

And she'd take clients like Karen Hartman over the corporate ones she'd seen in her fancy office. Karen's son had been injured by defective playground equipment. The case was complex, and her new firm, Hannan, St. John and Sawyer, had had to put up the money for investigation, depositions and discovery. Now, even though she'd won a judgment, the playground manufacturer was refusing to pay pending appeal.

Maggie's dream—her own law firm—would collapse unless some cash came in soon.

From behind her, Angela said, "Okay. I trust you." She sighed. "All we have to do now is get the word out about how good we are. In the meantime, we take on every client who asks us.''

''Everyone with money,'' Sharon Sawyer corrected, coming into Maggie's office through the open door, a file in her hand. ''No more *pro bono* work for a while. No pay, no work.'' She was blond and petite like Angela, but she lacked Angela's sense of humor. Life was serious business for Sharon.

Maggie reached for her coffee mug and took a sip. Sharon would be her sister-in-law when Maggie married Lewis, and Maggie was happy about that. Sharon—and Angela, for that matter—shared Maggie's desire to take on cases that interested them, all the cases where people desperately needed help. It was one of the things that had led the three to leave their high-paying jobs to start their own firm.

They all loved what they were doing, but Maggie had the most passion for her work. The other two women had families; Angela had her four boys and Sharon her husband and baby. Maggie swallowed hard. Many of her colleagues were mothers. Sometimes it seemed as if the whole world was having babies.

Of course, when she married Lewis, they'd have a baby. Meanwhile she had a ready-made family in Lewis's daughter. Someday soon she'd have everything—a baby and a stepdaughter and her own law firm. *If* she could keep cash flowing. ''Okay,'' she said somewhat reluctantly. ''From now on, we make sure that we take on plenty of clients with money. Preferably up front.''

''*Definitely* up front,'' Sharon said, shutting the file she held.

''I agree,'' Angela said, nodding. ''If they can pay, I'll take them on. Even big evil companies who make the canisters for germ warfare or have plans to pollute outer space.'' She looked straight at Maggie, her eyes twinkling.

Maggie put up her hand. ''Hey, wait a minute. I think we should still be able to refuse clients if we have a good enough reason. If I didn't want at least some small say in which clients I work with, I should have stayed in my old firm.''

Sharon went over to the credenza, where Maggie had left her coffee cup on top of a teetering stack of legal files. She picked up the cup, and summarily dumped the contents into the trash. ''Maggie,'' she said in the gentlest of tones, ''if you don't get some more paying clients, by the time the year 2000 rolls around, the firm simply won't exist.''

The three women looked at one another, sober and tense. Before anyone could break the silence, there was a light knock on the door frame. Maggie smiled at the sixteen-year-old who would soon become her stepdaughter. Tessa helped out after school with the clerical tasks.

''You've got a client, Maggie. He doesn't have an appointment, but since you were free I put him in the two-thirty slot.''

"Hey, does he have money?" Angela asked in a stage whisper.

"I'll go ask," Tessa said, making a quick turn, her long red hair fluffing out behind her.

"No!" all three women said at once.

Tessa frowned. Maggie walked over to her swiftly and gave her shoulders a squeeze. "We were joking, sweetheart," she said in quick reassurance.

"Oh. Oh, sure." The girl brightened. "I don't know if he has any money, but he looks really cool. Like Burt Lancaster. Or maybe even John Wayne."

"You don't say." Angela rolled her eyes at Maggie.

"Yeah, he's cool, all right," Tessa repeated, her forehead wrinkling with utter seriousness. Tessa had a fondness for Victorian novels and old movie stars. It drove her father mad, but Maggie understood. Her own dreams had once been equally romantic.

"And also some Harrison Ford," Tessa added.

"Harrison Ford?" Now Maggie was intrigued. "You know who Harrison Ford is?"

"Of course," Tessa said with dignity. "Just because I don't watch Harrison Ford movies doesn't mean I don't know he's kind of cute."

"Well, let's all clear out then and let her have at this movie star guy." Angela started to shoo them out.

Tessa was the last one out and started to close the door.

"Hey, wait a minute," Maggie said to the teenager.

"What's this client's name? And where's his contact sheet?"

"He wouldn't fill out a client contact sheet, said you wouldn't need one. He said you knew him from a few years ago. He said he was in trouble, and you'd know about that from the newspapers." The door was almost shut. "His name is Joe Latham. Too bad because that's not a very cool name."

Joe. Maggie's breath caught in her throat. Joe. Ohmygod. "Tessa," she called desperately toward the now closed door.

She took a few quick steps, intent on telling the girl to get rid of Joe Latham.

The door opened abruptly. Momentum carried Maggie forward, smack into her ex-husband's chest.

"Whoa," he said, and he grabbed her arm to steady her. Her nose pressed against his hard chest, and the scent of him hit her full force. In seven years, that hadn't changed, she thought with a little—unwelcome—thrill. He smelled of soap and man and Old Spice.

Quickly, she pulled away, feeling her cheeks grow hot. He wore black jeans and a new-looking twill shirt. He was as big, as broad shouldered as he'd ever been, she thought with a blur of recognition as images came back to her. It had been seven years, but she remembered the golden hair and the blue eyes under thick, straight eyebrows. She remembered how spare and regular his features were.

"That was quite a greeting," he said. "I admit, I didn't know how you'd take my coming here—"

She yanked and her arm came free of his grasp. "How did you think I'd take it?" she snapped. Their parting had been so bitter. *I never want to see you again,* she'd said at the courthouse on the day of their divorce.

Something flickered in those blue eyes, but if she hadn't been looking straight into them she would have missed it. When he spoke, his tone was quiet, neutral. "I expected you to react more like you just did." He tapped one fist into the palm of his other hand. "Look, I know you don't want to see me. But that's personal. I'm sure your receptionist told you I need to see you on a professional basis."

She nodded.

"I figure you've been reading the newspapers," he said.

She had. She'd opened her paper a few days ago to see that the *Plainfield Gazette* was running her ex-husband as front-page news. According to the newspaper, sources were reporting that Joe had made a mistake in firing his weapon and had killed an allegedly unarmed suspect. But she hadn't believed it for a moment. Joe was the best cop there was. She'd come to hate his job, but he was the best.

Under normal circumstances, few people would waste much sympathy on a twenty-year-old gang member who'd just held up a gas station. Unfortunately, the shooting had come on the heels of a year-long Ohio study that had been very critical of city police departments, especially those in smaller cities such as Plainfield. There had been allegations that the officers were poorly trained, even trigger-happy. Maggie knew there was a real chance that the department might decide to make an example of Joe. "You're in trouble," she said.

Joe was staring down at her with an intensity that had once been very familiar. "The suspect had a gun, Maggie. I had no choice but to shoot."

She nodded again. "I believe you."

He looked away and gave a small, caustic chuckle. "Well, then, you're the only person in Plainfield who does. Even my partner thinks I blew it, succumbed to the pressure of the moment."

"You would never do that," she said, and she heard the conviction in her voice.

He shoved his hands in his pockets and turned toward her. "Yeah. Well. So now I need a lawyer."

"I can give you some names—"

"I need the *best* lawyer. Especially if the best lawyer knows I would never have pulled a gun on an unarmed man. In other words, I need you, Maggie."

She squeezed her eyes shut for a moment as a wave of compassion washed over her. She shook her head and walked to the window. He needed her. Correction. His career needed her.

Pure irony. He wanted her to save the career that had helped drive them apart.

She said to the window, "I can't help you, Joe. There's been too much misery between us."

"But it's been seven years—"

Her throat got a little tight. "You think something as simple as time passing makes up for everything, and now it's all right for you to barge in here without an appointment and calmly tell me you want to hire me?"

Behind her there was a silence. A long silence. "No," he said finally. "I know damn well there are some things time doesn't take care of." The words sounded fierce, somehow. Unexpectedly heartfelt, and she told herself not to react to the hint of emotion. There was another pause. "But as you so gracefully put it, I'm in trouble, and I know what I need now. I need you. The *Gazette* might be flaying me, but they reported you won the Hartman case. You were really good. Everyone down at the courthouse talked about the case.

"Now," he continued. "Those guys at Internal Affairs will be questioning me, poking at every little detail. I need you to make sure the questioning is fair. I need you to make sure they conduct a full investigation, and aren't influenced by the politics of the situation. You know how important my badge is to me. I can't lose it. And I don't deserve to."

"I can't," she said again to the window.

"It doesn't have to be personal."

She whipped around to face him. "You're my ex-husband, and you say it doesn't have to be personal?"

"No," he said firmly, "it doesn't. Think, Maggie. Can you really afford to turn down a paying client?" He studied the office. "I bet this place is a far cry from your previous office."

She'd done the best she could to disguise their financial situation. She'd hung some nice, staid landscapes on the wall, put an Old-World globe on a stand in the corner, built some shelves for her collection of leather-bound law books.

She wouldn't look around and see her firm through his eyes. She couldn't stand here staring out the window all day, either. He'd put her off balance—literally—at first, but now she was recovering.

He spoke. "I have the money to hire you." Amazingly, he cracked a grin. His grin had always quirked higher on the left side than the other and revealed a row of blindingly white teeth. That grin had… Her hands tightened into fists.

What should she do? *Money,* Sharon had said just before Joe had walked in the door. Not ten minutes ago, Maggie had made a promise to her partners not to turn down a paying client unless she had a *very* good reason. Under the circumstances, Angela would undoubtedly let her out of the bargain, but she doubted that practical Sharon would consider the fact that the client was Maggie's ex a good enough reason.

She owed Joe nothing, but she owed her partners a lot. "I charge two hundred and fifty dollars an hour," she said coolly, doubling her usual fee. Either he'd be out of here fast, or she'd be very, very well compensated.

"Okay. I agree."

She faced him squarely. "With a twenty-thousand-dollar retainer."

He winced. "That's pretty steep."

"Yes, it is," she said with a certain satisfaction. "You said you wanted to keep this professional. You didn't expect a discount, did you?"

"Fine. Twenty thousand. Do you want it in cash?"

She'd been sure he'd walk out the door when she'd asked for that kind of money. Joe was probably comfortable enough financially, but he certainly had never been wealthy. Now she was trapped, on the verge of agreeing to represent her ex-husband.

"Joe, listen," she said, a touch of desperation in her tone. "From what the newspapers are saying, this case is pretty cut-and-dried. Either you were mistaken, or someone took the weapon before the police could search the alley fully. I'm a lawyer, not a miracle worker. I may take all your money and not be able to do a thing for you."

"I saw that gun in Hook's hand, right before the shooting. I saw the gun go flying out of his hand, too."

"Then where is it?"

"I'm thinking one of the other guys who was there somehow found it in the split second before they ran away. I wasn't watching too closely. I'd just shot an armed suspect. *That's* what I was focused on."

"Are there any witnesses to the shooting?"

"Sure are. At least two. I thought I heard a woman scream a second before Hook pulled the gun, but I don't know if she saw anything. Are you going to represent me?"

She paused, knowing it was her last chance to refuse.

He said, "Before you say anything, let me tell you that the only witnesses to the shooting that I know of for sure are fellow members of the Nightshade."

"Oh, Joe. Those guys aren't going to testify on behalf of a cop. Especially since you shot one of their members. They'll like the idea that you're going to lose your badge."

"I know."

There was a bleakness in his tone that she suddenly couldn't bear. "All right, I'll take you on." Her agreement had nothing to do with compassion. It was about money. And promises to her law partners. Nothing else.

His eyes lit, a fierce glow. He took her hands in his. "I knew you'd do it."

She willed herself not to react to the warmth and roughness of his palms. His hands had always been rough, and once he'd joked that he could give her back a scratch just by rubbing his hands on her skin. When he spoke, his voice was low and husky. "Only you know what this means. Only you know what that badge means to me."

Don't react, she told herself, hearing the vulnerability in his voice. To do her best on the case, she had to keep a certain distance. She was over him. He couldn't hurt her anymore.

"Here." She picked up a legal pad from her desk and shoved it toward him. "Go home. Get my retainer together. Then I want you to take that legal pad and write down every single thing that happened that night, starting from when you first saw your suspect until the police stopped searching for the gun. Think hard. Every feeling, every sight, every sound might be important."

He nodded. "Thanks again."

"Never mind." She was pleased at how brisk her tone was. "Your retainer will be plenty thanks enough."

"I JUST DON'T KNOW what Tessa's thinking most of the time." Lewis Sawyer tugged on his silver-and-blue striped tie. In the romantic, low candlelight of the small French restaurant, his starched white shirt gleamed.

He leaned toward Maggie, his thin, handsome face serious. "I took your advice. This time when I came home, I brought her a little present. A copy of *Jane Eyre*. So what does she do but take one look at it and burst into tears. 'I already *have* that book.'" His voice mimicked his daughter's dramatic emphasis on the word *have*. "'Haven't you been listening?' she asks. 'I've been talking about Rochester for weeks.' I can't win with Tessa, that's all."

Maggie impulsively reached across the tiny table and put her hand in his. "You're doing the right thing, just listening to her." But she couldn't help wondering how hard Lewis was listening if he'd missed all the talk about Mr. Rochester. Even Angela, who indulged Tessa at work as much as Maggie did, had been mumbling about how sick she was of hearing about *Jane Eyre*.

Lewis gave her hand a squeeze, then let go and sighed in utter frustration. "Maggie, she might have mentioned Rochester a time or two. But to me, Rochester is a city in New York. What do I know about *Jane Eyre?*"

"I think maybe you'd better listen a little harder."

"It's just that right now I'm so busy. That new plant in Italy—"

"I know." Maggie picked up her wineglass. Lewis was a manager for a firm that manufactured cookware, and he was often sent to help start up new plants overseas. "It's to your credit that you try at all. There are lots of men in your circumstances who would hire somebody to look after Tessa, or send her away to school." It was one of the things that had drawn her to Lewis. He'd lost his wife three years ago, and both he and Tessa had taken the death hard. But he was committed to his daughter. "Tessa's lucky to have you."

"Elizabeth was so wonderful with her. She understood Tessa so much better than I ever—" He cut himself off, looking embarrassed.

"It's okay to talk about her," Maggie said. But she wasn't being quite truthful. She knew Lewis and Elizabeth had been married for twenty years, and one didn't put aside that kind of commitment lightly. But Lewis seemed to mention Elizabeth every time they were together. Maggie sometimes wondered if she would have to spend the rest of her life hearing Elizabeth's name. How she longed to come first with someone!

Raised in foster homes since the age of five, she'd spent her childhood seeing the subtle but unmistakable signs that her foster parents favored their natural children. She'd longed for someone to say, "I love you best."

It was one of the reasons she'd succumbed to Joe's charms, swept off her feet by his endless silly, romantic gestures. She'd been his second wife, too, but when she married him, she was so sure she was first in his heart....

She pushed the memory aside and concentrated on Lewis. In his own way, Lewis loved her.

"Tessa doesn't understand how important work is," Lewis grumbled now. "Always lost in her own world. Her college costs are going to be huge, and corporations are cutting down on bonuses these days...." He went on for some length about his prospects for a bonus and then switched to a discussion of a new line of aluminum bakeware his company was introducing.

It was one of Lewis's less-than-desirable qualities

that he had a hard time believing the rest of the world wasn't as interested in cookware as he was. When he came home from a business trip, he was always wired, keyed up from having to solve problems.

Maggie knew she was being hypercritical. After all, Lewis always eased up on the business talk after he'd been home awhile. So the man was imperfect. Who wanted perfection, anyway? It would put too much pressure on her to be perfect back.

"Anyway," Lewis finally said, smiling at her. "What's new with you?"

After Joe had left yesterday, she'd vowed to be scrupulously honest with Lewis. "I have a new client," she began carefully. "He's given the firm a substantial retainer."

"That's terrific, Maggie." Lewis raised his own glass in a toast to her. His cuff links glinted in the candlelight. "I hope things are finally looking up over there at Hannan-and-such. You know, it was fine how you handled the Hartman case. Of course, you can't accept clients who can't pay very often, but since you insisted on taking on Karen Hartman, I was hoping you'd get some publicity out of the deal. Was that how you got your client?"

"Well, Joe had read about the Hartman case in the paper and—"

"Wonderful!" Lewis beamed at her. "I've often told you how important publicity is, and I'm not talking about paid advertising, either. I was worried about you, honey. Just the other day, I was telling Sharon that you'd have to get a good client in, one with a substantial retainer, and I admit I was hoping some of the corporate contacts I have might pay off—''

''The client is Joe. My ex-husband,'' Maggie cut in abruptly. Now that she'd started, she wanted to get this over with as quickly as possible.

Lewis's forehead creased. ''Your ex came to see you?''

Lewis had just gotten in from Milan, she reminded herself, so he wouldn't know anything about the shooting. ''He really needs a lawyer,'' she said, and she explained Joe's situation, careful to mention only what had been in the newspapers. It sunk in then, in a way it hadn't earlier, that Joe really was her client and was entitled to certain protections. Loyalty, regardless of her feelings. Confidentiality.

Lewis listened carefully. ''Well, at least you finally charged somebody enough,'' he said mildly, and signaled to the waitress.

''You don't need to know any more?'' she asked. ''You're my fiancé.''

''The only thing I'd want to know is if you suddenly discovered you still have feelings for the guy.'' He gave her a confident smile. ''But I know better. After all, he's the man who never wanted to have children.''

Trust Lewis to put it so bluntly. Even after seven years, it hurt that Joe hadn't wanted to have children. It hurt even more that he'd reacted with so little emotion, so little sadness, to her miscarriage. More than anything, Maggie had wanted a family.

Lewis, too, initially had balked at the idea of a family. Tessa, his only child, was sixteen, after all. But when he'd seen how important it was to Maggie, he'd agreed, and now he was quite pleased with the idea of a second family. That kind of flexibility beat Joe's unyielding stance any day of the week.

"Dessert?" Lewis asked, and Maggie knew that the subject of Joe was closed.

"No, thanks," she said, and Lewis signaled for the check. It had been a very expensive meal; Lewis liked nice restaurants. She suddenly wished Lewis had been just a touch jealous about Joe being a client. Not jealous, exactly, just maybe a little…concerned.

She scolded herself for being silly. It had been a stressful week even before the day Joe walked in the door. A tough motion hearing, a day-long trial, a decision about how to negotiate the Hartman appeal, the discussion about money—specifically, the lack thereof. So she was feeling a little blue, a little out of sorts.

Lewis drove her back to her house. She'd bought the bungalow two years ago and the first thing she'd done was paint it yellow and cream. The second thing she'd done was fill it with antiques. Everybody else's memories now making memories for her.

Lewis walked her to the door and stood with her on the wooden porch. He waited until she had fished out her key before taking her carefully in his arms.

He kissed her cheek, then moved over to her mouth. His mouth was warm and his tongue touched her lips lightly. His breathing picked up.

She felt herself start to respond. She liked Lewis's kisses, the way he always started out tentatively, as if to give her a chance to withdraw.

Unbidden, memories of Joe came into her mind. More than once he'd grabbed her just inside the door to their apartment, and pushed her up against the wall. Always ready for his lovemaking, she'd wrap her legs around his waist—

Ohmygod, what was she doing? Thinking about one man when she was kissing another. Abruptly, she pulled back.

Lewis stopped right away. "No?" he asked softly. "I admit, I'd anticipated—" He cut himself off, then gave a frustrated sigh. "But maybe you're right. Tessa is home alone so I can't stay the night."

Quickie was not a word in Lewis's vocabulary. Unless he could stay the night, he seldom stayed at all. Maggie was totally unsettled. She loved Lewis and enjoyed his lovemaking. He'd been gone ten days, and even before that, always aware of Tessa, they'd curtailed their lovemaking. Yet tonight she was relieved to be going into her house alone.

It was Joe's fault. Already he had disrupted her life, the nice, sane life she'd chosen and nurtured carefully. She was certainly over him, but his appearance had brought back memories—she and Joe had had a lot of problems, but sex had never been one of them.

She fitted her key in the lock and wiggled the old knob. She couldn't tell Lewis what she was thinking. Though she'd decided to be honest, there was no point in telling him she found her ex-husband as physically attractive as ever. She'd been hurt enough times by Lewis's references to his late wife to know that some things were better left unsaid.

Especially when they meant nothing. Joe Latham was a client, and tomorrow she'd get going on his case right away.

The door opened, and she said good-night to her fiancé. As she stepped over the threshold alone, she sent up a silent prayer that Joe's case would be over soon.

CHAPTER TWO

MAGGIE PERCHED on Angela's desk and watched her partner and friend stuff files into her briefcase. "Are you sure you can't reschedule?" she asked.

Angela snapped her briefcase closed. "It's Judge Carroll. You know how he is. Once he's decided to see you in chambers, he expects you there. Pronto. Besides, if we can get a decent plea that will settle this case, we'll get our fees. Sorry, kiddo, you'll have to go without me."

Maggie nodded, although she was frustrated by the change in plans. Joe had dropped off his notes yesterday afternoon. In them, she'd read that there was a tavern on the corner where the street met the alley. It seemed as good a place as any to begin her investigation.

She planned to interview the bartender and anyone who might have been around that night. She knew that Pierce Street, the street that fed into the alley where the shooting had taken place, was a rough area. She knew it would be prudent to have Angela accompany her.

A small city, Plainfield had always had its share of both serious and petty crime. But in the last several years, the city had begun to see more of the kind of crime that plagued its bigger neighbors: more drugs, more prostitution, more auto theft. It also had one thing it hadn't had five years ago: a youth gang called the Nightshade.

But surely if she was careful, she could go down and ask a few questions.... Besides, it was afternoon; the Nightshade operated mostly after dark.

"Ask Sharon to go with you," Angela suggested on her way out the door.

"Sharon's in court," Maggie replied.

"Well, then, I guess you'll have to go on Monday." With that, she was gone.

Maggie thought about waiting but decided against it. She'd been in a few tough situations before.

She could handle herself so there was no need to wait for an escort. She needed to get Joe's case rolling.

But when she stopped at the receptionist's desk in the outer office to tell Tessa where she was going, the teenager's mouth dropped. "Oh, Dad'll have a fit if he knows you're going there."

"Your dad's a great guy, but I don't tell him how to run a cookware factory and he doesn't tell me how to practice law."

"You could be murdered down there, Maggie." Tessa gave a dramatic shudder and Maggie smiled.

"Give me a little more credit than that for getting out of situations."

"But really, isn't it dangerous?"

The door to the office opened. "Is what danger-ous?" Joe asked, stepping inside.

"Never mind," Maggie said, trying not to react to his abrupt entry...and his rumpled good looks.

"Maggie is going to this really crummy bar down-town," Tessa said.

Joe frowned. "No, she isn't."

"Hello to you, too, Joe." Maggie picked up a small yellow legal pad and stuffed it into her briefcase. "Excuse me," she said, starting to pass him on her way out the door.

"Just a minute." His arm shot out and grabbed hers.

She shook free. "You're my client, not my hus-band anymore. It's not your job to watch out for me." She heard Tessa give a sharp exclamation and real-ized that no one had told the girl who Joe was. Rats. She'd hoped that any necessary explanations could be handled gently.

"I might not be your husband, but I'm still a cop, and I know those streets aren't safe."

"I'm going to be careful."

"You bet you are, because you're not going."

Maggie felt her temper rising. But Joe was a client now and that meant he got a modicum of respect. "I've got twenty thousand dollars of your money. I'd think you'd be grateful if I actually did something to earn it." She paused. "I'm just going to say I'm an attorney and ask a few questions. Nothing dangerous. I'm not Nancy Drew, looking for clues."

He was still gripping her arm. "I doubt those thugs will care that you're a lawyer."

"Don't go," Tessa said.

"I'm going," Maggie said.

"Then I'm coming with you."

"Oh, for heaven's sake—" Maggie started, then she shut up. She wasn't going to win the argument, anyway. And maybe having Joe along wasn't such a bad idea.

"We'll take my car," Joe said when they were on the street. His Jeep was parked at the curb, and he opened the passenger door for her. The Jeep's seat was high and her skirt was straight. She had to let him help her up. She shot him a quick glance, feeling suddenly uncomfortable. He was looking away, she thought in some relief. He'd always said she had terrific legs.... She shook off the thought.

He was also always overprotective, she reminded herself. In the early days of their two-year marriage it had felt rather good. But that had been a long time ago. And there had been times when his overprotectiveness had annoyed her. Like the time he'd offered to intervene on her behalf when a law professor was giving her a hard time.

And now, right on form, he was going downtown with her to protect her from bullies there, too. He'd always been there for her physically. But emotionally—well, he'd always been reluctant to talk about his feelings. Then after her miscarriage, he hadn't been willing to talk at all. He'd volunteered for a dangerous undercover assignment that took him away from home for weeks.

They'd become more and more distant from each other, until Maggie's grief over the loss of their baby had turned to anger and bitterness toward her husband. Even then, he hadn't been willing to talk, to share. That was the story of her marriage.

She decided to take control of the situation today. As soon as he put the car in gear, she said, "When we get there, I'm asking the questions."

"I'm a detective."

"You're the client. I'm your lawyer. I'm asking the questions."

"What am I supposed to do? Stand there and hold up the wall? Be an ornament?" His voice sounded put out, but she looked at his profile and saw that he was smiling. It struck her that Joe would make a heck of an ornament, and her cheeks heated a little.

They drove the rest of the way in silence. As they neared Pierce Street, Joe thought about how Maggie had always been able to make him smile. Until, of course, he'd made her so unhappy there'd been no more smiles for either of them.

Well, he wasn't about to make her unhappy now. Once the case was over he'd honor her wish never to see him again.

Besides, he'd noticed that big diamond on the third finger of her left hand on that first day. The sight had practically dropped him in his tracks. When he was getting up the nerve to go see her, he'd told himself she surely had a husband by now. Children. All the things she deserved. But then he'd seen the ring, and there had been nothing at all rational about his reaction.

Maggie was still so pretty. Still so smart. And he still got a jolt every time he looked at her. Helping her into the Jeep just now, he'd touched her for the first time in seven years. He'd had to turn away so she wouldn't see how having her so close—touching her—had affected him.

There was no way to deal with that except ignore it. He slowed as he turned the corner. The place looked even worse in the daylight. It had once been a retail area with stores below apartments. Now it was a mess of decaying brick, crumbling curbs, windows boarded with plywood, green and black—Nightshade colors—graffiti everywhere. "You still sure you want to do this?" he asked, hearing a gruff, authoritarian note in his voice. Oh, hell. She wasn't going to like that.

"You bet. You planning to stop me?"

He eased the Jeep alongside the curb. "No. But please stay within sight of me all the time."

He had to lock the Jeep and he was a few steps behind her as she headed into the tavern.

Inside, the place was dark and reeked of old smoke and new booze. A couple of young men were at the bar, drinking in earnest, engaged in low conversation with the bartender. A third was over by the jukebox, feeding in quarters. None wore gang colors. Otherwise, the place was empty. So Joe should have no trouble keeping an eye on them all.

But his relief was short-lived, because all four men turned to stare at Maggie. In the split second of silence, he could hear a few coins hit the floor over by the jukebox.

Maggie's suit was modest, but it was bright blue. Eye-catching, especially with Maggie in it. Her coil of dark brown hair gleamed richly. The glint of her tiny gold earring was like a beacon. She had on silk stockings and designer high heels, and she had legs that a guy would have to be blind not to notice.

Joe's back tensed. He knew Maggie's wide eyes and her air of innocence—qualities that had drawn him to her—would play big in a place like this.

"Well, hel—lo." It was the bartender. Joe gritted his teeth and took a few steps toward her. Maggie gestured for him to stop. He finally chose a place off to the side where he could see her in profile and hear all the conversation.

Maggie said coolly, "Hello. I'm Maggie Hannan and I'm an attorney." The guys at the bar put down their beer mugs.

"You're way too pretty to be an attorney," one of them—the one with the greasy ponytail—said. He laughed, a low, suggestive sound. "My last lawyer was so young he still had zits and his voice cracked. How come the county never gives me a girl like you? I'll bet you could get me off." The sexual double meaning was unmistakable, and there was a laugh all around.

Joe felt murder in his blood. It took every ounce of self-control he had to say nothing.

Maggie ignored the comment. She pulled out her legal pad and said, "I'm investigating the shooting here in the alley on August twenty-seventh. The one where the cop supposedly shot a Nightshade gang member nicknamed Hook."

There was a short silence. Then the bartender said quietly, "That shooting took place at two in the morning. The bar was closed."

"Was it?" Maggie pulled out a pen.

He leaned forward. "By law, a tavern closes at one."

Maggie just smiled. "Maybe you really are going to need a lawyer then. My firm has a couple of clients who'd be glad to testify that you're open all night quite often. But I have no intention of asking for testimony like that. Not if my questions are answered."

The bartender eyed her for a long moment, and Joe read a dawning respect in the guy's eyes. Then the bartender's gaze slid to Joe. "This punk your boyfriend? Or your bodyguard?"

"Bodyguard," she said smoothly. "Do you think I'd come in here without one? Do I look stupid to you?"

"Honey, you look anything but stupid."

"Yes. Well. I know you were open that night, so

let's cut to the chase. How crowded was the bar at the time of the shooting?''

"Why should we tell you anything?" This time it was the guy from the jukebox, who came over with a definite swagger and leaned against the bar. A little younger than the others, his leer at Maggie ticked Joe off.

"Because of the reward," Maggie said.

"How much?" Jukebox again.

"Two thousand dollars."

These guys were tough, not used to showing what they were thinking, but there was a small gasp from Ponytail. Joe knew that around here, two thousand dollars might as well be two million. These were the kind of guys who mugged people for twenty bucks.

"Two thousand. No shit." The bartender straightened from his slouch. His own earring, a cheap silver hoop, also gleamed. His smile showed yellowing teeth. "Hey, honey, you want something to drink?"

"Just a couple of answers. Did anyone see anything at all that night? Hear anything? Smell anything? Anything at all?"

"We were open," the bartender acknowledged quietly.

"And?" Maggie's voice was calm, in control, but Joe felt his heart start to pound. He'd checked out plenty of places like this in his career. *Finding a witness is never this easy.*

"The curtains were drawn," the bartender said with some regret. Joe turned slightly and looked more closely at the window. The curtains looked like old burlap sacks. If someone were standing by the juke-box and happened to look up and out the window, he'd be able to see right through the torn fabric. If he turned even slightly, he could see the Dumpster at the end of the alley. Hook had been standing in front of it, spotlighted by the streetlamp. The pounding in Joe's heart got harder.

Would Maggie really get him his badge back? He'd always known she was brilliant, from the very first time he'd met her. She'd tracked him down because she'd had a million questions after he'd spoken to her law school class about lie detector tests.

"You can see through the curtains. If you were looking," Joe said now.

"Hey, who is this guy?" the bartender asked with new suspicion.

Maggie shot Joe a quelling look before turning back to the bartender. "I told you, my bodyguard. Did you look through the curtains?"

"If I did, what would I have to do to collect the reward?"

"Say what you saw, to the Internal Affairs Department of the police. Also you might have to testify in court."

"Just say I saw a gun, right?"

"You'd have to give enough detail about that night to convince someone. If you didn't see it, you can't testify to it."

Joe's heart sank. This guy hadn't seen a thing. He

was only interested in the reward. "Let's go," Joe said, despair making his voice a growl. That shooting had taken place in the middle of the night. The street had been basically deserted. Besides, only punks and criminals roamed this part of town at night. The chances of anyone seeing anything—much less telling the truth in a matter involving a cop—were slim to none.

Maggie nodded. "I think you're right. It's time we got going." She put a stack of her business cards down on the bar. "Listen. You're the bartender. You know people. If you hear anything, you could get part of the reward as a sort of finder's fee. If you hear anything, call me."

"Call you what?" One of the guys at the bar sniggered.

Joe had had enough. "Maggie, you've done what you had to do. Now let's go."

She nodded decisively and went ahead of him out the door.

A couple of whistles followed her.

MAGGIE WAITED for Joe at the door to the Jeep. "Thanks," she said quietly as he came up to her.

His eyebrows arched in surprise. "No chewing me out for interfering? For acting like the protector?"

"I was glad you were there." She shuddered. "The way those guys looked at me…"

"Don't worry about them," he said gruffly. "I would have kept you safe."

She swallowed hard.

He unlocked the door and she got in, using her fingers to tug on her skirt so that it didn't ride up as much as it had before. When he got in on his side, she said, "I've been in tight situations before. But there was something about how that man from over by the jukebox leered—" She cut herself off and changed the subject. "I hope we planted some seeds today. Guys like those lie to cops and lawyers all the time. We've got to give them time to think about the money."

He put the Jeep in gear. "Just where is that money coming from?"

"From your twenty-thousand-dollar retainer."

He was quiet for a few minutes as he drove. Finally, he said, "That's your money."

"It was your money until a couple of days ago."

"You know what I mean."

She did. She and her partners needed the money. But the retainer had been substantial and she'd known that she'd need leverage to get the case moving. "Let me worry about how I spend my money," she said quietly.

"But—"

"Joe." She took a deep breath. "You came walking into my life a couple of days ago after a seven-year absence. We never resolved any of the issues between us. I'm trying to be adult about all this, but your controlling tactics make it hard, because it's one of the things we used to argue about."

He nodded. "I knew I was too close to my own case to do all my own investigation. That's why I came to you in the first place. But Maggie, how you investigate something like this is, you go downtown in the middle of the night and you offer the street people, the hookers and the dopeheads a few bucks. Ten or twenty dollars, not two thousand."

She winced. "Well, two grand might be overkill, but it'll get the job done. Assuming anybody saw anything."

"I told myself when I hired you that I'd let you handle the case your way. I'll do my own investigation, but I have to let you do your job, too."

She felt a spurt of surprise—and something else? Disappointment? She had to admit her heart had jumped when she heard him coming to her defense in the bar.

She shook her head, annoyed at herself. That annoyance grew when she saw he had pulled up in front of a small restaurant. "I thought you were taking me back to the office."

"It's after one. You have to eat lunch sometime."

But this place looked romantic. Intimate.

He said, "I'm buying."

"I'll buy."

He slapped his palm against the steering wheel. "For Chrissake."

Okay, she reminded herself. *He's compromised once today.* "You can buy. But let's just pick up a sandwich instead. She spied a hot-dog vendor set up across the street. "You can buy me a hot dog."

He didn't argue. After he'd paid for a couple of hot dogs and Cokes, he headed for a nearby park.

It was a fine day, one of those days in early fall that looked and felt more like summer, but the air had an underlying bite to it that was refreshing. This park was small and near downtown, and it attracted mostly office workers on lunch hour. Those who were lunching late had taken up seats near the river. Joe headed toward a picnic table nearer a copse of trees, away from the crowd.

They unwrapped their hog dogs. A silence settled between them, and nervously, Maggie tried to fill it. "That restaurant you had picked out for lunch," she began. "It was too fancy."

He cocked his head. "You didn't think you were properly dressed?"

His expression was grave, but his eyes twinkled. She'd always liked his sense of humor. She eyed his threadbare jeans and cotton shirt and couldn't help smiling. When they'd been going together, it had taken Joe a little while to show that dry humor of his. And in the end, it had died, like everything else about their relationship.

"Going to that restaurant would have felt like a date," she said impulsively.

"Oh."

She felt her face flame. She concentrated on opening the little packet of mustard and slathering it on her hot dog.

Joe stretched out his long legs and took a bite. After he'd swallowed, he said, "It wouldn't have been like one of our dates. We never had the money for a restaurant like that."

When they'd met, Joe was still a uniformed officer with a modest salary. After they'd started dating, he'd said maybe he would start saving for a down payment on a house. She'd agreed wholeheartedly. In addition to a family of her own, she'd wanted her own house.

So they'd done things that didn't cost too much. Gone to the library. Seen old movies at film festivals, rented videos. Traveled a little way out into the country to auctions and flea markets, picking up furniture for the house they planned to buy. Walked in the park. A hot dog in the park had been very much their style.

She felt a twinge in her heart. Once, it had all seemed so romantic. "Lewis—my fiancé—likes to go to little restaurants. French ones."

He eyed her ring, and she found herself babbling, the way she always did when she was nervous. "We're going to be married next June." Joe was watching her, his half-eaten hot dog in his hand. "He's a widower," she hurried on. "His daughter is Tessa. You've met her. She's that redheaded teenager who works for us when she's not in school. The work is good for her. She's learning a lot about getting along in the adult world and she doesn't have as much time to miss her mother who died three years ago.

Tessa is a sweet girl. She's kind of emotional, the way teenage girls can get sometimes. She likes books and movies just as much as I do. We're very close.'' She finally had to stop and take a breath.

''It sounds like you think a lot of her,'' Joe said finally.

''I love her.''

''Right.'' He gave his head a quick shake and took a couple of bites of his hot dog. He wadded up the paper wrapper and sent it sailing toward the trash can.

Maggie wrapped up what was left of hers.

''Finished?'' Joe asked quietly.

''Yes.'' She stood, proud of herself. All in all, the lunch had gone well. She'd managed to be alone with Joe and keep up her end of the small talk. She'd even discussed her upcoming marriage. A polite conversation between two people who no longer knew each other very well.

But as she stood and reached for her bag, she saw the balloon vendor out of the corner of her eye. She froze, then swallowed hard against the sudden prick of tears in her eyes.

Coming here had been a bad idea. Because she remembered a lot more than those few dates in a park like this. She remembered her birthday, a month after they'd been married. Joe had bought her everything pink, because pink had been her favorite color. Pink bubble gum. A pair of absurd pink slippers with kittens printed on them. A pink comb and brush. And a dozen pink balloons. She'd felt so…cherished. For the first time in her life.

She got up quickly, walked over and plunked her hot dog in the trash can. "Joe, I've got a hearing this afternoon. Technical stuff, so I need to get back to the office and look at my brief again."

He didn't argue. But as she picked up her briefcase, he asked, "Is pink still your favorite color?"

"Let's just say I'm more of a red woman now," she said, striving for a light tone and hoping she'd succeeded.

She looked over at him. The tightness of his jaw, the pain she saw in his eyes startled her. He'd said so little when she'd told him she wanted a divorce. *You never talk to me,* she'd railed then. Now she wondered if in her insistence that he talk to her about everything, she'd been missing subtler clues.

"Are you happy nowadays?" he asked, and there was a gruff note in his voice that she remembered well.

"Of course. I'm getting married."

"It's just that…" He paused. "When we were talking a few minutes ago, you hardly even mentioned your fiancé. Not even what he did for a living. Just so much talk about his daughter, Tessa, and I wondered if you really were…happy."

"Of course I'm happy," she snapped. "Lewis is a fine man. And by the way, he's in cookware." The spurt of anger felt good. He was asking about her happiness seven years after he'd broken her heart. "What else do you think you have a right to know?"

"Nothing," he said immediately. "I know I have a right to nothing."

CHAPTER THREE

"MOVE!"

"Make me!"

"I'll make you. It'll be a blast."

"Go ahead, try it. Try it!"

Joe quickened his pace to a jog. He rounded the corner to the locker room of the gym just in time to see Jeff Collane and Rick Williams shove Kenny Sheets into a row of lockers. Metal clanged and the back of Kenny's head thunked hard.

Joe grabbed Jeff by the neckband of his T-shirt and pulled. "Hey, who do ya—" The kid whirled, fists up. But when he saw it was Joe with a hand on his shirt, he stopped.

"Got a problem?" Joe asked with deceptive mildness.

Jeff tried to shake him off. Joe held on. "I said, got a problem?"

With a bitter look at Joe, Jeff subsided. "No problem, man."

Rick and Kenny stood still, too. Kenny had a purplish bruise developing at the corner of his mouth, and his T-shirt was torn. All three kids were breathing hard. Joe knew they would have been in the middle of a ruckus right now if he hadn't shown up. Jeff and Rick especially welcomed a fight. That was one of the reasons they were standing in the gym with Joe right now. They were part of his Kids at Risk group.

The program, set up in a downtown building that had once housed a men's club, served ten- to twelve-year-olds who'd been in trouble with the law. Though their offenses were minor, these were kids who would soon be moving up to bigger crime if they didn't get some help. The juvenile court had referred Jeff, Rick and Kenny to the program, which emphasized after-school sports and good citizenship. The Kids at Risk was staffed with volunteers from the police department. A couple of Joe's buddies—former cops—ran the place.

Supposedly a good example and sports would help counteract the effects of a street culture that offered kids such as these a quick buck and an early death.

Joe gave Jeff's collar a shake. "You going to settle down now?"

Jeff nodded in exaggerated compliance. "Yessir, Mr. Detective Man."

Joe held the boy for a second more, then let him go. Jeff danced a couple of feet away and then added, "Mr. Detective Man who ain't got no badge no more."

"Just get out of here," Joe said wearily. "Go home and try to stay out of trouble tonight, you hear?"

With some grumbling, Jeff and Rick left. As they closed the door behind them, he could hear them laughing. Mocking laughs from a couple of wiseass twelve-year-olds.

Kenny stayed where he was, flat against the lockers, looking at Joe. "You didn't have to come in here. I was doing okay."

"Yeah, I heard."

"I coulda beat them by myself," Kenny insisted. His clean, but poorly cut hair hung down his forehead. The corner of the lens of one of his eyeglasses was cracked. It had been cracked for months. "You think just 'cause I'm small, I couldn't have taken them both. But I could. I can take care of myself."

Kenny was twelve, too, but small for his age. It was one of the things Joe figured had given the kid an aggressive attitude. But over the last three months since Kenny had entered the program, Joe had seen differences between him and most of the kids who came here. Kenny was intelligent, well-spoken. And Joe sensed a vulnerability that Kenny tried desperately to hide.

Joe put a hand against the locker and leaned in a little. "All I know is, it was two against one. Those aren't very good odds."

Reluctantly, Kenny nodded. "But you could go two against one, couldn't you, Joe? With a gun, anyway."

Regret and sadness washed over Joe. He was trying to protect Kenny and the others from a fate like Hook's. "The trick is to handle things without a gun. With your head, instead of a gun or your fists."

Despite the bruise marring his lip, Kenny grinned. "I knew you'd say that. I coulda, you know, put the words right in your mouth."

"Yeah." Joe pushed his sad thoughts away. "Listen, I was about to go for a burger. You want to come?" He made a casual offer of a meal nearly every day. Sometimes he could get Kenny to join him, but not very often.

"My mom packed me a big lunch. And she'll have dinner for me when I get home," Kenny said, putting his chin up. "She always makes homemade. Chicken. Mashed potatoes and gravy."

"I want some company is all," Joe said carefully. Kenny wasn't simply small for his age, but skinny, too. In the locker room after basketball games, Joe had seen the kid without a shirt. His ribs stood out.

"Like I'd be doing you a favor?" Kenny asked dubiously.

"Yeah. Just hanging out."

"Doing a favor for a cop," Kenny mumbled, shaking his head. He ducked under Joe's arm. "Okay. Since I'm in this program, I guess I gotta suck up to the cops." He opened his locker and took out a battered backpack with a broken zipper. Joe could see a couple of books in the bag.

At the fast-food restaurant, Kenny decided he could have a double hamburger with cheese, just to keep Joe company. "Make it two," Joe told the counter person. "And fries."

At the table, when Joe tried to engage him in conversation, it was the same as it always was. Kenny said little as he wolfed down his food.

"Hey, you going to eat that?" Kenny asked, looking at the rest of Joe's burger.

Silently, Joe passed his plate across the table.

Kenny polished off the food, then said he'd better get home. "I guess I was a little hungry," he said as they were going out the door.

"Well, I'm glad you came. I was glad for the company. I hate eating alone." Joe was always careful to let Kenny keep his pride. Joe understood pride; sometimes it was the only thing that kept a person going.

He put the Jeep in gear and scanned the sky. "Looks like we're in for rain. It's getting a little colder, too. Why don't I drop you off at home?"

"Yeah, okay."

Great, Joe thought, pleased. Kenny had never let him take him home before.

But when they got a few blocks from home, Kenny said, "Drop me off here. On this corner."

"I've got time. I can take you all the way." He had plenty of time these days. He wasn't allowed to set foot in the door of headquarters since his suspension, so he was spending even more time at the gym.

"Hey, I said drop me on the corner. I've got a couple of things to do, you know?"

So Joe dropped Kenny on the corner and sat watching him for a few seconds. The street was littered. A chain-link fence surrounded the parking lot of a business long gone. Yellowing weeds grew through the cracks, only emphasizing the concrete and grit. Graffiti highlighted the plywood covering the windows of the old storefront. Joe scanned the words. Profanity. *Shelly loves Jeff. Wanna ball me?* But there were no gang symbols painted on this corner. Yet.

Kenny was several feet away, but now he turned around and looked at Joe, still at the curb.

Joe looked back. He was getting way too involved with Kenny, and he knew it. He cared about this kid in a very personal way, and the thought made him uncomfortable.

At first the volunteer program had been a way to fill his days after Maggie had left him. At least, that's what he'd told himself when he'd originally read the memo on the bulletin board at the station house.

But he knew the real reason he kept going back to the gym. It was his attempt to pay back, to somehow make up for what had happened to his Alex. The son he'd failed to protect.

The son he'd told Maggie had died, but he'd never told her how.

The son he could barely manage to think about, even twelve years later. The only way to deal with those thoughts was to immerse himself in his job. To absorb himself in working the clues, dealing with the people, processing the endless, mind-numbing paperwork.

What was he going to do now that he might not have the job? His hands gripped the steering wheel.

Up ahead, Kenny hadn't moved. Joe could sense

the kid's impatience, his need for Joe to leave so he could be off toward home. Even after all this time and effort, Kenny didn't trust him enough to let Joe even see the inside of his apartment.

Joe finally waved and pulled away from the curb. Kenny would go home to whatever awaited him. Whatever it was that the kid didn't want Joe to see. And when Joe went home, there would be nothing. Nobody. No wife, no family.

With a pang as sharp as those he'd felt seven years ago, he suddenly missed Maggie. Her smile. Her laugh. That brief soul-warming time of sharing, of knowing someone would be there when he came home from a shift after dealing with crises and squalor.

She'd said she loved him. But she hadn't known him then, not really. She'd come to know the real Joe Latham when she'd lost their baby, and he hadn't been there for her.

He'd always known she wanted children. Kids of her own. When he'd been dating her, he'd been so caught up in loving her, in having her love him back, that he thought he could handle the idea of their having children. He really thought he could handle it, or he would never have asked her to marry him.

So he'd married Maggie. And found out how wrong he'd been. She'd become pregnant and the thought of fatherhood again had scared him to death. Then her miscarriage had broken his heart. More importantly, it reminded him of exactly what he couldn't have, what he didn't dare let himself have. One of their last conversations as a married couple had been his admission that he didn't want her to try to get pregnant again.

In marrying her, he'd done the unforgivable: in deluding himself that he could have a normal life, he'd hurt Maggie, an innocent woman whom he'd loved.

So he had to resist his attraction to her now. He owed Maggie that much.

ON THE CORNER by Kenny's apartment, a cocky rich kid in a yellow car was making a drug buy. Kenny felt a sharp stab of envy. If he had a cool car like that, a good pair of shades like that guy wore, he'd *never* come to this part of town. He sure wouldn't come to buy coke. A guy like that didn't need to get wasted. He had everything.

As Kenny watched, one of the hookers who hung out on this street approached the car. The guy flipped her the bird and laughed, and then peeled out and turned the corner, tires squealing.

Kenny felt his fists clench. Not because *this* hooker had had a guy flip her the bird. No, it was the idea that guys might treat his mother that way. He felt even worse when he thought of the guys who might take her up on her offer.

His mom. He quickened his step. Now that he was a Kid at Risk, he had to spend a lot of time at the gym. He couldn't be there when she woke up in the afternoon. He wasn't around to take care of her as much as he used to be.

"Hey, Kenny, how ya doin'?"

It was the hooker, the one who'd gone over to the yellow car. "Okay."

"Just okay?" She let out a shrill cry of laughter. "When you're a little older, I can make you feel better than okay."

"Yeah, sure." He was finally at the door to his apartment building.

The hallway to the apartment was dirty, stuff just ground into the floor until the beige carpet was black in a wide stripe down the middle. He could hear music coming out of some of the doors. He hated this place, but it was better than nothing. He knew people who had lost it all and lived in boxes and only got to go to shelters sometimes when it got cold. He knew some of them died.

His mother swore nothing like that would ever happen to her and Kenny, but he knew his mom had a kind of horror of it, just like he had. Kenny's father was long gone. Kenny's brother, Craig, had taken care of them all until three years ago. Then he'd gone and got shot dead over some girl, and now it was just Kenny and his mom.

When he got into the apartment, he realized that she was up. He breathed a sigh of relief. He was always afraid Joe would come into the apartment and find out how much she slept. Joe might be kind of a friend, but he was a cop. He'd tell child welfare for sure, and then maybe they'd take him away from his mother. His mom was in the kitchen, stirring soup on the stove. "Hi, Mom."

"Kenny." His mom turned to him. Her voice rose. "What happened to your face?"

"No big deal," he said. "Just some pushing."

He squirmed as she studied him. Finally she sighed and said, "I'm making some soup. Chicken noodle. Doesn't it smell good?"

It did, even though he'd eaten so much with Joe. It seemed like some days he couldn't get filled up. He was going to offer to set the table, but she'd already done that, real pretty.

When she served up the soup, he noticed that her hands were shaking. "You okay?" he asked.

"Why wouldn't I be okay?"

He could think of about a hundred reasons, but he just shrugged. She was acting really funny today. He was surprised she hadn't taken her nerve pills or at least a drink. He was really glad she hadn't but...something was weird. He didn't like things weird.

For a few moments there was silence. Kenny spooned up his soup.

"How did school go?" his mom asked.

"Okay."

"Just okay?" She sounded concerned now. He figured she was thinking of Craig, and how he'd graduated from high school with honors and got a great job doing the books in a muffler shop. He knew she wanted the same for him.

Only it couldn't be the same. Back when Craig was in school, his mom didn't dye her hair that ugly kind of red to get the guys to—

"School went good," he said quickly. He had to lie a bit because he really didn't like school. He didn't mind social studies, because that was the class Celeste was in. And he liked English, too, because he liked to read. "We're doing a book called *Oliver Twist*." He liked the books about rich people a whole lot better.

"Then I went to the gym," he said. "Then Joe and I got a burger and talked some."

"Joe?" His mom was frowning.

"Yeah, me and Joe."

"What did you talk about?" she asked, and she was kind of staring at him.

He played with his spoon. "I don't know. Stuff. Basketball. Stuff on TV."

Kenny liked talking with Joe. He always made it seem like what you said was important. Of course, there were a lot of things Kenny couldn't tell him. Like about his mom and the booze and pills, and especially the times when she got dressed up and went out at night.

Most of all, he couldn't say, *I want to be a cop someday*. Joe had made being a cop seem like the greatest thing in the world. Not just carrying a gun and giving orders, but helping people, talking them down when they were high, protecting little kids, that kind of stuff that made you feel proud somehow.

They said Joe shot a guy who was unarmed, but Kenny knew that he hadn't. Joe was too good and he never lost his cool. Never, no matter how many rough kids were hanging around the gym.

He got up and took his bowl to the sink. He ran the warm water and squirted some soap in to start on the dishes.

"I'll do those," his mom said from behind him. "You go do your homework."

"Okay." He dried his hands.

He was almost at the door when she said, "Kenny, I don't like you hanging around with that cop."

"I've gotta go to the gym. It's part of the court order. If I don't go, I violate my probation, and then I get locked up."

"I know." There was something in her voice....

He turned to look at her. She was standing by the sink. Skinny, like he was, kind of pretty except for the hair.

She bit her lip. "Just don't get too friendly with that cop."

"His name is Joe."

"I know that!" Quickly, she added, "I'm not mad. It's just that around here, it doesn't make sense to be friends with a cop." She was looking at him the way she did when she meant business. She hesitated again, said more softly, "Any cop."

Oh. Now he understood. Kind of. Even though the

Nightshade guys weren't on this block, it was a rough neighborhood; lots of people didn't like cops, that was for sure. But his mom had always wanted him to be nice to the police, just like she told him to respect his teachers.

Weird, he thought again, stopping in the living room for his books.

His homework took almost two hours. Finally, he went out to tell his mom he was done, but she wasn't in the kitchen or the living room. Her bedroom light was on, her door partway open. He paused there. "Hi."

"Oh! You startled me." She looked up, into her mirror and saw him in the doorway. "I thought you were asleep."

"What are you getting all dressed up for?" But he knew. She'd been out last week, too. Now she'd teased up her hair until it was kind of like a bush around her head. She had on a shiny purple top that was as tight as her skin and cut way low. "Don't go," he said suddenly, desperately. "Don't go."

"I'm just going out with Roger." She averted her eyes as she clipped on big, dangling earrings full of rhinestones. There was a can of beer on the table next to her, and, not looking at him, she raised the can to her lips and drained it.

Kenny squeezed his eyes shut. There was a pause, then his mom said, "We need the money. I don't have rent money, Kenny, and I should have paid it on the first."

Why can't you get a job? he wanted to ask. But he knew the answer. Who'd hire his mother when she kept taking pills and drinking? "Don't go tonight," he whispered. But in a way, he was scared if she didn't go. If they didn't have rent money... They had to have it. And he couldn't do anything to help.

He hated being a kid.

THE FOLLOWING MONDAY night, Tessa emerged from the fitting room at the Bridal Bower. She was dressed in a filmy lavender gown with a hem that hit the floor. She had twisted her long red hair and now held it in a fist to the back of her head.

Her face was alight. "What do you think?"

"I think you look beautiful. Just like a Gibson girl," Maggie said fondly.

Tessa's smile grew wider. "Really?"

"Really."

"So I can wear this to the wedding?"

Maggie sighed just as the consultant who was helping them bustled forward with some silk roses on a comb. "Here, let me pin this in place," she said helpfully. She used the comb to secure the hair Tessa held off her neck. A lot of hair didn't make it into the comb and tumbled around the girl's face. But still it was obvious that Tessa was stunning.

Maggie said as much, then added gently, "But it isn't going to be that kind of wedding."

Tessa said, "Why not?"

Maggie sighed again. "Sweetheart, we've been

over this before. Your dad and I have planned a small wedding. A nice day, all our friends, but not a lot of fuss.''

''Weddings are for fuss,'' Tessa said. Both she and the consultant shot Maggie an accusing look.

''My fiancé wants something simple,'' she explained to the consultant.

''I know that. I realized it when I ordered your wedding outfit. I was just thinking…'' The woman's eyes went dreamy, the way Tessa's often did. ''We could cancel the order for that cream-colored suit you'd planned to wear.'' She shot Maggie an assessing gaze. ''Your hair is perfect for a turn-of-the-century style. I think—'' She cocked her head. ''Yes, a hat.'' She marched over to a hat stand and took off a broad-brimmed lace hat. ''We could trim this with silk flowers in the same shade of lavender as the maid of honor's dress.''

''I look awful in lavender,'' Maggie said weakly.

Tessa turned a pleading look at Maggie and clasped her hands together in a supplicating posture.

The saleswoman said helpfully, ''A couple of lavender flowers on a hat won't hurt your coloring. And every bride looks good in antique white.''

Maggie's eyes were on Tessa. Seeing the girl she loved with her hair askew with that rose spray in it… *Come on,* a tiny inner voice said. *You've always wanted old lace for your wedding.*

''Try this on.'' The saleswoman was coming toward her with the hat. In the woman's hand, the brim looked even larger than it had on the stand. Lewis would fumble, hit the brim when he kissed her.... She held out her hands, warding off the woman.

"Come on, Maggie," Tessa said.

"Here, let me do this." The woman pulled the hat down firmly on Maggie's head and started stuffing her hair up under the brim.

Maggie felt herself succumbing. The combination of Tessa, the bridal consultant and her own silly yearnings for a romantic wedding straight out of a past she'd never had...

She looked in the mirror and was lost. The lace of the hat brim cast dainty shadows over her forehead. It made her eyes look large and mysterious, her mouth rosy. She could almost feel the scratchiness of lace at her throat and wrists, the heaviness of her cascading gardenia bouquet. "All right. Cancel the order for the suit," she said impulsively. "When I can manage an afternoon off, I'll come back in and try on bridal gowns."

"Yesss!" Tessa shot her fist into the air.

The consultant was smiling. Her future stepdaughter was smiling. Maggie was smiling as, a few minutes later, she looked at her watch. "We're going to be late meeting your father."

"You're going to tell him it's going to be a real wedding, aren't you?" Tessa asked as they got into Maggie's car.

"It *is* a real wedding, no matter what we wear," Maggie assured the girl. "I know what you mean, though. I'll tell him I've changed my mind, that I want to wear a gown instead of that suit. He won't really care what I wear. Men never do.''

But he did, Maggie discovered twenty minutes later at the coffee shop. Her fiancé abandoned his double latte, leaned toward her and said flatly, ''This whole thing is ridiculous.''

Something in his tone irked Maggie. ''I don't think it's ridiculous at all.''

''The next thing you know, you'll be expecting me to wear an ascot.''

''It's an evening wedding,'' Tessa said, a spoon in her hand.

Lewis turned toward her. ''What's that got to do with—''

''Dad,'' the girl said in a patronizing voice, ''an ascot is for morning wear. At night, it'll be white tie and tails.''

''Tails!''

''Okay,'' Maggie said, striving for calm. ''This is between your dad and me, Tessa.''

''But you said—''

''I know what I said.''

Tessa slammed her spoon down on the table. ''All right. But Dad, Maggie wants this. She really, really does. How can you say it's ridiculous?''

Looking beleaguered, her father turned to her again. ''Listen, Maggie's right. It's between her and me.''

''Right,'' Tessa said dramatically. ''I'm just the

daughter. Out of the loop. I'll wear a burlap sack if you get your way about what we're going to wear to this wedding." She balled up her napkin. "I'm going to the ladies' room," she announced before flouncing off.

"Good God," Lewis said quietly. "When did she ever get to be such a brat?"

Maggie shook her head ruefully. "It's her age, they tell me."

He turned to gaze at her fully. "Sometimes I wonder why you agreed to take us both on." There was a softening around his mouth that made him younger somehow, and very endearing.

"Because I love you both," she said simply.

Lewis smiled at her. She longed for him to take her hand, but he didn't. She wanted him to say he loved her, too. But she knew he wouldn't. Lewis didn't show his feelings too often. She told herself that she shouldn't be hurt by his silence.

"I'll talk to Tessa," Maggie said, earning her an even broader smile from her fiancé. One tinged with relief.

"Good. You'll know what to say to her. Just tell her she's being romantic and silly. That the whole thing is ridiculous."

That…word again. In a flash, Maggie went from wanting this man to hold her hand to having to bite her lip not to snap at him.

Lewis took a long sip of his cooling latte. Obviously, he thought the subject was closed. Maggie knew they should get going. It was nearly ten, and it was a school night for Tessa. When Tessa came back, Maggie would just suggest the three of them leave.

"You don't like your coffee?" Lewis asked when he saw she wasn't drinking her damn-the-calories caramel cream.

"Just what's so ridiculous about me wanting to be married in a more formal wedding?" The question was out before Maggie even realized she was going to ask it.

Lewis looked pained. "I'd feel—"

"Don't say it," she warned.

"What? Ridiculous? It's what I'd feel."

"Why?"

He looked a little startled. "Why? Gosh, maybe because I'm so old."

"Forty-three is not old."

Lewis sighed. "I'm not a juror, Maggie. You don't have to argue so hard."

Maggie didn't apologize. "Is it because of Elizabeth?" she asked quietly.

Lewis looked pained. "No."

She didn't think he was lying, exactly. But the way he averted his eyes made her know that he was remembering his first wife, perhaps his first wedding. He sighed again. "Look, I don't want to spoil anything for you. But this is…well, you've always been sensible, and the wedding you're describing seems like so much fuss for two mature people. After all, I was married before."

"So was I," she pointed out, and right then and there an image of Joe popped into her brain. Joe of the plastic-cup-and-instant-coffee, Joe of broad chest and scratchy beard. She had a past, too, and the trick was not to let either Joe or Elizabeth interfere with the present. "This big, fancy wedding was something I let Tessa talk me into, I guess," she admitted. "It's not that important." Mentally, she kissed visions of old lace and tea roses goodbye and gave him a determined smile. "What's important is that we're together."

Lewis smiled back. "Thanks for understanding." He reached out and squeezed her hand.

"I'm sorry," Tessa said quietly, and Maggie and Lewis looked up to see she'd rejoined them. She was standing at the side of their table. "It's your wedding. Only— Never mind. Like I said, it's your wedding."

"Right," her father agreed.

The girl bit her lip. "It's just that I've spent so much time looking at that big photo album of your and Mom's wedding, and you looked so happy, and I thought it would be fun to dress up and have everybody happy again—" She caught Maggie's eye and went abruptly silent. Then, "Oh, Maggie, I didn't mean—"

"It's okay," Maggie said. She stood up and put her arms in the sleeves of her blazer just as Lewis made a belated move to hold it for her. She picked up her purse.

From behind her, Tessa was still trying to explain.

"I only meant that I like you, Maggie, and I wanted you to have as much as my real mom had. Oh, I didn't mean that you wouldn't be my real…ah, stepmother…." her voice trailed off.

When they got to the car, Maggie touched the teenager's cheek. "I know you loved your mom. I appreciate it that you like me so much that you want me to be like her, to have what she had."

Under the garish lights of the parking lot, Tessa's eyes filled with tears. "I miss her," she said in a young, high voice.

"But we have Maggie," Lewis said, and the false joviality in his voice pricked her heart again.

Tessa nodded once, quickly, and got into the car.

Lewis walked Maggie to her own car. "We'll follow you home."

"That's okay."

"No, really. I don't want anything to happen to you."

Maggie nodded her assent. Lewis leaned over to kiss her cheek, and then abruptly took her in his arms. He held her tightly for a moment, and pressed his cheek to hers.

"I need you," he whispered. "So does Tessa. Don't ever think we don't know how lucky we are."

She thought of Lewis and Tessa alone these last three years. She thought of filling Lewis's big, lonely house with babies. Warmth shot through her. He needed her.

He kissed her gently on the mouth. When he lifted

his lips from hers, he said gruffly, "I love my little girl, but sometimes I wish she weren't around so much. I'd like to come home with you right now."

She wished that, too, wished to make love so that she could feel close to him, know he didn't just need her, but wanted her, too. "Tomorrow?" she whispered.

"I can't. I've got to go to Milan a day early. I was going to tell you tonight, but we got sidetracked with all that wedding talk. I've got to figure out what's gone wrong with the aluminum alloy we've contracted for over there."

"How long?" Maggie asked with resignation.

"Ten days at least." He kissed her again, longer this time. Firmer, the kiss now filled with sexual desire. When he lifted his mouth from hers, he said, "I plan to remember that kiss when I'm lying awake in some strange hotel room these next few days."

It was one of the sexiest things he'd ever said. Maggie kissed him hard herself. "I'll miss you."

He let her go gently and pulled open her car door.

He was a good man, she thought, seeing his headlights in her rearview mirror as she drove home.

Lewis was probably right. They didn't need a big wedding, where the guests on his side might remember his first wedding and compare her with Elizabeth. Lewis would move on with his life more easily if she kept showing him she was just as loving as his dead wife, only different.

She wasn't out to test Lewis's love or commitment to their relationship. She wasn't asking for more than Elizabeth had had. She only wanted her share.

CHAPTER FOUR

IF SHE HADN'T KNOWN him so well, Maggie would never have realized Joe was nervous. As soon as she entered the hallway from the elevator at the police station, she caught sight of him. He was sitting in a straight chair and stood up just a little too quickly to meet her. "Maggie." He came down the hall and took her briefcase from her. "They haven't called us yet."

"That's because we still have ten minutes before your interview." She gave him a smile. She'd been working with him for several days on his case. She still had to warn her heart not to kick up its rhythm each time she saw him, but at least she was used to the sensation. "You're going to be fine. All you have to do is tell the truth."

"Right." His mouth thinned. "Tell the truth. Like that works."

"It's a lot better strategy than the whoppers some prisoners use." She strove for a lighter tone, and she noticed it worked when he finally cracked a small smile.

"Yeah. Let's see. 'I was framed by the mob.' 'The cops really want my identical twin, or my surgically altered brother.' Or, 'I was standing outside in that alley, right in front of that bar because I was trying to sell them printing services.'"

"Printing services. There's a new one."

"Not really. One of my last collars used it to explain himself. Might even have worked if it hadn't been four in the morning." He paused, and the little smile died. "Want some coffee?"

"Police station coffee? No, thanks. But go ahead."

He shook his head and leaned against the wall.

Very aware of him, Maggie took her briefcase from the chair he'd set it on. She sat down in the chair and got out her file. Out of the corner of her eye she assessed him.

He looked good. His hair was brushed carefully back, and he'd had it trimmed around the ears. His white shirt was so crisp she was sure it would crackle if she touched it, and his charcoal suit looked more lawyer than cop. A red silk tie projected both conservative and confident. It said, *Do I look like the kind of guy who could have lost my cool in an alley in the dead of night?* It might be easier to believe that James Bond habitually lost his cool. Maggie allowed her mind to stray. Joe looked a whole lot better than Bond, more masculine, actually....

Professional assessment, she reminded herself, opening her file and making herself concentrate.

As they waited, a few of the officers Joe worked with came by. A young uniformed officer passed by and nodded respectfully, then stopped. The young man said to Joe, "You tell those Internal Affairs sons-

of-bitches that they need to come on the street sometime, see what it's really like out there.''

''No kidding,'' Joe said.

The young man looked up at him and added ear-
nestly, ''But it doesn't matter how rough it was out
there that night. I know you didn't lose your cool.
Remember my first day on the job, you came over
and helped me talk to that guy holding a gun to his
wife's head? I was shakin' in my shoes, but you never
missed a beat.'' He paused, swallowed. ''You're
good. Really good.''

''Thanks,'' Joe said, his voice gruff. He looked
away, a little flush of red highlighting his cheekbones.

''You need a character witness, I'm here.''

Maggie stood up. ''I'm looking for character witnesses.''

The young officer drew himself up to his full
height. ''Well, you got one in me.''

''The department might be looking to make an example of me,'' Joe said. ''You sure this is something
you want to get involved in?''

He nodded. ''Yes,'' he said quietly, and he suddenly didn't look quite so young to Maggie.

''Thanks,'' Joe said briefly, that little flush of red
still on his skin.

Maggie understood how tough this was for Joe. All
the cops she knew considered themselves strong
enough to go it alone, and she knew full well how
hard it was for Joe to show his feelings.

She took the young officer's name. Terry Allerton.

He was extremely cooperative. Maggie was still asking him some questions and taking notes when Joe was called into the Internal Affairs office. Joe paused to let her go ahead of him. She flashed him a look of encouragement. She'd gone over his story, but she hadn't coached him in any way. Joe had the best defense of all—the truth—and she didn't want him to appear rehearsed.

The officer in charge of Joe's case—a detective from a different precinct—stood up from behind his desk and introduced himself as Randall Smithers. He was dressed in a somber suit and tie, and looked about fifty. Maggie looked him in the eye as she shook his hand, but she could get no real feel for the man. Maggie seated herself next to Joe.

They waited for the other detective who would be questioning Joe. Maggie looked around. The room looked as though it had once been part of a hallway that had been blocked off when more office space was needed. It was windowless and brightly lit by a flickering fluorescent fixture in the ceiling. The walls were institutional green and badly needed a coat of paint. There wasn't a landscape, a calendar or even a clock in the room.

She shifted, suddenly nervous herself. She knew the procedure. The detectives would conduct an independent investigation. As part of that investigation, Joe would be subjected to one or more interviews. This was the first, though he'd given a statement at the scene of the shooting. Maggie would be allowed to ask questions afterward. It should have been routine. But she'd never represented a police officer before. And there was so much at stake here. Her ex-husband was depending on her to get him back his career.

Joe sat up straight in the hard chair, his pose deceptively relaxed, his hands open and resting, palm down, on lean, powerful thighs. He seemed to feel her glance; he turned to look at her briefly. There was a kind of flicker in his eyes.

I'm glad you're with me, those eyes said.

The look unsettled her further. She pulled out her file and pretended to take a few notes. Finally, the other detective arrived, full of apologies. It dawned on Maggie then that forcing her and Joe to wait might have been a tactic. Were these officers subtly trying to intimidate Joe? The thought brought her chin up.

Detective Smithers introduced Detective Garrick, who was much younger and seemed a tad warmer. Smithers explained the procedure, which Maggie already knew. Maggie could object to the questions the detectives asked Joe, but she could not keep them from being asked, and Joe could not avoid answering them. Afterward, she could ask Joe questions of her own to clarify his story.

It was all supposed to be fair and aboveboard. But this wasn't a courtroom, and there were no real protections for the accused.

Garrick pushed the button on a small tape recorder that sat prominently in the middle of the desk and began. He asked Joe a few questions; Joe answered. Then Joe described what had happened the night of the shooting. Maggie listened intently. When Joe got to the part about seeing the necklace near the dead man's hand, Smithers said, "Describe it."

Joe said, "It was pewter, I think. There was a pendant in the shape of a skull hanging from the chain, with crystals where the eyes would be."

"Isn't it possible that what you saw Hook pulling out of his pocket was this necklace? That it had a sheen or gleam to it that made you think, 'metal' and then 'gun'?"

There wasn't the slightest pause. Without inflection, Joe said, "No."

Smithers pasted a look of sympathy on his face. "You only had a few seconds to react."

"Is that a question?" Maggie said.

Smithers shot her a look of open hostility and said to Joe, "Okay, I'll reframe it into a question." He paused, then, "Isn't it true that in situations such as you've described, you only have a few seconds to react?"

"Yes."

Maggie almost smiled. Joe was a good witness; he'd testified often. It was hard for witnesses to simply say yes or no to the kind of questions Joe was being asked. People always wanted to explain themselves. It took a lot of self-discipline and experience not to do so. She felt a warm pride in him.

She wanted him to win back his badge. Not just

because he was a client and he was telling the truth. But because he was Joe. Because he was a good, compassionate cop. Because he wanted it so much.

Whoa. It had been a long time since she'd wanted to please him. Getting emotional over her ex wasn't smart, and it sure wasn't good lawyering. With determination, Maggie pulled her notes toward her and read while she listened. Garrick was doing the questioning now.

Finally, the officers were done. Smithers asked her if she had any questions for Joe. She turned in her seat toward him. She asked him to detail his years on the force, especially the fact that he'd never fired his gun before.

"Not even in the hostage negotiation of 1990?" she asked. Back in 1990, a frustrated, suicidal man had taken his girlfriend and child hostage. It wasn't the kind of thing that happened very often in Plainfield. SWAT teams had been called in from neighboring Cleveland, but they hadn't been needed.

The guy had asked to speak to Joe, who had arrested him several months before the hostage incident. Joe had stayed on the telephone for four grueling hours, persuading the man to release the woman and child unharmed.

"I was able to talk the suspect into surrendering peacefully," Joe said.

She saw Smithers and Garrick exchange glances. "You won a medal for that, correct?" she asked quickly.

"Yes."

Okay, she thought. So far, so good. If the department wanted to make an example out of Joe, they were going to do it knowing full well that they were taking down a good officer. "Now, let's go back to the night of the shooting, and let's assume a few things." She paused, then went on. "You've told these detectives that you saw this Hook character pull a gun. Let's assume for the moment you're correct."

"I *am* correct." Joe's already straight spine seemed to stiffen slightly.

"Of course you are," she said, willing him to bear with her. "What do you think happened to the gun?"

Smithers studied his watch, and seeing him do so made Maggie grit her teeth.

As if he hadn't noticed Smithers's gesture, Joe said calmly, "I wasn't alone in the alley with Hook. Two other men who were wearing Nightshade colors were there. I assume, since Hook was also wearing gang colors and has since been identified as a member of the Nightshade gang, that these two others were his buddies. The gun wasn't found in the alley or anywhere between the site of the holdup and the alley. So I assume one of his buddies must have taken it. But, regardless of what happened to it later, there was a gun in Hook's hand when I shot him. And I saw it fly through the air after he was hit."

Smithers shook his head impatiently. "You don't recall seeing anyone actually *take* the gun, do you, Detective?"

Joe said, "No." Smithers shot Garrick another look, this one clearly tinged with impatience.

Maggie lost patience herself. "As you detectives have both emphasized, there was only a split second for Detective Latham to react." She turned back to Joe. "At the precise time that Hook pulled the gun on you, were you looking at either of the other members of the Nightshade in the alley?"

"No. I never took my eyes off Hook."

Maggie turned to Smithers and Garrick. "Detective Latham didn't have an opportunity to observe everything that was happening in that alley. He was too busy protecting himself and any innocent people who might be around. After all, he heard somebody scream just before the shooting, and he thinks it was a woman."

"Did she ever come forward?" Smithers asked.

Maggie shook her head. "Not yet."

"Well, we have a gun that doesn't seem to exist and a woman who doesn't seem to exist, either." Smithers made a quick note on his pad. "So let's get on with this proceeding."

Garrick threw his pen down on the desk. "This isn't going to be a witch hunt, damn it. Ms. Hannan, ask all the questions you want."

Maggie smiled and turned to Garrick. "I'm done with my client, but I have a few questions for both of you. First, when will this investigation conclude?"

Smithers said, "We have most of the facts now, and—"

Garrick interrupted, "When we've done a full investigation, which will include making every effort to track down any witnesses."

Maggie sensed some conflict between the two reviewing officers. She turned to Smithers. "Isn't it true," she asked sweetly, "that the governor's office has decided to make an example of Joe Latham and the situation in Plainfield?"

Smithers colored. "Of course not."

"Do you deny that you've talked to the governor's office about this?"

"This isn't about me. And the procedure permits you to ask questions only of your client. I'm not the one in trouble for discharging a weapon."

At that, Joe leaned forward. His voice went deadly quiet. "That's because it's been a long time since you've been on the street, hasn't it? Let's face it, you're a paper-pushing cop. You don't have a clue what it's like out there."

Smithers went beet red, and Maggie knew that the detectives who didn't pull street duty were sensitive about the fact. She wasn't sure that Joe should have gone after Smithers so directly, but she couldn't help admiring the courage and calmness with which he defended himself.

Red-faced, Smithers stood.

Joe stood.

From across the desk, they assessed each other. Quickly, Maggie stood also. On the whole, the interview hadn't gone badly. The thing to do was end it before Joe said any more. She reached out and pressed his hand to caution him into silence. His hand was hard and warm. He didn't move. She pressed again, digging a fingernail into his palm.

Slowly, he looked at her and nodded.

She motioned for the door. Garrick thanked them for coming, told them there would be a decision soon and held the door for them. As Maggie passed through, he said, "Ms. Hannan, no matter what, I promise you that this investigation will be conducted fairly."

Maggie looked into intelligent hazel eyes. "Thank you. So you think Detective Latham is telling the truth?"

Garrick looked Joe over, his eyes troubled. "I have to go on evidence. Just on evidence. So far, we have no evidence that there was a gun in that alley. And even good cops make mistakes. So…" His voice trailed off.

Joe shook his head and went out the door.

Maggie followed. Fourteen years as a good cop wasn't going to be enough. Her legal skills weren't going to keep Joe's badge, either. They needed evidence.

"I'M A COP, Maggie. What the hell am I going to do with the rest of my life if I don't have my badge?" An hour after the interview, Joe sat across from Maggie in a booth at a corner diner and posed the question.

Maggie pushed her coffee aside. ''What kind of talk is that?''

''You heard them in there. Smithers is after my ass to make some kind of political point, and even Garrick thinks I blew it.''

''And now you've decided it's over.''

''It is, isn't it?''

He looked across the table toward her. Though she knew how important it was for Joe to be a cop, the utter bleakness of his gaze momentarily shocked her. She was so used to him hiding his feelings. She had the strongest urge to soothe him, to pull him toward her and lean her head against his broad chest and make him promises about his career that she might not be able to keep.

But if she did that, if she got up from her side of the booth, and sat beside him and touched his chest, leaned her cheek against that starchy shirt, what would happen to the new life she had created for herself?

She was going to help Joe, but she was determined not to get involved emotionally.

''You did great in there,'' she said. ''You sounded confident and honest. I know Garrick wanted to believe you. He won't let Smithers walk all over you.''

''But Garrick is obviously a stickler for evidence, which we don't have,'' Joe pointed out with more spirit. ''I've been doing what I can to help myself.

I've been going down to the area talking to a few of the street people who hang out there at night. I've offered a few bucks on my own. But...nothing.''

They hadn't had any serious calls from anyone in the bar, either, despite Maggie's offer of a reward. But Maggie knew that if they were to find a witness, it would probably come from that area. The bar had been open that night. Someone must have seen something.

Of course, the Nightshade didn't rat on each other. And even non-gang members could be just fearful enough of the Nightshade to turn their backs on any reward money. And trying to track down the woman who screamed seemed an exercise in futility.

Maggie took a sip of her coffee, thinking. She couldn't sit around and wait for a witness to come forward; she had a case to prepare. She looked over at Joe. ''What I'm going to do now is develop a sort of fact sheet on you. Some character evidence, a package to present to Internal Affairs along with the testimonials of your reputation that I've gathered.'' She got out her legal pad and a felt-tipped pen.

Joe's hands tightened around his cup. ''Do you have any idea how hard it is to ask for stuff like those testimonials? To say my lawyer will be calling? To admit you need people to vouch for your character?''

She bit her lip. ''It has to be done, Joe.''

He nodded, drained his cup. ''Right. So what do you want to know from me?''

''Tell me about your condominium.'' Maggie knew

the place from the address he'd given her, and also knew he'd lived there since shortly after their divorce. The complex was trendy, upscale, and she was pretty sure no children were allowed. He'd certainly picked a pretty sterile place to live.

That's not your concern, she reminded herself. "I mean, tell me if you live there alone, and how you're spending your time. If you're…involved with anyone. A woman, I mean." She knew he hadn't remarried. She realized with sudden clarity that she didn't want to know about his "involvement" with other women. But she had no choice.

He leaned back and studied her. "I'm not seeing anyone right now. Over the years, I've dated a few women. But I've never considered remarrying."

She digested that information, thinking about how some men were meant for marriage, and some weren't. She blinked hard. Her eyes were suddenly stinging with remembered hurt.

She had a case to build, and if the man who'd been responsible for causing that hurt sat across from her, well, she'd decided to take his case and she owed him her best effort. So she listened as Joe recited his daily routine. When he got to the part about helping out at the gym with a crime prevention program, Maggie said, "Why didn't you tell me you were doing that before? That's important character evidence."

He shrugged.

"What kind of program is it?"

"Referrals from the juvenile court. Kids at Risk, they call it."

She was astonished. Joe working with kids? "How long have you been doing this?" She wasn't taking notes anymore. She certainly wouldn't have trouble remembering this information.

"Seven years," he said quietly.

Seven years. He'd been working with kids since they split up. A shiver skittered up her spine.

"It's no big deal," he said, his hand curling around his coffee mug.

"But you don't like kids," she said flatly, embarrassed that there was still a bitter edge to her voice.

There was a pause. "Not true," Joe finally said quietly.

"But you didn't want children." There was another pause. "You said you didn't want children."

"No. I didn't." He was staring at his mug as though the cup held the secrets of the universe. Suddenly, she noticed that his knuckles were white. Joe wasn't as cool about this conversation as his stance and voice indicated.

"But you didn't want children," she repeated. "At least, you didn't want them with me." Her throat got tight.

"Working with someone else's kid is a lot different than having your own," he said softly.

He sounded as though he was trying to convince her of that. Or maybe himself? "I know," she said.

He finally looked directly at her. "There's a kid at

the gym. Kenny Sheets. Somehow, I think he's different. He could have a chance if someone paid attention to him, helped him sort through his choices. I seem to be the one he's picked for that.''

She heard the conviction in his voice, and asked some questions about Kenny. Though he didn't come out and say so, she realized Joe cared about this kid. So he *had* changed.

Well, maybe he had changed in that he was now involved with kids. But he'd always helped others. She remembered when she first met him. He and another cop had kind of adopted an older couple, taking them groceries and checking on them. He hadn't wanted to talk about it. That was the way he was.

Suddenly, she flashed back to an incident in their marriage. They'd just made love and were lying side by side. Joe was quiet; he always was after they'd made love, but the silence felt full of meaning. She'd reached out, touched his hand, traced his knuckles with a fingertip.

Somehow, they'd got to talking. Joe had started to tell her things about his childhood.

She'd lain there, hardly daring to breathe for fear he'd stop talking, stop telling her things. He'd said something about how rough his father had been. How he'd insisted Joe be a man, take it like a man, put up with a good cuffing across the mouth from his old man. And not talk about whether it hurt.

She'd stiffened in horror, but Joe hadn't seemed to notice. Instead, he'd taken her hand, gripped it so hard her palm ached. He'd finally whispered, "Once, when I was sixteen, my father slugged me right in the face. I was so upset, I gave him a push. Just to get him away from me, you know? But he fell backward, over a chair, hit a table and landed on his butt."

He'd paused. "I just stood there, shocked at what I'd done. He was my father. There was a cut on the side of his head, and he was bleeding. I started to say something, some kind of sorry, because I was sorry and scared as hell. He sat there and wiped blood off his head with his knuckle, and he said, 'Shut up, don't say you're sorry.' And then he got this grin on his face...." Joe had paused, and a heartbeat later had added even more softly, "He said, 'Don't apologize for being a man.'"

Her own existence, precarious as it had been, had never involved this kind of abuse. When she was a kid, she'd fantasized about real parents, the ones who loved you unconditionally, gave you hugs and bandaged your hurts. The reality for Joe had been so different.

She'd said something sympathetic. Abruptly, Joe had disengaged her hand, mumbled something about her being a romantic. Then he'd got up from the bed and headed for the bathroom. She'd lain there, hurt and confused, wondering what had happened to their closeness.

Over the years she'd learned that every time they talked about something emotional, Joe would withdraw. While she'd had an almost compulsive need to talk, to share the pain of her own childhood, Joe preferred to keep his pain to himself.

One more memory. He'd come home exhausted. She'd said, "You work too hard. Don't keep volunteering for the hard assignments. Coast awhile, at least until my bar exam is over." He'd said, "I can't afford to coast. I've got some wrongs to right as a cop."

She'd been too naive to know exactly what that meant. She did know that his determination to prove himself as a cop had something to do with his father's career on the police force. But she resented the fact that he'd volunteered for a dangerous undercover assignment while she was pregnant. When she'd miscarried, there had been no way to reach him quickly, and she'd gone to the hospital alone. Even when he'd finally come with two dozen pink roses, he hadn't been able to talk about what had happened to their baby.

Looking back on it, Maggie knew that the day of her miscarriage had been the real end of their marriage. After that, Joe had talked to her less. He hadn't bought her any more silly presents. He kept volunteering for dangerous assignments. Then, one night, he'd said he didn't want her to become pregnant again.

And he'd refused to talk about it.

Well, he was talking now, at least about his volunteer work. She forced her mind back to the task at hand. When she was done compiling her case, Internal Affairs would know every good deed he'd ever done.

"Kenny Sheets has become more than a project for you." She said it as a statement.

"Yes." He told her about taking Kenny out to eat, and about the time he'd bought a couple of tickets to one of the Cleveland Indians baseball games.

"Tell me what else you do with your free time," she said.

He talked about golf, the police softball league, running on the track at the gym. She took notes. Everything he was saying was important. She wanted to show that he was a normal guy with normal interests.

Joe talked about a movie he'd seen recently, some books he'd read, and Maggie thought how much their tastes were the same. Well, their tastes hadn't been the problem.

When he paused, she flipped the top pages of her legal pad back down. "That's enough," she said decisively. "I need to get back. I have a client coming in this afternoon." She stood.

Joe rose with her. He was tall, and she had to look up into his eyes. "I'm going to do my best," she said sincerely.

His eyes were very blue and very intense. They guarded secrets. She had to remember that. Her eyes traced his mouth. So hard, but it would soften just before he kissed her. As they moved away from the booth, they came within inches of each other.

His sheer…bigness overwhelmed her for a moment. She longed to move even closer to him.

Don't even think about it, she told herself. *You're engaged to be married.*

She already had what she wanted. She had Lewis and Tessa. In fact, Tessa was staying with her for a few days while Lewis was in Italy. These days Tessa often stayed with Maggie. She seemed more comfortable there than with her aunt.

Maggie and Lewis had a lot of plans. Simple plans, important plans that involved one child already and would—if things went according to plan—include others. There was no reason in the world for her to let a little physical attraction to her ex-husband get in the way of the life she'd chosen so carefully.

CHAPTER FIVE

TWO DAYS LATER, Joe put down the newspaper with a snap and walked over to the sliding doors that overlooked the pool and tennis courts at his condo. The blinds were drawn back. Though the days were getting shorter, it was still light at seven o'clock in the evening. There were people down on the tennis courts.

Now he shifted restlessly, and told himself to forget the editorial he'd just finished reading…for the third time. But he couldn't. He could remember nearly every word. The headline was burned in his brain, two simple words on the editorial page of the *Plainfield Gazette*: Bad Cop?

The damn article went on to speculate about what everybody else was speculating, and didn't even mention the good things he'd done or the medal he'd won a few years ago.

He thought about going down and whacking a few tennis balls into the boards to get rid of some tension, but he didn't want to face his neighbors. They would have read the papers.

He didn't feel like hanging out with his friends on the force; the shoptalk would just remind him of all he was missing. And he wasn't up to listening to sympathetic comments about his suspension even over a couple of beers.

Mentally, he ran through his other options. The Kids at Risk office had closed two hours ago, and he figured there'd be no way to catch up with Kenny now.

Once, he would have gone down to the station, even if his shift had ended. There was always paperwork to do. There were always suspects to trace. It was amazing how much free time you had when you weren't allowed to go to the office.

He let out a long breath. He thought he'd been so careful to make a life for himself after Maggie, and look at him now, standing at the window, nowhere to go, feeling sorry for himself.

Disgusted, he closed the blinds and changed into a pair of jogging shorts and a sweatshirt. As he headed out the door, though, his stomach rumbled. It was past dinnertime.

He wondered if Maggie was home, if she'd eaten dinner yet.

Over on his credenza, there was a stack of papers he'd picked up from the personnel department, detailing his employment history. Maggie had asked him to get them as soon as possible. He'd planned to drop off the papers at her office tomorrow, but he could take them to her house tonight.

Maybe he could buy her dinner. Despite their history, she was trying so hard to save his badge. Maggie loved Chinese food.

Just dinner, he warned himself as he grabbed the stack of papers on the credenza and headed out into the hallway of his building.

He made a stop for Chinese, and then he was at the front door of Maggie's yellow bungalow. The bright red roses that still bloomed on the porch posts made the air smell good.

Maggie came to the door. Her hair was down, the first time he'd seen it that way in seven years, and it gave him a jolt of pure sexual attraction to see the dark silky waterfall over her shoulders. He quelled the sensation. *Just dinner, buddy. You owe her a thank-you dinner because she's your lawyer.*

Maggie wore jeans, and her long-sleeved T-shirt was bright red. The color highlighted the drama of her features. A pair of gold hoops made her face exotic, Gypsy-like, and the toenails of her bare feet were painted red, too. He suddenly remembered her saying *I'm more of a red woman now.*

And how. Maggie sure didn't look like his lawyer tonight.

But it was too late to beat a retreat. "Hi," he said, holding up the brown paper bag. "Have you eaten?"

"Joe—"

"I brought Chinese. Chicken chop suey and beef chow mien. And I've got those personnel records you wanted. You said you needed them as soon as I could get them." He kept his eyes on her face, not on those little red-tipped toes.

"Maggie? Who's here?"

Startled, Joe looked over Maggie's shoulder. A teenage girl was standing behind Maggie. He remembered her. Tessa. Lewis's daughter. Oh, hell, why hadn't he thought about Lewis being here?

Maggie said, "Tessa's staying with me for a few days. Her father is out of town."

Maggie turned her head slightly and said, "Tessa, you remember Joe Latham? He's my client."

Tessa stood a little behind Maggie. "Hello, Mr. Latham."

Maybe it was the cool tone or "Mr. Latham" that did it, but Joe knew he had no business being here. He'd wanted to see Maggie, and the dinner and the papers were just lame excuses for stopping by. He said, "I brought you dinner, but I didn't realize you had company. Why don't I leave this for you both?" He held up the bag again.

Maggie opened the door a little wider. "Have you eaten?"

"That's okay," he said, avoiding the question, intent on leaving.

Maggie took the bag. She bit her lip. "This feels heavy. I think there's enough for three. Why don't you come on in?"

Joe hesitated. He really didn't want to eat alone tonight. Besides, Maggie's fiancé's daughter was here, so there was no way he could do anything that might complicate Maggie's life.

Like kiss her.

In the living room, he stopped for a second and looked around. The walls were a bright peach color and the furniture looked old and gleamed with polish. There were little silver picture frames and vases, and one had a big bouquet of roses in it, the same red roses that scented her front porch. Here in the warmer air, the scent was stronger.

Maggie held the bag of Chinese food and took the manila folder Joe handed to her. "We were going to get in a pizza for dinner," Tessa said. "Maggie brought home a tape from the video store. *The Philadelphia Story*. We were going to watch it together." Joe didn't think he was imagining the touch of resentment in her tone.

He knew the film; he remembered that Maggie had liked it a lot. But *The Philadelphia Story* seemed an odd choice of movie for a teenager.

He liked movies, even the old stuff. Both he and Maggie had, but he liked action pictures, westerns in particular. He said something to Tessa about seeing a lot of movies.

The girl brightened. "A lot of people think these old movies are overacted, but that's not true." She plunked herself down on the floor, sitting cross-legged.

"You've seen it?"

"Oh, sure. I've seen every Katharine Hepburn

movie there is. Even the ones where she's old. You know, like *The Lion in Winter*."

Maggie came back down the hallway with plates and silverware. "Tessa has seen them all, and I mean all." She gazed with obvious affection at the teenager.

She set the place settings on the coffee table. Joe unpacked and dished up the food. Tessa went on and on about the movie they were about to watch. Joe had a hard time paying attention to the kid's chatter. He was too busy watching Maggie. All three of them were sitting on the floor.

Tessa struggled with her chopsticks. "I'll never get the hang of this," she said. Joe watched as she tried to keep her chopsticks together long enough to pick up a water chestnut. Instead, the tips skidded on the plate.

Maggie smiled at the girl. "The trick is to use three fingers for support," she explained.

Tessa nodded and tried again. This time she succeeded. Maggie applauded. Her eyes were twinkling. They were dark and shiny and happy.

Happy in a way he'd never made her. He quickly looked away, and caught a glimpse of her bare toes again. Focusing on his food, he quickly took a bite. With a fork.

"I think it's important to know how to behave in other cultures," Tessa said absently as she stared down in wonder at a morsel of food that was actually caught between the ends of her chopsticks.

After dinner, they settled down to watch the movie. Tessa remained seated on the floor, her back to the sofa. Maggie had chosen the old oak rocker and Joe sat on the sofa that faced the television. The movie was engaging. They all laughed at the banter. If Tessa had resented Joe's presence, she seemed to be over it now.

It had been a rotten day, but Joe felt finally comfortable here in this small yellow bungalow. When the credits rolled, Joe said to Tessa, "So you think you know all the Hepburn stuff, huh? What about *Woman of the Year?* What year did that come out?"

"Nineteen forty-two," she said promptly.

That sounded about right, and Tessa had said it with conviction. "Ah-ha. But do you know your westerns?"

"Try me."

"*High Noon.* Name the actors and tell me the plot."

"Grace Kelly and Gary Cooper. One man against a gang of outlaws, and he only has a few hours to beat them. It was a pretty good movie with a bit of symbolism."

"Symbolism. Okay." He raised his eyebrows at Maggie.

Tessa said, "You want westerns? Who starred as Wyatt Earp in the 1950s in *Gunfight at the O.K. Corral?*"

Joe thought for a moment. "Gregory Peck? No, wait. Burt Lancaster."

"Well, you almost missed. Let me think of another."

Maggie listened to the two of them try to stump each other, waving her hand in protest when Tessa tried to lure her into the game. Instead, she watched Joe.

Movie trivia was a game they'd played often in the early years of their marriage. Joe's memory was good and his eye for detail was great; after all, he was trained as a cop. In desperation, she'd once gone to the library and surreptitiously checked out a book on old movies. She'd beaten him soundly after a week's study.

He'd "rewarded" her that night by carrying her to bed and making love to her. He'd grinned and commanded her to just lie there. She'd kept her own hands to her sides as he touched and kissed every inch of her. She could vividly recall how he'd used his tongue, first to wash her skin, then to flick over it until she'd moaned.

Her body went hot. Why had he decided to play movie trivia tonight?

She eyed Joe; he didn't seem to be paying much attention to her, so surely he didn't remember that night.

She took a deep breath and thought for a moment. "What Hitchcock film featured Laurence Olivier in the male lead?"

Joe and Tessa answered as one. *"Rebecca."*

"Okay, maybe that was too easy." She asked another question and both Tessa and Joe got it right away. They asked her a more difficult question, and she got it on the second try. Joe tossed her a fortune cookie as a reward. She broke it open and took out the little strip of paper.

She read aloud. "You have much to learn." Tessa giggled. "Never mind this lousy fortune," Maggie said, her competitive spirit kicking into overdrive. "Here's one for you, Joe. What movie about a playboy who becomes a surgeon starred Rock Hudson and Jane Wyman?" Joe wouldn't be able to get this one. It wasn't his kind of movie.

Joe thought hard. Tessa had gone silent, watching him closely. Finally he said, *"The Magnificent Obsession."*

"Wow," Tessa said, giving him a thumbs-up signal. "That was a hard one. You're really great at this." She looked at him, clearly surprised and just as clearly impressed.

Joe chuckled and Maggie smiled at Tessa's open admiration.

Then Tessa said, "How'd you know that, anyway?"

There was a small pause, just one beat. "Maggie and I saw it together," Joe said quietly.

Maggie looked at Joe. Joe looked at Maggie.

"Oh." Tessa frowned.

The telephone rang. All three of them started. "I'll get it," Maggie said. She made a quick dash into the kitchen and pulled the receiver off the wall unit.

"Hello, Maggie."

It was Lewis. As she recognized his voice, nausea rushed through her, strong enough to cause her body to go weak. Her fiancé was on the phone. The man she loved. The man she hadn't thought about for hours as she'd played trivia games with her ex-husband.

And enjoyed the experience.

From somewhere, she found her voice. "Lewis. How are you?"

"Fair to middling. You know Italian food doesn't agree with me, but this northern Italian is a little milder. I found a hotel that deals with Americans regularly, and a concierge who recommended I try a nice little restaurant that has a way with beef. Actually, my workday yesterday didn't go too well, because of all the labor trouble over here. There're so many layers of bureaucracy, you don't even know who you're negotiating with—"

"Joe's here," Maggie blurted out. Another wave of guilt washed over her, and she had a childish but profound need to confess all. To blurt out how much fun she'd had. Lord, to blurt out that she had been thinking about how Joe used to make love to her.

There was a long pause. Finally, Lewis said in very measured tones, "Joe Latham was over?"

"He's here now," Maggie said quickly.

"Oh." There was another pause. Then, "Tessa's still staying with you, isn't she?"

"Of course. She's here, too," Maggie said quickly. "We watched a movie."

"Listen, I trust you," he said right away, and perversely, his words made Maggie feel worse than ever. "If you had something to talk over on the case, well, then of course it's fine for him to come over."

"He did bring me some paperwork on the case. He brought dinner—Chinese takeout." She still had that absurd urge to tell all.

There was another pause, and then Lewis said in a hearty tone, "Fine. So how's my daughter?"

They talked about Tessa for a while, and then Maggie asked him again about his day. She tried to relax, but she couldn't. Joe and Tessa had turned on the television to some comedy. Once in a while she could hear the low rumble of his voice. When Lewis asked to speak to Tessa, Maggie went in to get the girl.

Tessa went past her to the phone. Joe got slowly to his feet.

"So that was your fiancé calling," he said. It wasn't a question.

She nodded and stood in the doorway, listening to Tessa's chatter, realizing that if Joe had been listening closely, he could have heard every word she'd exchanged with Lewis. That felt disloyal. "I told him you were here," she said defensively.

"I think that was a good idea."

"Yes. Honesty is always a good idea. Lewis and I talk things over all the time, and I wouldn't want him to get a false impression." She bit her lip; she hadn't meant to use that lecturing tone. "Well, it's getting late—"

"I should be going," he said at exactly the same time. He fished in his pockets for his keys, jingled them a moment in his palm. "Look—never mind. Thanks for a fun time. Tessa is a nice kid."

That made her smile a little. "On her good days she is." She went toward the door and held it open for him.

He was just about to go through it when he turned, hesitated, then spoke. "Listen, I just want to say something, okay?"

The little foyer was dim, lit only by the light coming from the lamps in the living room. She looked up into his eyes. They were dark, the area around them in shadow. The light all coming from one direction threw his features into stark relief, highlighting his ruggedness, and also the tense lines around his perfectly shaped mouth.

He cleared his throat. "I'm not going to screw this up for you."

She didn't pretend not to understand. "*I'm* not going to screw this up."

"I can tell you'll be a good mother to Tessa. I know you've always wanted a kid. And Tessa loves you a lot. I only hope she's not the only reason you're marrying the guy. You deserve so much more."

Maggie felt her temper rising. "I'm marrying Lewis because I love him," she said. "Anyway, how would you know what I want? You don't even know Lewis.''

He cleared his throat. "Okay, I overstepped the boundaries. What I'm trying to say is, I'm not going to cause trouble. I only wish the best for you.''

"Thank you," she said stiffly. "Everything's fine. Thanks for dinner.''

He nodded and went through the door. She didn't say goodbye.

How dare Joe question what she and Lewis had? She loved both her fiancé and his daughter. Besides, there was nothing wrong with wanting to be Tessa's mother.

KENNY'S MOTHER SAT before the mirror and struggled to pile her hair high on her head. She fumbled with the handles of the hair clip, trying to get its jaws to open. Kenny stood in the doorway and watched. She did it slowly, staring in the mirror and concentrating. She got the clip open and tried again, both arms quivering above her head, a bright red lip held between her teeth. The clip clattered to the floor.

"Shit!''

"Mom—''

"Shit, shit and double shit.'' She bent to pick it up, but she had to hold on to the edge of the table.

She was drunk.

Kenny had known that as soon as he'd come home from the gym. He hadn't said anything then; he didn't say anything now. Her drinking was something they never talked about.

So he said instead, "You don't have to go out."

She started to cry, big blubbery tears, the clip held in a limp hand.

"Don't cry," he said, feeling desperate.

"Don't end up like me," she said. "Promise me you won't end up like me." She stood, grabbed the edge of the table and faced him. "Promise me." Her voice rose. "Promise me!"

"All *right*."

She looked mollified for the moment. Then she reached for him. Her hand shook. "I love you, you know."

"I love you back."

"Don't get in trouble."

He tried to laugh. "Mom, I haven't been in trouble for months. I go to school. I go to the Kids at Risk like almost every day."

She scrubbed at her lips with a tissue, then just held it. "That's what I'm talking about. Don't get in trouble with the cops. Don't hang around the cops." Her voice had gone low, a little less slurry. Her eyes were wide. "I want you to stay away from Joe. Promise me."

"What's wrong with Joe?" Even though he knew not to ask because her mind didn't work right when she'd been drinking, he couldn't hold back the question.

"He's trouble."

"He's not trouble. He's a cop, Mom."

"I know that!" She took a couple of steps toward him and grabbed his arm. Her nails hurt as they dug into his skin. He tried to get loose, but she gripped harder.

"Got to tell you. Got to…keep you safe." Her grip never lessened. "I'm so scared," she whispered. "They'll kill you, or they'll kill me and then you'll have to go with social services."

He could hear the fear in her voice. Not the drunk kind of fear. This was the real thing, and she was scaring him, too. "What's wrong, Mom? Tell me what's going on," he begged. "Come on, Mom." He shook his arm, so that her own arm shook. "If you want me to be safe, you've got to tell me."

"You've got to promise not to tell."

"Okay."

"Swear to God promise."

God? Kenny could have laughed, but he didn't. "Swear to God promise."

She let go of him abruptly, sat down hard on the bed and began to cry. He sat beside her.

She finally whispered, "I know what happened, see? That cop, I know what happened. I saw it all. I saw him shoot that guy." She took a deep breath. "I saw your cop shoot that guy."

His cop? "Joe?" he asked, stunned. "You saw Joe the night he killed that man?"

"Yeah."

"Did that guy have a gun?" He knew the story

from the newspaper he'd filched from the desk of one of the cops who ran the Kids at Risk. The paper had had an article and picture of Joe on the front page. He knew the whole trouble for Joe was that he'd said the guy had a gun but the cops hadn't found the piece on the dead guy.

There was a little silence. Finally, she said, "Yeah. I saw the gun."

Kenny just sat there. His *mom* had seen the shooting? *His mom had seen the gun?* "Are you sure?" he whispered. Jeez, even drunk she wouldn't make this up, would she?

She was so stiff and scared, and suddenly, he knew she wasn't making it up. "Tell me what you saw."

She talked slow; it was hard not to tell her to hurry up. "Well," she began, "I was outside this bar, that one on the corner. I wasn't drinking," she added defensively.

Right, Kenny thought.

"I was just standing there."

Waiting for some horny guy to show up, he thought.

"I was standing there, and a guy came running between the buildings. He was a Nightshade." She shuddered.

"Then a guy came running after him, yelling that he was a cop and the guy should stop. Then I looked down at the end of the alley and there they were. All Nightshade…and I knew…they were going to kill that cop and if they saw me they were going to…kill me, too, and I screamed…I couldn't help it…and then I tried to hide but there weren't too many places to hide but I stood behind this sort of opening between the buildings and I saw it…'' She began to cry in earnest.

Kenny took her hand. Jeez, she'd seen all this and kept it secret for two weeks. He couldn't believe it. "What exactly did you see, Mom? Tell me exactly, okay?''

She rubbed the back of his hand. "You're a good kid. I rely on you now, since your brother's gone. I love you.''

"I love you, too. What did you see?''

"The cop—that Joe—he was talking to them, quiet like. The one that ran into the alley pulled out a gun real fast. Joe shot him. And the gun went up high.'' She paused. "I didn't know it was Joe, just that it was a cop. Then in a car a few days later, when some guy was kiss—when I was in a car, I saw a newspaper on the seat and I saw his picture and it said Joe Latham and I knew that was the name of your Joe and I got so scared….''

"Where's the gun?'' He shook her arm a little. "Tell me what happened to the gun.''

She worried her lip. "I don't know where it went. I never saw that part.''

"But you saw the gun in that guy's hand, the one who got shot.''

"Yeah, I saw it all right.'' She shuddered again. "I saw him pull it out and aim it right at your Joe.''

"You've got to tell that to the cops," he said.

"No! We'll get killed for saying that. The Night-shade…they're bad." She started to blubber again.

Kenny knew that the members of the gang hated cops. But…he forced himself to think. His mom had only seen a gun on the dead guy. He was dead. Telling what she'd seen wasn't like ratting on a *live* member of the Nightshade—that would get you killed for sure. But this…? He didn't know. You never knew what would piss them off.

The thing to do was tell Joe and let him handle it. "Joe will take care of you," he said to his mom.

"No!" Then, more softly, "No." She raised a hand and smoothed it over his cheek. "You promised. I know I…I know I make you be a man too much, give you too much resp…"

She struggled with the word, and he said, "Responsibility," for her.

"I know I give you too much of that. But I'm the mother. You promised. You *promised*."

He didn't know what to do. Joe was going to lose his badge if his mother didn't tell. And he was worried about her, too. What if the Nightshade did come after her? She was too messed up to watch out for herself. Kenny had to go to school and to the Kids at Risk if he wanted to stay out of juvenile hall. He couldn't watch her all the time, and she wouldn't let him anyway.

He'd promised.

He swallowed hard. He couldn't tell. He'd just

have to let Joe go down. At the thought, his gut churned. He wished— Oh jeez, it didn't matter what he wished. It *never* mattered.

He got his mom to lie down, then he convinced her to take off her shoes and stay home for a while. That was about all it took. Pretty soon she was asleep, and Kenny finally relaxed and shut off the light and got in bed himself. The clock said 2:00 a.m.

He couldn't sleep.

His mom had seen Joe.

She'd made him promise not to tell. Well, that didn't mean anything, did it? After all, *she* never kept her promises to *him.*

Swear to God promise.

He couldn't tell.

He thought of Joe slapping him on the back. He thought of how Joe always came just in time to prevent the bigger kids from picking on him. Kenny could fight good, but if he fought, he'd be in trouble. So Joe kind of kept him out of trouble.

If he lost his badge for good, would Joe still come to the Kids at Risk? The funny thing was, Kenny kind of thought he would. And that thought made him feel worse for not telling what he knew.

At three o'clock, he finally got up and turned on a light, just enough to see as he rummaged in his bottom drawer. Yeah, there it was, the article he'd cut out of the paper. He read down it, looking for that lady lawyer's name, the one that was working for Joe. When he found it, his heart started to pound real hard.

CHAPTER SIX

MAGGIE WAS LATE for work the next morning. After Joe left last night, she'd taken the telephone from Tessa and talked more to Lewis. She'd encouraged him to tell her about his labor trouble in some detail, then asked him about the chemical formula for the newest alloy, the one that was giving him so much trouble. She could hear in his voice that he was pleased that she was interested in his work, but there was strain, at least on her part. Then just before they'd hung up, Lewis had said, "I love you."

She'd said, "I love you" back, but somehow that hadn't seemed like enough. So she'd added, "I miss you." As she replaced the receiver, she suddenly realized that she'd lied. She didn't miss him desperately when he was gone.

But that was all right, wasn't it? she wondered now. Didn't that signify that theirs was an adult relationship, based on respect and kindness?

Well, it might be all right not to miss her fiancé desperately, but it wasn't all right to have been lying in bed imagining another man touching her, kissing her. At that moment, she'd resolved to have as little contact with Joe as possible.

She sat at her desk, downing several mugs of coffee and checking out the citations that Tessa had pulled off the computer. Maggie had a brief due in a few days. She had just begun to concentrate, when Angela tapped on the open door frame.

Maggie looked up, pleased to see it was Angela. Her partner's cheerfulness was just what Maggie needed this morning.

"This is for you," Angela said, handing Maggie an envelope. "Mrs. Hannan" was printed on the front. Maggie frowned, looking for a postmark or stamp.

"It didn't come through the mail," she explained. "It was lying on the floor of the office when I got here at eight." She chuckled. "It must've been shoved under the door, like a love note. Except, of course, your intended's gone away and he isn't the type for love notes anyway." She grinned. "And he'd call you Mrs. Sawyer if he was going to do the 'missus' thing. Hey, maybe you've got a secret admirer."

Just like that, Maggie's mind conjured Joe. Impatient with herself, she pulled a letter opener out of her pencil holder and slit the envelope carefully. Angela said, "How come I never get mysterious love letters shoved under the door?"

"It doesn't happen to me all that often," Maggie said dryly, unfolding the paper. She read and her heart skipped a beat.

Their is a witnes to the crime. The lady who is around the bar.

"Hey," Angela said softly, her hand out for the note. "What's the matter? You look white."

Without comment, Maggie held out the note to Angela. Her friend read and took in a sharp breath. "Joe Latham's case."

Maggie nodded. "It's got to be." Swiftly, she considered the possibilities. "None of my other cases have anything to do with a bar."

She paused, then tapped her knuckles on the desktop. "I knew there was something going on down there! I had a feeling somebody saw something, knew something. But not a soul's tried to collect my reward. Oh, God, Angela, I'm a lawyer, not some amateur sleuth. This is so…cryptic. Can you make any sense of it?"

"No, but maybe we shouldn't have handled it so much. The police could have checked it for prints or something." Angela handed the note back to Maggie, who was careful to hold only the edge as she laid the paper out flat on her desk. They studied it. The paper was white and lined, with one rough edge, as though it had been torn from a spiral notebook. The pen was blue ink, and whoever had printed it had pressed down hard.

"Do you recognize the handwriting?" Angela asked, her blond head bent as she traced the words with her finger.

"No." Maggie picked up the plain envelope by the edge and put it down when it yielded no information.

"Whoever it is thinks I'm married, so it isn't some-one who knows me very well."

"No, but you wouldn't expect a witness to know you, would you?"

Maggie shook her head. "And then there are the spelling and grammar mistakes."

"Which could be anyone. This is a street crime, Maggie, not a white-collar one. Most of those guys on the street can hardly read, much less write."

"Or women. It could be from a woman. 'The lady who is around the bar.' Maybe it's the woman who Joe heard scream right before the shooting."

She paused. "I'm going down to that corner," Maggie said decisively. "The bar won't be open, but maybe I can spot this 'lady.'"

"I'd come with you, but I've got court again. It seems any time you need me these days, I'm in court."

"Making us some money," Maggie noted with a smile. Her eyes met her friend's. "That's okay. You're with me when you can be. I'll just have to go myself. Or I could—"

"Call Joe," Angela finished for her.

"Yes," Maggie said shortly.

There was a little pause. Finally, Angela said, "You were glad he was with you when you went down there before."

Maggie nodded. If she'd decided last night that she'd have as little contact with Joe as possible, well, this morning's note had changed that. "I have to go over the note with Joe anyway. He's the client. Besides, he might recognize the handwriting."

She picked up the phone receiver. "I'll call him and have him meet me in front of the alley."

She'd thrown her blazer over one arm and was already at the door, the note and envelope in her hand, when Angela called her back. "Maggie."

She turned. Angela paused, then said, "Are you all right?"

"Of course."

"I just thought…" She paused again, which was unlike her. Angela usually said what she thought, and there were no constraints between her and Maggie. Finally, Angela said slowly, "You look pale and tired. I know Joe is your ex. Just now when you said you'd call him, you looked… Oh, I don't know. You aren't having…thoughts about him, are you?"

"He's a case," Maggie said, feeling the heat in her cheeks.

Angela eyed her, and Maggie was sure her friend could see how pink she must be. "Yeah, but he's one sexy guy, and I know how much you loved him once upon a time."

Angela fiddled with the cuff of her own blazer. "Stuff happens between ex's. You know that."

"Angela," Maggie said quickly. "Nothing's happened. No way." The warmth of her cheeks spread until her whole face felt hot.

"But it does happen. You know as well as I do from doing domestic-relations work that people sometimes get lonely after they split up. A lot of couples sleep together after their divorces.''

''I'm not lonely,'' Maggie said. ''I have a full life. I know how fortunate I am.'' She raised troubled eyes to her friend's gaze, and added, ''I know what I'm doing.''

''I hope so. In every way.'' Angela sighed. ''Well, if I don't go, I'm going to be late. That jerk of a prosecutor, Brett Langer, will be late for sure. I hate waiting for him, but it makes points with the judge if I'm not the one holding things up.'' She headed for the door, and as she passed Maggie on her way out, added briskly, ''You'll do the right thing, Maggie. Whatever that is.''

After Angela left, Maggie paused to put on her blazer. Angela had been the first to congratulate her on her engagement to Lewis, and her words stayed with Maggie.

You'll do the right thing. Whatever that is.

SHE'D INSISTED on meeting Joe in front of the alley instead of having him come to the office and drive them both. When she got there, she waited in her car until she saw his Jeep pull up. They both got out of their cars.

He didn't look as though he'd had a great night, either. He wore a navy sweatshirt and a pair of tight, faded jeans. He wasn't wearing socks with his running shoes. His hair fell over his forehead as if it had been styled with impatient fingers; he needed a shave.

The cool, early-morning sun made his golden stubble of beard glisten.

She was careful not to look at him too much as she gave him the note. She apologized for touching it so much. "I never thought about it being used as evidence."

"It probably wouldn't have made any difference. We seldom get good prints off something like this." Nevertheless he held the note carefully as he studied it. Finally, he shook his head. "There's a witness, a woman apparently, but I've got no clue who sent the note."

Maggie looked around. The corner of Goshen and Pierce looked the same as it had the first time she'd been here. It was early and there was nobody around.

She looked more closely at the upper stories of the buildings. The apartments might be occupied, but all the windows facing the street were covered with plywood. If someone had seen anything, they would have had to have been standing on the street or in the bar, looking out the window from there. The note had said "The lady who is around the bar."

But if the witness was hanging around the bar, she wasn't doing it at ten o'clock in the morning. At least not this morning.

She and Joe walked toward the alley. It was litter-strewn, similar to police photos of the scene that Joe had shown her. The end toward the Dumpster looked dark and dingy even by daylight. She walked toward the large receptacle, conscious of a silent Joe beside her. She scanned the brick walls, the Dumpster itself, looking for…she didn't know what.

She got to the end of the alley. It smelled here, a sour-sweet scent of garbage, of warm air that didn't circulate. No breeze stirred the rubbish. Broken pop and beer bottles, a few beer cans. Crushed fast-food cartons and greasy pizza boxes, empty cigarette packages, a used syringe over by the curb. A dead rat; she shuddered.

It was in this spot, this place that spoke of hopelessness and hate and crime, that Joe had pulled the trigger of his gun, a shot that was probably going to end his career.

She felt a pinch of disappointment and frustration. What had she expected? That she'd walk into the alley and find "the lady around the bar," just waiting, like some angel of salvation?

They had their first real clue, but Maggie was damned if she knew how to track down her witness. She'd taken the damn twenty thousand dollars and she couldn't do a damn thing to help him.

Beside her, he said, "Let's go home."

"I'm not done here," she said stubbornly.

"This alley is just as I remembered," he said. "Just like it was the first time we came here and you offered that reward. Unless we can get somebody in that bar to talk, we don't have anything. We'll have to come back when the bar is open."

"We don't have time to mess around," she said sharply.

He touched her, then took her arm and gave it a quick tug. "Hey," he said quietly. "Are you okay?"

Suddenly, she wasn't okay at all. "It's this place," she tried to explain, but she didn't really know how to explain the sense of hopelessness she felt. The sense that everything was getting away from her. The sense that in the last two weeks, her safe, quiet life had been turned upside down. She looked up into Joe's eyes. They were bleak, too, and she suddenly couldn't stand it.

"How hard did the police look for the gun?" she asked.

"Hard. They searched for hours."

She shook off his arm and turned abruptly, heading toward the Dumpster. "You didn't see anybody take it, so maybe it's still here." She struggled to open the lid.

From behind her, he said, "Maggie, you're going to wreck your suit."

She got the Dumpster open, and he said more firmly, "The cops went through the contents that night, and it's been emptied by the garbage company several times since."

"Oh sure, they do a lot of garbage pickup in this place." But she let the lid fall back and started pacing. Her good high heels hit some paper and sent it flying. "He had a gun, and nobody found it, so it's got to be here."

Something just…snapped in her then, and hopelessness and determination became one emotion. She gritted her teeth so tightly they ached, and she kept pacing, a little more methodically, letting her feet kick up the trash. She grabbed a small box, looked in it briefly, tossed it aside, picked up another one.

"Maggie, stop it."

She ignored him, and when she heard him behind her, she picked up her pace. She grabbed an old blanket and threw it aside, not pausing to think what might come scurrying out. A trickle of perspiration ran down her side. "How can you do this kind of work, Joe? For God's sake, how can you stand it? How...can...you...stand...it?" Another kick.

He grabbed her arm and swung her around. "Maggie, come on, quit that!"

"Oh, sure. Just stop looking, just wait until they take your badge permanently, that badge that always meant more to you than I did." To her horror, she felt tears gathering in her eyes. "All those years as a good cop, and you'll just stand back and let this place be the end of your career."

He grabbed her shoulders and shook her a little. "That's not what we're doing. I can't stand to see you searching through all this crap, so stop for a minute, okay?"

Maggie made an attempt for control.

"That's better," Joe said. He looked into her eyes, his own expression grim. "I should have known better than to involve you in this."

"Well, you *did* involve me."

For a second, they just stared at each other. In a

gritty voice, Joe said, "I wouldn't have if I'd thought it would hurt you. I swear, I never would have come to see you if—" He cut himself off.

She let out a tight little sigh. "I don't want you to lose your badge forever. I know how much it meant to you. And you're a good cop. The best. The people out here—" she gave a tiny gesture to indicate the alley "—they need you. At times it hurt that you thought more about them than you did me, but I was always proud of you." A tear threatened to spill over, and she started to blink it away.

His hand came up, and a rough fingertip touched the corner of her eye. He pulled his hand back and stared at the wetness on his fingers. "I can't stand hurting you." More softly, he said, "I never could."

His mouth looked soft, vulnerable, as he stared down at his hand.

"Then why did you?" Maggie asked quietly, unable to help the question. She'd vowed seven years ago not to ask it again, but here she was, doing exactly that. "I thought you loved me. But you didn't even care when I lost our baby."

His hand abruptly fisted. "I cared."

Had he? Had she been mistaken all these years? Had he grieved as much as she had? There was something about his stillness, the almost painful way he held himself that made her think that maybe he'd felt far more than he'd ever let on.

Somewhere, there was the sound of a bird, incongruous in this filthy place, as incongruous as the conversation they were having. She told herself it would do no good to go over this old ground. But her throat ached and she needed this acknowledgment that he'd felt the same pain.

She couldn't help it; she touched him then, fingertips to fist. He uncoiled his fingers. She lifted her hand and touched his cheek. It was rough, just like it looked. Helplessly, she traced her fingertip along his jawline, touched the corner of his mouth.

He said, "Don't."

But she didn't stop. She'd lain awake last night and thought of Joe's mouth and now she couldn't help touching...

She felt his breath on her skin as he spoke. "I cared about our losing our baby Maggie," he said. "And I cared about you, too." His voice went gruff. "Always."

She went straight into his arms. Her throat felt so tight. *Hold me for that time seven years ago,* and then, she thought, *Hold me for now.*

She buried her face in his chest as his arms tightened around her. His sweatshirt felt warm, and the scent of him made her inhale deeply. She lifted her head and, almost without conscious thought, she met his mouth with hers.

She'd had some dim thought of needing comfort. Now she didn't think at all. He made one sound, low in his throat, and he was instantly kissing her, his lips moving and pressing with unmistakable hunger. Another sound, and heat rushed through her. His arousal was hard against her belly. She opened her mouth. His tongue thrust inside, and she melted against him, suddenly boneless.

He never stopped kissing her as he pushed his hands up under her blazer, to the small of her back, and pulled her even closer. His hands burned through the thin silk of her blouse. Maggie put her own arms around his neck, then touched the back of his head, running her hands frantically through the short, strong strands of his hair.

She moaned. It had always been like this with him; she always got so soft and needy so fast. Desire clutched her. It had always, always—

Dear Lord, what was she doing? Shock ran through her as she realized she was in his arms, and that she was so greedy for more than this one incendiary kiss. He must have felt her stiffening. His hands, which had been making frantic circles on her back, abruptly stilled. He lifted his mouth from hers. For a long second, they stood, clutched together. Then Maggie took a deep breath and pushed him away.

He stepped back immediately. He shoved his hands in his pockets and looked away. Her own hands shaking, Maggie smoothed her blouse. She looked over at him, noticed the lean muscle of his back, his broad shoulders. Always—

There was no always.

She said, "We can't do this."

He turned finally, studied her. She had an urge to

smooth her blouse again, but resisted it. He nodded. "I'm sorry."

Honesty forced her to say, "It wasn't your fault. I'm the one who's sorry." She wanted to lick her lips, to keep the taste of him on her tongue.

Lewis had never been able to make her go breathless in an instant, make her want to rub up against him until his skin became hers. He'd never been able to make her moan with one thorough kiss.

Horror washed her anew as she realized she was actually comparing Joe to her fiancé. The fiancé she'd slept with less than a month before.

"I have to go," she said, and she hated how weak she sounded.

He nodded again. Why didn't he say something? Anything. He didn't look at her, but he didn't seem particularly ruffled, either. In fact, without another word, he turned and began a purposeful stroll from the alley.

She fell into step with him. She had an insane urge to analyze the kiss, tell herself—tell *him*—that it didn't mean anything. And it was beginning to annoy her that he didn't seem to be affected as much as she was. There was no denying he'd been fully aroused. But he always got his self-control back easily.

As they came out from the alley, the sun almost blinded Maggie. The September sun still had a lot of warmth left in it, and she was sweaty under her blazer. She shaded her eyes with her hand.

Next to her, she felt Joe look around. She did the

same and spotted the bartender with his keys in his hand, preparing to unlock the tavern door.

Joe picked up his pace.

Maggie hurried to keep up with him.

Just as the bartender thrust the key in the lock, Joe reached him. "Wait a minute. We need to talk."

"About what?" the guy said. Maggie would have bet that the bartender had perfected his combination of belligerence and lack of interest in prison somewhere.

"About the lady who hangs around the bar."

The guy went absolutely still. Maggie leaned forward.

"I don't know nothing about a lady. What would I know about any lady." He started to turn the key.

Quick as a wink, Joe had the key out of his hand. In a lightning move, he turned the guy around and pinned his shoulder to the wall. "Don't mess with me, okay? Not this morning. I'm not in the mood for it. Tell me who the lady around the bar is."

The bartender kept his back to the wall and brought up his hands in a supplicating gesture. "Hey, take it easy, okay? I don't want any trouble." He turned his head toward Maggie. "You've got a hell of a bodyguard."

Joe didn't move a muscle. "The lady," he repeated.

"I don't know what you're talking about."

"The note."

The guy's eyes opened a little wider. "I don't

know nothing about it. I swear.'' His gaze included Maggie.

"Look at me," Joe commanded. "Only at me."

The man swallowed, and his Adam's apple bobbed. "I said, I don't know nothing about the note."

"But you know about the lady."

The guy tried to crack a grin, but couldn't seem to quite manage it with Joe holding him so effortlessly against the wall. "Ain't no *ladies* come around here, you know? 'Cept your lady, of course." His eyes went to Maggie as if seeking rescue. When Maggie said nothing, he turned back to Joe. "Listen, man, I don't know who you are, but I don't know a thing about what you want to know. Not a thing. So let me go and do my job."

Joe gave him a good, long stare, then let him go abruptly. The man sagged for a split second, then straightened. When Joe stepped out of reach, the bartender grinned, showing his yellowing teeth. Then he shrugged at Maggie before quickly fitting his key into the lock and going inside.

Maggie and Joe were left alone on the street. For a moment, neither said anything. Then Joe said, "He's lying."

Her stomach felt a little queasy. "How could you tell?"

"Did you see how every muscle went still when I mentioned a woman? And there was something about the way the guy just stood there and took it. Guys like him are pretty tough."

"Yeah, but you pinned him so fast I don't think he had time to be tough."

"Sure. But still, I don't think he was telling the truth. Not the whole story, anyway. I believe he didn't write the note, though." Joe scratched his jaw as he thought. "A guy like him wouldn't refer to a woman from around here as a lady. And he looked downright confused for a second there when I mentioned the note. But I think he knows the woman we're looking for. Did you see his reaction when I mentioned that?"

"He looked very shifty to me the whole time." She paused. "I don't know, Joe. When I've got a witness on the stand and they're forced to answer my questions, I can usually trip them up if they're lying. But out here—well, this is your world. If you say the guy knows something, then I guess he does."

Joe added, "But he's not going to talk easily. We'll have to figure out a way to get at him. For a start, I'll get my partner to run his rap sheet. Maybe I'll come up with something that'll put a bit of pressure on him to talk."

She nodded.

"But there's nothing more we can do here for now. Come on, I'll walk you to your car."

They walked the short distance to the car in silence. When they got to Maggie's car, she opened the door. She hesitated, then said, "I'm glad we're making progress on your case."

I'll be glad to see this case end, glad when I don't have to see you anymore. Their official business here in this alley might be finished for the day, but she had to make Joe understand where her loyalties lay.

"Joe, I—" She stopped as she realized her voice had gone suddenly low, almost pleading. More strongly she said, "What happened in that alley cannot happen again."

He looked directly into her eyes for the first time since she'd gone into his arms. His mouth was tight and grim. When he spoke, his voice was gruff. "Don't you think I know that?"

CHAPTER SEVEN

"THIS WAS THE BEST I could do." Henry Muff shrugged. Joe and his partner were standing in front of a bar called Craig's Place, under an overhang. A cold autumn rain was falling, giving the night air a definite chill. Craig's was a neighborhood establishment, not one frequented by the cops, and Joe had chosen this meeting place for that very reason. Henry handed Joe a small sheaf of paper.

"There's got to be a whole lot more than this," Joe said, using the light from above the tavern door to see the papers. He'd asked Henry to do him a favor—to pull arrest records for him. He wanted the name of every person who'd been arrested in the area in the last six months. Then he'd start trying to track those people down, ask some questions, try to shake loose some information.

Henry put his hands into his pockets. "I can only pull a few at a time. You know I've got to wait until there aren't too many people around. You aren't allowed to have that stuff while you're on suspension."

"I know that," Joe snapped. Then he studied his partner. Henry was in his fifties, with a paunch in the gut, and deliberate in his movements. The bottom line was, Henry played it safe. He was a decent guy, but a bureaucrat. "You're my partner, Henry. I'm not trying to pull something here with these records. I'm only trying to clear my name."

"Yeah, I know." Henry let out a long breath. In the cool night air, it made a stream of fog.

"I need them all, and I need them fast," Joe said. "It's already been over two weeks."

"I owe you," Henry said now.

Joe made a sound of dismissal, one note. But he knew what Henry was talking about. Joe had been all alone in that alley the night of the shooting, his partner far behind. Henry hadn't stayed in shape and he was slow because of his excess weight and lack of exercise.

If Henry had been right behind him on that night, he might have seen Hook pull that gun. Joe didn't blame Henry. Stuff happened out there in the streets. But he'd sure thought he could count on his partner to help him out now.

Joe folded the papers and stuck them in the inside pocket of his jacket. Then he took a couple of restless paces. A few drops of cold rain hit his face and some ran down the back of his neck. Quickly, he stepped back under cover.

When he spoke, he was blunt. "Are you going to get me this stuff, Henry? Are you going to get me the records before Internal Affairs fries my ass?"

"I want to. But I've got to be careful. I'm up for my pension in six months, and face it, Joe, they want you on this rap or it'd have been smoothed over before now.''

Joe bit off an expletive. "Listen, Henry, all I'm going to need are the female reports. Think you can manage that?''

Henry smiled for the first time. "You've found something out?''

Joe told him about the note, then about his conversation with the bartender. "The guy had no intention of telling me anything, but he gave me a clue without knowing it. He said, 'What would I know about any *lady*.' Makes you think of a certain kind of woman, doesn't it?''

"She's a hooker.'' Henry looked pleased.

"So he implied. So I'm not just looking around for all kinds of street people anymore. I heard a woman scream. We got a note to the effect that a woman witnessed the crime. And I figure she's a prostitute. So if you could pull me all the female arrests, I might actually be able to get somewhere.''

Henry said, "I'll do it, you know I will, but it's going to take some time.''

"I'd appreciate your doing your best," Joe said.

But he wouldn't wait for Henry, he decided in the same instant. He'd have to pull in some other favors, he guessed. He'd talk to the vice cops, see if one of them had arrested a hooker in the area. Talking to vice would give him something to do until he got what he needed.

He pulled out his car keys. Henry extended his

hand; Joe shook it. Unexpectedly, his partner put out his other hand, gripped Joe's arm. "I want you to beat this, Joe. I really do. Even if I—well, I want you to beat it."

"Thanks," Joe said briefly. Then he headed home, planning to sift through the reports Henry had given him. Maybe he'd have some luck for a change.

He got into the Jeep and drove through the rain. He thought about calling Maggie to tell her what he was going to do. He'd already spoken to her earlier today to share his theory that the missing witness was a prostitute.

But he didn't call her, much as he longed to hear her voice.

Instead, when he got home, he went into the kitchen and opened the refrigerator door. Then, leaning his butt against the kitchen counter, he stood drinking a can of beer. The kitchen was white, almost institutional in its plainness, white cabinets, white laminated countertops, the grids of white ceramic tile on the floor. Even the clock on the wall was rimmed in glossy white plastic. Stylish, the condo owner had said, just right for a single guy.

Joe liked Maggie's house better. She had always had a good eye for color. Even their first apartment— with its secondhand furniture and faded quilts and those crocks and things she'd picked up at auctions— had looked better than this.

He crumpled the can and tossed it into the waste-basket beneath the kitchen sink.

Maggie had a way of exposing his soft side. When he first met her, he hadn't really been sure he had one. Not after he'd lost Alex. But Maggie *had* found it. And now he wished she hadn't. He didn't dare let her that close to him again. If his soft side ever bled again, it might never stop.

He went back out into the living room and picked up the arrest records. He'd been a damn good cop. It was time to concentrate on becoming a good one again. Nothing else mattered.

"DEAR LORD," Sharon Sawyer said softly. Lewis's sister looked Maggie and Angela over and her mouth got very round. The three of them were standing in Maggie's living room almost a week after Maggie had found the note.

It was ten o'clock at night, and Maggie had switched on all the lamps. Under the bright light, Angela struck a vampish pose. "'Dear Lord'? That's all you can say when I went to all this trouble?"

Angela wore a tiny, pleated skirt in black, with a shiny purple top. Her pixie face was very made up, and her blond hair now sported a purple streak.

"Your hair." Sharon put fingertips to her mouth and almost moaned the words.

"Oh, this?" Angela touched the purple area lightly and grinned. That smile showed a couple of lipstick stains on her teeth. "It'll come off the next time I shampoo."

"Or you'll give Judge Osborn a good shock when

he sees you in court day after tomorrow.'' Maggie found herself grinning, too.

Sharon snapped, ''You're both out of your minds. Stop smiling, Angela. You, too, Maggie. Something dreadful might happen to you.''

''That's why Angela's coming along,'' Maggie explained for the tenth time. ''Besides, nothing's going to happen. I've been there before, remember?''

''You haven't been there in the middle of the night. Besides, Maggie, you look even worse than Angela does! If Lewis were here, he'd have a fit.''

Maggie knew that. It was one of the reasons she'd decided to go tonight. Lewis would be home from Milan tomorrow night, and she didn't feel like having to justify her actions. Better to just do it. If the evening went well and she got her witness, Lewis would be pleased that she could finish Joe's case.

''You know what Lewis would do if he saw you like that.'' Sharon was still pressing the point.

''He'd drag her off to bed,'' Angela said, looking Maggie over with a twinkle in her eye. ''That shirt of yours is cut to here—'' she made a slashing motion across her middle ''—and you aren't exactly small in the chest department, kid.''

Maggie's shirt wasn't cut that low, but she knew what Angela meant. Her breasts were full and she usually dressed to try to disguise that fullness. Tonight she was deliberately flaunting it. She gave her shirt a tug, bringing the edge of the collar up higher, but it felt uncomfortable.

Her legs were a little wobbly; the heels she wore were awfully high. She didn't want to be mistaken for a prostitute, but she still had to look different enough from her workaday self to fit into the rowdy atmosphere of the tavern on Pierce and Goshen.

She went to the table to pick up her purse. It was hard not to scrub at her face. She'd used so much makeup that she felt as if her cheeks would crack if she moved them. Her hair was curled and teased and pulled in a heavy ponytail over one ear. She wore huge glasses in a final attempt to disguise her appearance.

Tonight wasn't for fun, but Maggie felt a high anticipation nevertheless. And Angela's color had been bright even before she'd put on all that makeup. There was a sense that something was going to happen.

From behind her, Sharon was still fussing. "Lewis would not take her off to bed. What a thing to say! For heaven's sake, he'd be worried sick if he knew what she was up to."

Maggie shot Angela a helpless look. Everything Sharon said was true. She also knew that if she represented the corporate clients that Lewis favored, she'd be home, comfortable in her sweats, watching television.

But corporate clients weren't the reason she'd wanted to practice law. She wanted to help real people with real problems.

Joe was a real person with a real problem.

A real person she had kissed.

Her mind skittered away from dangerous territory. She'd deliberately concocted this scheme to get his case moving. There was a woman witness, and she was "around the bar." So that was the place to start, and going there in her official capacity had gotten Maggie exactly nowhere. As Joe had said, all the action in that part of town was at night.

She took a deep breath. "It's after ten. Let's go, Angela. It's show time."

"Okay." Angela shot a thumb in the air.

Sharon took one more long look at them both and then said abruptly, "I'm coming, too."

"You?" Maggie was astounded. "You?" she repeated.

"Who's going to watch your kid?" Angela asked.

"My husband's home. I'll just tell him that I'm going out for a drink with the two of you. To talk business." She shook her head. "I can't tell him the complete truth. He'd think I'd lost it." She glanced down at her own outfit. Her jeans were new and unfashionably crisp, and her checked blouse was modestly loose and buttoned high. She shrugged self-consciously. "I can't let you two do this without me. I've been thinking about it all day. If we're going to have trouble, we're going to have trouble together."

Maggie smiled. Sharon could be difficult and stubborn, but she was there for you when you really needed her. "Thanks," she said softly.

Sharon's cheeks went a little pink. "I'll just use your phone," she said briskly, hurrying off.

IN MAGGIE'S CAR on the way to Pierce and Goshen, Sharon sat next to her, dabbing on blusher by the light of a tiny flashlight, looking in the mirror of a compact. Behind her in the back seat, Angela urged her to "load it on," pointing out that they weren't going to the barristers' ball.

"You know, I know where this place is, but not the name of it," Sharon said, scrubbing at her cheeks with a fingertip.

"Easy," Angela said. "It's the eer."

"The eer? What kind of name is that?"

Maggie explained about the neon beer sign with the missing *B*. "This kind of place doesn't need to display a name. Believe me, people find it. And the drinking that goes on there is hardly casual. When I was there, I noticed that there was a kind of…desperation in it. In the whole place."

Maggie's words sobered her companions. Despite Angela's and Maggie's kidding around earlier, they all knew this was no game. In fact, by the time they entered the tavern, Angela had to remind them to relax.

Maggie pasted a smile on her face. She glanced at the bar. The bartender was not the same one who'd been on duty when she'd offered the reward. Instead, there was a young guy with red hair and bad skin mixing drinks. She let out a sigh of relief. She most definitely didn't want to be recognized as an attorney tonight. She was also relieved to see that none of the patrons wore Nightshade colors.

The three of them made their way to a booth near the back. Their presence was noticed immediately by men; there were more than a few catcalls.

Maggie looked around as Angela went to the bar for beer. There were only a few women, and all of them were with men. A beefy-looking guy came over to their table. "Hi, sweetheart," he said to Sharon. She eyed him and moved into the place vacated by Angela, blocking his entry into the booth.

"Why don't you scoot over again and I'll sit beside you, and we can kinda get to know each other?" He grinned and put his hands on the table. "I'm Pete."

"No thank you," Sharon said.

The guy laughed. "Kind of prissy, aren't you? I like that in a woman." He started to slide into the booth, nudging Sharon a little. His hands were still flat on the table, and even in the dim light Maggie could see the tattoos that ran up his forearms. She tried not to shudder.

Sharon stood her ground, putting her own hands on the edge of the table and holding on. "I said no thank you."

"She's not in a good mood. She had a fight with her boyfriend," Maggie explained quickly.

"Well, I could make her feel a whole—"

"But we're getting back together," Sharon cut in.

Pete shifted his gaze to Maggie. "You might look good without those glasses," he said hopefully. "I mean, your upper parts aren't bad, you know?"

"Here we are," Angela cut in jovially, the handles of three beer mugs in her hand. Without missing a beat, she took a quick swerve to avoid Pete and slid into the booth next to Sharon, who hurriedly made way for her.

Another man summoned Pete. "I'll be back," he promised. "Don't go anywhere without me." He flashed a grin and was gone.

"Oh my." Sharon almost moaned the words after the man was out of earshot. "Did you see his tattoos? The guy's probably an ax murderer." She grabbed her beer and gulped.

"I don't know about an ax murderer," Angela said. "But I'll bet there are plenty of guys in here who've spent a long time in prison."

Sharon said something about being glad she'd always stuck with estate and trust work and real estate law.

"I'll handle these punks," Angela said. "I've had plenty of experience." And indeed, the next guy who offered to buy them all a drink was dispatched almost before he'd got the offer out. Angela had a way of discouraging attention without making anyone angry.

Relieved, Maggie sipped her beer and kept watch. A few women came in and were almost immediately absorbed by the crowd. As the night wore on, the place filled up.

"How long are we going to stay?" Sharon asked Maggie after a couple of hours.

"For a while longer at least."

"Any one of these women could be a prostitute," Sharon said.

Angela said, "Maybe, but I don't think so. I've represented a few prostitutes. For one thing, they like to work alone."

For quite a while, a group by the door had obscured Maggie's view of the doorway, but she could see the counter of the bar clearly. She kept her eyes there.

She finally had to excuse herself. As she came back from the ladies' room, a man caught her eye.

She almost did a double take as she recognized him. Joe.

He was standing with his back to the wall near the door. A deceptively casual slouch that she knew wasn't casual at all. He was watching her; she knew it.

Across the bar they stared at each other. The air was blue with smoke, and it smelled rank, a persistent undertone of poorly washed bodies. People moved, cut in front of her. They passed and still he was there. In a pair of jeans and a dark T-shirt and leather jacket. He raised his hand in a silent greeting, but his expression never changed. Unsmiling. But tantalizingly so. The kind of…thrill of having him within range hit her full force.

Now he was affecting her from across a crowded room! She'd never believed in that cliché, and now—

She stomped back toward her table. "Joe's here," she announced. "Isn't that just great." She sat down. "I wonder how he knew we were here—" She stopped as realization dawned. "Sharon, did you call him?"

Sharon nodded without the slightest bit of guilt in her expression. "You were bound and determined to come here tonight. It was dangerous, and we needed a police presence. Joe didn't think he could talk you out of it."

"So he came to be the big protector," Maggie stated.

Sharon shot Maggie a curious glance and Angela kicked her under the table. She knew she was reacting too strongly. After all, Sharon's telling Joe had been a reasonable thing to do.

It was just that now she knew he was there, she couldn't stop looking in the direction where he lounged by the door.

She could almost feel him here. She didn't want to see him, she didn't want to talk to him more than absolutely necessary. She wasn't going to betray Lewis in any way.

"Fifteen minutes," she announced. "Fifteen minutes and then we're out of here. We can come back some other time.'' And next time she wouldn't be foolish enough to share her plans with Sharon.

Maggie looked at her watch, marking the time. She had fifteen minutes to find her witness, then she could solve her case, exonerate her client and get on with her life.

CHAPTER EIGHT

THE MINUTES FELT like hours.

With only four left to go, a woman, a redhead, approached the bar. Alone. Maggie tensed. She said in a low voice, "Did you see her?"

"Yes," Angela said in an equally low voice, standing partway out of her seat to get a better look.

All three of them stared. The woman's hair was a garish, chemical red, and it was piled high on her head. She was small and slight, and her top left a lot of skin bare. The hoops in her ears were so large and glittery Maggie could see them from across the bar.

As they watched, the woman sat down on an empty bar stool and struck up a conversation with the man next to her.

"A prostitute," Angela theorized.

"Are you sure?" Maggie asked.

"Pretty sure. She has the look."

"She looks the same as us," Sharon muttered.

Angela ignored the comment, craning her head to see better. "Actually, I think she's in negotiation with a potential john right now."

The woman was leaning toward her companion, her

head bobbing as she spoke, her hand on the back of his neck.

"Let's go," Maggie said, standing up.

"If you're going to interfere with the…ah, their business arrangement, you're going to have to be real careful," Angela cautioned her quietly as they approached.

They stopped when they were within a few feet of the woman. Maggie was in front. In her pocket was a twenty-dollar bill. She had more cash in her purse if necessary. She was conscious of Joe, off to the side, but she focused on the woman. For a few minutes, they just watched the conversation.

The man finally shook his head, threw a couple of bills down on the bar and vacated his stool.

Maggie headed there and slid onto the stool. The woman eyed her with open suspicion. Now that Maggie was close, she could see that the woman was older than she'd thought at first. In her mid-thirties, perhaps, and her skin had an unhealthy gray cast.

"Hi," Maggie said quietly.

"Hi," the woman said back, and then reached over and downed the dregs of the drink the man had left.

"I want to talk to you," Maggie said still in a low voice.

"So talk," the woman said, and laughed a little, a kind of giggle. Drunk or high, Maggie decided. "But make it fast, because I got work to do."

Maggie could feel the press of bodies here by the bar. The bartender came up and asked her for her drink order. Several men offered to buy the drink…and her.

"Come outside," Maggie suggested.

"Gotta work. Don't have time for coming outside."

Maggie extracted the twenty-dollar bill. "Consider this business."

The woman cocked her head. Then she said with suspicion, "What do you want?"

"I've got twenty bucks," Maggie repeated. "I guarantee you all I want to do is talk."

The woman hesitated, some instinct for self-preservation flickering deep in her eyes. Then she shrugged. "Five minutes."

She went ahead of them through the doorway of the bar, but it was without the sashaying of hips that she'd done when she'd first come in. Maggie looked around for Joe as they passed, but she didn't see him.

Outside, the four of them stood on the sidewalk. The woman's back was to the brick wall of the bar, and she shivered, rubbing her hands up and down her bare arms. The streetlight picked out the sequins of her top and made the whole scene surreal and theatrical. Quelling an attack of nerves, Maggie asked, "You didn't bring a coat?"

She shook her head and started to lose her balance before righting herself. The earrings bobbed. "Ruins the show, you know? Gotta show the skin." She didn't smile. "The sooner I make my pay, the sooner I get home to my kid."

"Here, take this," Maggie said impulsively, handing the woman her own sweater.

The woman took it, looking surprised. She pulled it over her shoulders, her arms crossed over her chest, holding the sides close to her.

"You have a child?" Maggie asked, hoping to make some connection with her companion. Angela and Sharon hovered, but they were silent.

She nodded. "A real good kid. Going to school, going to be somebody someday. I had another kid, but he died."

Her words went a little slurry, but Maggie heard the sorrow in them. She put out a hand to touch the woman's arm.

She jerked away. "Where's my money?"

Maggie sighed and put the twenty in her hand. "I'm Maggie." The woman didn't say anything, so she added, "And your name is...?"

The woman hesitated, then said, "Rose."

"Rose, that's a pretty name. Can you help me? I'm looking for a lady who comes around to this bar."

Next to them, the door opened, and several men spilled out. They were having an argument, but it ended with nothing more than a couple of shoves.

"I don't come to this bar." Rose spat on the street, then swiped at her mouth with the sleeve of Maggie's sweater.

Maggie tried not to wince. "Well, you're here tonight, so you do come sometimes?"

"That's true. But I'm not what you think. I only do it when I have to."

Maggie ignored the comment. "Well, I'm trying to find out if you might be the woman who saw a shooting in this alley three weeks ago." She was watching Rose carefully. The woman's eyes widened.

Maggie's heart missed a beat. Rose had definitely reacted to the mention of the shooting. Now she was turning away. "I don't know nothing."

Maggie reached out and grabbed her arm.

Quick as a cat, Rose turned on her, jerking her arm away and reaching for Maggie's face. Maggie took a quick step back.

Rose started to cry. "I got a good kid," she said, blubbering.

"Hey." It was a new voice, a male voice. "You're the broad from the bar." Coming toward them was the man Rose had been talking to in the bar. He was big, tall with frizzled hair and a handlebar mustache. "Wait."

Maggie straightened her spine. He came right up to them.

"You were too expensive, baby Rosebud, but I changed my mind." His eyes were intent and leering, and Maggie's heartbeat accelerated another notch. "Or, I could maybe change my mind if you gave me a little discount. Or a two for one." His gaze encompassed them all and he took a step closer. A little too close for Maggie's comfort. "What do you say to a little group action?"

"No thanks," Maggie said quickly.

"Stay a while." His voice was deadly quiet, and he grabbed her upper arm. She saw a flash of silver. It was the blade of a knife.

"Take your hands off me," she said, furious at herself for not noticing the knife before.

"I'd do as she says." A voice Maggie recognized seemed to come out of nowhere.

Joe.

"Oh, yeah!" The guy sounded a lot less confident.

In a split second, Joe had backed the man up against the wall and twisted the knife out of his hand. It fell to the ground. "Call the cops," Joe directed. He wasn't even breathing hard.

Without a word, Sharon ran for the door of the bar.

Rose was backing away. Maggie said, "Stop! Stop. Please. Just wait a minute. Everything's fine and I still need to talk to you."

From his place beside the man, Joe said to Rose, "Don't be afraid. I'm a cop myself."

Rose looked momentarily uncertain, then she took another step.

Joe said, "I'm not going to do anything about your soliciting. Just wait a minute, okay?"

The guy started to twist, but Joe quickly subdued him with a knee in the stomach.

"You keep doing that," he said, "and I'm going to have to get rough."

For a second Maggie and her friends were focused on the guy who was now doubled over. Rose turned on her heel and fled. Maggie could see a flash of sequins, and then there was only darkness.

"How did she get away so fast? Where did she go?" Angela asked.

"There're openings between buildings, doors that don't lock, loose boards everywhere," Joe said, still holding on to his suspect. "You won't find her if she doesn't want to be found."

When the police arrived, Joe, Maggie and her partners gave their statements. Then they all stood by the curb, Joe next to Maggie. "Listen, everyone," Maggie said. "We have to find Rose. She could be the 'lady around the bar.'"

"You think?" Angela said eagerly.

"It was her expression when I asked her. Scared. More scared than if she'd just heard about it. If she does her soliciting anywhere around here, she'd be used to the rough stuff on the streets. She knows something's different about this shooting."

Like the others, Joe had been listening in silence. Now he said abruptly, "I'll find her. For you, this is the end, Maggie. Do all the legal work you want, but you're not coming down here anymore. I want your promise on that."

"I just told you that woman knows something—"

"Okay. You've told me. Now I'll find her and talk to her. That's what I do for a living, after all."

"She didn't want to talk to you. As soon as she found out you were a cop, she took off."

"Promise me."

She said firmly, "I can't do that." Angela and Sharon were looking from her to Joe. Maggie added, "She was talking to me. I think we'd made a bit of a connection. I'm not sure she's really much of a hooker. She seemed more sad or something."

"Don't romanticize this," he warned.

"She talked about her kid, Joe."

"Many of these women are mothers. Coming down here's dangerous and I won't have you putting yourself in danger. That's not what your taking this case was supposed to be about."

"I had Angela and Sharon with me," Maggie pointed out, trying to be reasonable.

Angela finally waded in. "It was all right until—"

"It wasn't all right." Joe's voice went grim. "And we're not going to leave this street corner until I hear that you, Maggie, agree to work on my case in your office or down at the station, and only in those places."

"I'm sorry," Maggie said quietly. "I'm not going to do that. You don't have the right to demand that, even if I'm your attorney."

He took an abrupt step toward her. "For God's sake, this doesn't have anything to do with your being an attorney! It doesn't have a damn thing to do with our professional relationship. It's dangerous down here and I'm not going to let you get hurt."

"I'm your attorney and I have a respons—"

"If you come down here again, you're fired."

Her mouth opened in shock. Anger washed over her.

Joe lifted his hand, as if to make a quelling gesture. "My badge isn't worth this." His voice was hoarse. "Maggie, for God's sake. Don't you know I'd die if something happened to you?" He stared at her, and his eyes were intent and vulnerable.

Here, where harsh light washed the world and made it all shades of black and white and gray, she could see into their depths. She stared, unable to look away.

He cared about her! Really cared what happened to her, even was willing to lose his badge if it would keep her safe. Her heart hurt, a physical pain, for him and all he was willing to give up. The sounds of the city faded, the light of the streetlight became more concentrated until it shone only on Joe. His features were thrown into high relief—the wells of his eyes, the thin, straight nose, the tough, unsmiling mouth.

She shivered, started to reach for him, unable to stop herself.

On her other side, Sharon cleared her throat.

Maggie jumped. She'd actually forgotten for a second that her friends were with her. Joe shoved his hands in his pockets and looked abruptly away, as if he, too, had only just remembered.

"I think," Angela said quietly, "that we'd all better get home. It's getting late." She touched Maggie's hand lightly. "Come on, Maggie."

"Yes," she said obediently.

Joe said he was going to follow her home, and when they got in the car, they waited for him to return with his Jeep. After she saw his headlights in her rearview mirror, Maggie sighed and started the car.

She felt... She didn't know what she felt. It had been a roller coaster of an evening—sitting there in that tavern with all her nerves on edge, the excitement of finding Rose, the even greater excitement of deciding the woman might know something. Then that knife... She tried not to shudder.

"Joe's a hero," Angela said quietly from the back seat. "I don't think I remembered to thank him."

"I think he knows we're grateful." Sharon's voice was tart. There was a pause. "Maggie, you know I don't want to get into your business, but I need to say something here. I know this was an awful night— I was scared myself—but your behavior with Joe wasn't—"

Angela made a sound of impatience. "Sharon, Maggie was just grateful to Joe."

"He's her ex-husband, and for a second he was looking at her like she belonged with him. He didn't say he'd die if anything happened to you or me, did he?"

Maggie stopped at a stop sign and then turned. She felt awful, her stomach sour, and she had the sensation that her heavy makeup had gone gooey. Now a hot wash of embarrassment heated her cheeks. "He said that because we have a past, Sharon. It's complicated. You knew it was complicated when I took him on as a client and explained who he was.''

"The firm needed the money, and I thought I could count on you. I thought you hated the guy.''

"Well, I don't hate him anymore,'' Maggie admitted.

Sharon let out a shocked sound. "Oh, my Lord, you're not falling in love with him, are you?''

"No!'' she said quickly. She thought of him hanging out at that bar, watching over her, subduing a violent man. She thought about him playing old-movie trivia, smiling as Tessa tried to use chopsticks. She thought about him saying not even his badge was worth her getting hurt. "No,'' she said a little more quietly.

"I'm not stupid. I know what a mistake it would be to allow myself to have some feelings for him.'' But she didn't sound convincing even to herself.

Angela said, "You can't always use your head to decide what's in your heart.''

"That's crazy!'' Sharon slapped her hand on the armrest. "Maggie has a good life now. What did this guy ever bring her but heartbreak?''

Maggie's hands tightened on the steering wheel. "Sharon, do you mind not talking about me as if I weren't here?''

"Sorry,'' she said quickly. "It's just that I'm worried. I know you wouldn't do something dumb, it's *him* I don't trust. It would really hurt Lewis to know that your ex-husband is hanging around, making big, dramatic statements about his feelings.''

"Lewis has always been understanding,'' Maggie said, hoping to forestall the lecture. She'd feel guilty enough when Lewis came home tomorrow.

"I don't want my brother to get hurt.''

"Neither do I,'' Maggie said quietly. "But it's between him and me, okay?''

"Okay.'' Sharon turned finally and shot a sympathetic glance Maggie's way. "I know I'm butting in. It's just that I know you, and I know how good you and Lewis are together. I know what's right here.''

Like brother, like sister, Maggie thought, her mind flashing on Lewis's tendency to tell her what to do. But while that thought once would have brought wry amusement or irritation, now she analyzed herself. Was she looking for faults in her fiancé to absolve herself of her own guilt?

Maggie slowed, then stopped in front of Angela's house. Angela got out, and on her way up the walk, kicked a soccer ball that had been left in the driveway to a spot nearer the garage. "See you!'' she called before heading up the walk. At her house, every window was lit.

Maggie and Sharon were quiet on the short ride to Maggie's bungalow, where Sharon had left her car parked in the driveway. Once there, Maggie got out of the car and unlocked the door. Joe tooted his horn and went on by. "Do you want to come in for something to drink before heading home?'' Maggie asked

Sharon, who'd followed her to the bottom of the steps. She really didn't want her to. She needed to be alone.

"No thanks. I'd better get home and spell Bill. It's late, and there's no telling whether the baby slept or not." Sharon smiled, a smile very like her brother's. A serious smile but a kind one.

Maggie walked Sharon to her car. Just as Sharon was about to get in, she said to Maggie, "I hope I didn't overstep the boundaries of friendship tonight."

"Of course not."

"I hope I didn't overstep the bounds of what a future sister-in-law ought to say." She paused. "I *am* still going to be your sister-in-law, aren't I?"

"Of course!" Fresh guilt washed over Maggie.

Sharon let out a sigh of relief. "I thought so, I just… Tonight didn't really mean anything. So the guy let his heart show a little. So maybe he's remembering old times, got a little screwed up in his thinking. You haven't done anything wrong."

Only kissed him.

"I'll talk everything over with Lewis as soon as I can," Maggie promised. She knew she'd spend a sleepless night formulating the right words. Words that were honest, but not intended to alarm. Words that were kind, the ones that would restore equilibrium to their relationship.

Sharon paused with her hand on her car door. "It's really great that you're going to be in a family. That you and Lewis and Tessa will be a family. I don't want Tessa to be hurt either, you know. She's very attached to you.''

Maggie saw the girl in her mind's eye, Tessa of the dramatic sweep of arm, Tessa with her warm smile. ''I don't want to hurt her either. Believe me, I'd never want to do that.''

Sharon reached out and hugged Maggie.

Maggie was astonished, but she hugged her friend back, feeling an awful need to cry. She blinked it away.

What she needed to do was see her fiancé again, she decided. Of course Joe was appealing. He was handsome, they had a history, and she was discovering he was a much more emotionally complex man than she'd ever realized. He'd always been able to make her heart speed up.

But sex was most certainly not everything in a relationship. Was it?

Of course it wasn't.

Anyway, she'd always liked Lewis's kisses.

In bed an hour later, too keyed up to sleep, she allowed herself to think about the night's events. She thought about Rose, and the fact that Joe had let their witness get away without a second's thought, because he was busy protecting Maggie and her friends. No matter what happened, she owed it to him to try to find Rose once again.

Turning the pillow to its cool side, she thought of Lewis. She told herself that all she needed to do was see Lewis. Surely, when her fiancé came home, she'd have a visceral reaction to his presence. When he kissed her, she'd respond as she always did. She'd lean into his reassuring arms and know that she was content. That she was very lucky to have him and his daughter, and his sister.

THE NEXT DAY started out fine. Maggie had a new client, the owner of a small antique business who'd picked Maggie because the firm had been mentioned in the newspaper account of Joe's case. Maggie was the only lawyer the older woman could think of to call with a couple of routine problems. It wasn't the best way to choose a lawyer, but Maggie was glad to help her.

But that had been this morning, and things had gone downhill from there. This afternoon, she'd been in court with a difficult judge and a jury from hell, the kind where you could look over at the jury box and just tell they weren't paying attention. Her client had been on the verge of losing, but she'd managed to settle the case with a bit of tense, last-minute bargaining while the jury was on a break.

She had dinner plans with Lewis, but the trial had made her run late. So she'd had to arrange to meet him at the restaurant instead of having him pick her up. He'd grumbled that they were going to lose their reservation. He'd apologized as soon as he'd seen her come in, but the incident didn't add anything good to her day.

Now Maggie played with her little seafood fork, stabbing listlessly at a shrimp on her plate.

"Could you please stop that?" Lewis asked sharply.

She looked up over the candle in the middle of the table. Lewis looked tired. His handsome face had lost some color and he needed a shave.

When Joe needed a shave, he looked ruggedly handsome, but Lewis only looked tired—

Enough! "I'm sorry," she said, genuinely contrite, and laid down her fork.

Lewis frowned. "Are you okay?" He peered at her more closely.

"I'm fine."

"Well, why in God's name do you keep poking at your food—"

"I'm just tired," she said, and it was true. Her feet felt like lead, her shoulders ached. "I had a rotten day in court."

"Poor Maggie," Lewis said in genuine sympathy. "I didn't realize. You should have told me. Well, don't worry. We'll make it an early night. No problem."

"Thanks." She gave him what she knew was a wan smile. Her stomach hurt a bit, too, because she'd been so sure she'd have an emotional reaction to seeing him after this absence.

Instead, the only real emotions she'd felt were guilt and regret. Perversely, his kindness now made her feel worse. And the ease with which he just promised her an early night made her uncomfortable. Surely they should have more to talk about. They should be eager to share all that had happened to them while they were away from each other.

In fact, she should be dying to touch him.

When the silence got a little long, Maggie said, "Tessa had a good time while you were gone."

He perked right up. "School was okay?"

"School was great. She had to do an essay on the Middle Ages. She had a blast doing knights and the rules of chivalry. She went to the library four times and was on the computer until one in the morning. You know how she's always liked the Victorians. Well, I think now we might go back a little way in history."

Lewis cracked a tired smile. "I'm glad you two get along so well."

"Yes." The conversation lagged again.

Maggie became a little desperate. She leaned over her plate of shrimp and said, "I read a good book the other day." She named a book and mentioned a few of the parts she liked.

The waitress brought more coffee. Lewis smiled at her and said, "I wish I had more time to read. You know, other than *Fortune* and *Forbes*. I can't think how long it's been since I've read a novel or watched a good movie."

Her mind flashed to that night when she and Joe and her fiancé's daughter had done just that. Now Maggie knew it was time to tell Lewis the truth. She hated to hurt him. She'd thought about how to be gentle. "I've been seeing quite a bit of Joe since you've been gone."

Lewis had been patting his mouth with a napkin. Now he stopped, watching her.

She said, "We've had a lot to do on the case."

Rather carefully, Lewis smoothed the napkin in his lap. "I think we had this discussion before. You've also told me he was over at your house. I've told you I trust you. So, unless you have more to tell me—"

"I think about him," Maggie blurted out. She plunged ahead, her eyes focused on her plate. "I think I have feelings for him." Oh, no, she hadn't planned to tell him this way. But she couldn't stop herself. "I think about what we used to—used to do together. Activities, I mean, not doing—not that." She stumbled into, "But I did kiss him." Her cheeks went so hot. Then her whole face flamed.

She raised her eyes to her fiancé's. His were stricken. Lewis finally said quietly, "Is that all?"

"Isn't that enough?" she asked miserably.

"Yes. Yes, it is." He started doing things with his hands. Folding his napkin and laying it down. Rearranging his knife and fork at precise angles on his plate. Finally, he said, "Look, he's only been back in your life a few weeks. You're just…reacting to unfinished business between you, I think. We can work this out."

A curious wash of emotion went through her. Relief: *Maybe I didn't hurt him too much.* Gratitude:

He's a good man. Irritation: *I kissed Joe! Don't you want to yell at me and…and challenge him to a duel?* Her cheeks got hot again as she realized how childish her emotions were. Lewis was handling the issue rationally, better than she'd dared hope. Their relationship had always been so adult. So…rational.

He repeated, "We can work this out," then added, "You're so good with Tessa."

As gently as she could, Maggie said, "Tessa is very important to me. But we need to have more in common than Tessa. In a couple of years she'll be going away to college."

"But we'll have our own family. He can't give you what you want. He tried once. Well, I don't know how hard he tried. It seems to me that he took what he wanted without any thought to the future. He said he wanted a family and he didn't, and he hurt you. Are you ready to face that again?"

His bluntness hurt, but it was a sort of cleansing slap, the kind she needed when she got all cloudy on the subject of Joe. Very quietly, she said, "Of course not."

Lewis put a fist lightly down on the table, one small rap on the linen tablecloth. "Thank God, you haven't taken leave of your senses. You're so good for us, Maggie. Joe didn't need you, but we do. I don't have to say one more time how good you are with Tessa. You make her laugh. You get me out of the house, too. I was in there moping for over two years, Maggie! So sad and so lonely."

It was not a declaration of undying love. Maggie struggled to understand what was happening. She had no idea what she wanted, so she struggled to understand her fiancé. "And you're...happy?" she asked.

"Of course I'm happy. I have a good job, a good daughter and my fiancée. I like my life orderly. I'm good for you, too, because you need a little order in your life. I've always thought, once we were married, I'd offer to get your firm on track with billing and a business plan, get some more corporate clients that you and Sharon could split..." Maggie tuned him out. Here she was, confessing her sins, he was hearing her sins, and he was talking about a business plan for her firm.

All of a sudden, the truth hit her. It was hopeless.

As gently as she could, she interrupted. "Lewis, I need to say something here." He stopped immediately, waved for her to go ahead. "I think we need to break off our engagement."

He looked absolutely stunned. His mouth opened, then closed.

She waited, her heart pounding. When he didn't say anything, she started to pull off her engagement ring. The ring had always been a little tight. She tugged harder on the wide band, trying to slide it over her knuckle. *Come on, move,* she thought, wanting to get this over with and get out of here before she burst into tears.

Tears for mistakes made, for opportunities lost, for

having to hurt a kind man and for not knowing where her life was going.

She dipped a fingertip into her water glass, thinking if she wet her finger the ring might slide more easily.

Lewis finally spoke. "I won't hear of it," he said flatly, with more force than he'd used all evening. It was the kind of voice he must use for labor trouble in Milan.

He wouldn't hear of it? She'd tried to do the right thing and he wouldn't hear of it? Of all the things Maggie had expected, this was the last. Now what?

He said, "I'll be anything you want, Maggie. We need to try harder. Give us a chance."

His sincerity brought sudden tears to her eyes. He reached across the table, his hand covering hers, stopping her efforts to remove her ring. "Just listen to me. You left Joe Latham because he didn't share your values. You still have things about your relationship you've never understood. You've told me how you think he kept his emotions from you, that he'd never really explained why he didn't want a family. True?"

It was true. Joe had once had a family, Alex, the son who'd died. So obviously he'd once been willing to have children. He'd never explained why he'd changed his mind. Maggie nodded, looking at Lewis through a sheen of confused tears.

"I imagine women find the guy good-looking, if you like the type. I don't blame you for thinking he's attractive."

Guilt squeezed her again. She wanted to say she

found Lewis far more appealing than her ex-husband. But she couldn't. She'd been honest tonight. She needed to stay honest. It was hard not to reassure Lewis, especially when she saw his lips tighten and knew that was what he'd been hoping she'd say.

He continued in a forceful tone. "So what's changed? What makes you think you could have a relationship with him now?"

"I don't think that," she said quickly. It was one thing to confess. It was one thing to have fantasies. But she hadn't said she was thinking about a relationship with Joe. "I want to be fair to you," she said.

"And you have been." His mouth finally softened. "You're fair and honest and I admire that about you."

Her eyes misted again.

"We've made so many plans. When you said you'd marry me, you sincerely thought we could make a go of it. This guy broke your heart once. Don't let him do it again."

"I won't." She wasn't going to do that, was she? No. She definitely wasn't going to let Joe into her heart again.

"You can't get involved with him anyway. He's a client." Was there a small note of triumph in Lewis's voice?

Well, what if there was? She'd dealt him a heck of a blow tonight.

"Think about us," Lewis said. "Let's leave things as they are for now and just think."

"Okay," she said. She didn't know what else to say, because every word he'd uttered was true. Her finger was swollen and tender from her efforts to force the ring off. She wasn't a superstitious woman, but that seemed to be some kind of a sign.

Somehow, she had to think about her relationship with Lewis, independent of any thoughts of Joe. But her relationship with Joe *did* have an impact on her relationship with Lewis. Because she hadn't been aware of the cracks in her relationship with her fiancé until Joe had come back into her life.

But she'd made a commitment to Lewis, a commitment that had once made her very happy. Shouldn't she give Lewis a chance? Shouldn't she put Joe firmly from her mind and search for common ground with her fiancé? Shouldn't she use her head as well as her heart? For one thing, if she made a mistake, Lewis wasn't the only one who would be hurt. There was Tessa to consider.

Maggie's heart wasn't the only one at risk.

CHAPTER NINE

ON MONDAY NIGHT, Joe stood on another rain-washed street. This one was different from the one he'd stood on with Henry Muff over a week ago. It was also colder out, because autumn had arrived in earnest. It was darker and later than the time he'd met with Henry, because Terry Allerton got off his shift at 11:00 p.m. But one thing hadn't changed: Joe Latham still hated to ask anyone for help. Especially another cop.

In fact, a couple of years ago, he might have gone it alone, no matter the consequences. Hell, a couple of weeks ago, he might have gone it alone.

Joe was trying to clear his name because he wanted his badge. He'd been a good cop, unlike his father whose behavior on the force had been less than exemplary. Citizens needed to be able to count on their cops.

His thoughts flashed to Kenny. The kid was finally beginning to open up to Joe—last week he'd wanted advice on how to act around a girl he liked. Joe took the responsibility seriously. How would Kenny feel if Joe was thrown off the police force? The boy desperately needed someone to look up to, needed to see an adult successful at his job, and proud of the work he did.

Joe turned up the collar of his leather jacket and put his hands in his pockets. Then he took a quick walk to the corner through the drizzle. It was wet, but the walk got his blood pumping.

He needed to track down Rose before Maggie got it into her head to go back down to that bar. Joe had gone to the bar every night since Maggie had been there, and sat in his Jeep, waiting for Rose to appear. She never had.

A small black Honda stopped at the curb. Joe stepped toward it in the drizzle. In the back seat was a child carrier. But when the young cop got out, he was alone. He'd changed from his uniform and now wore a college sweatshirt. Joe hated to involve Terry. Terry was young, had just really begun his career. But he'd offered to help the day of Joe's interview with Internal Affairs.

Terry slammed the car door, lifted a hand, then came up onto the covered walkway.

"I've got most of them," Terry said. "There're just a few more to run, sometime when the station is quiet."

"Be careful," Joe cautioned, taking the sheaf of paper Terry handed him. It felt a whole lot thicker than the one Henry had given him.

"I will. I know what I'm doing."

"Thanks." Joe meant it.

"Yeah." Terry kicked at a place where the pavement had heaved. "I was glad to do it, you know? Really glad."

"I don't want to get you in trouble."

"Give me some credit." He grinned, an infectious smile, and Joe found himself smiling back. "The thing is," Terry went on, "sometimes you just gotta do the right thing. Not the thing regulations say, but the right thing. You gave me that chance, the chance to help out somebody who deserves it."

"Well, thanks."

"Listen, if these records don't tell you what you need to know, I'll help you figure something out."

Terry got back in his car and drove away. Joe walked to his own car, which was parked a few buildings away. He discovered that he'd begun to hope again. If the description on one of these arrest reports matched the description of Rose, he'd know her real name.

He thought about Terry helping him out. It felt good to trust someone. Sometimes the right thing to do was to let another person help instead of going it alone. Maybe if he'd been that way with Maggie...

But Joe knew his limitations. He'd be the best cop he could, he'd be a good friend to Kenny, and he'd ask for help when he needed it. So when the case was over, he wouldn't see her again.

His mind's eye flashed to the modern white condo he lived in, and he thought of the years ahead. Bleak.

Well, he'd known all along that he couldn't have more. If he ever thought differently—and sometimes when Maggie was with him he did—there was only one name he needed to repeat in his mind. Alex. There were no second chances when you'd blown it as badly as Joe had. After all, his son hadn't had a second chance, had he?

"WE'RE AGREED THEN," Maggie said, standing on the steps outside police headquarters. "We won't mention Rose to Internal Affairs."

Joe shook his head. "Not with these guys. Not until we have more. I've reviewed everything I got from my contact, all the arrest records he's been able to pull so far. Nobody who was arrested for solicitation in that area matches Rose's description. But I'm still waiting for the rest of the reports, and I don't want the, ah, pipeline closed before I do."

He said the words quietly, because there were people coming and going. In ten minutes he'd have a final questioning by Internal Affairs. Then the I.A.D. officers would presumably finish whatever investigation they were doing and issue their report.

Maggie nodded. "I hope you turn up something soon. Angela knows a lot of police officers, and she put the feelers out, looking for any gossip about what's going to happen on your case. Her sources say that the chief is looking at this investigation very closely. Given that study by the governor's office, he can't look soft on internal investigations. Seems Smithers isn't the only one with political aspirations."

"I'm being set up," Joe said bitterly.

"Let's just say there's some pressure. Garrick has been sticking up for you, and all that character evidence we submitted may be giving them some pause. The bottom line seems to be, if you can clear your name, fine. If you can't, you're not going to get any benefit of the doubt from I.A."

"You aren't telling me anything I didn't suspect, especially after our first hearing. So we don't say much, we just find out what they came up with. Ready?"

"Ready," she said. They climbed the steps together. He held the door for her, then put a hand on the small of her back to guide her through it.

She felt that casual touch right to her bones.

Although this was not the time to be thinking about her own life, she knew that pretty soon she was going to have to make a decision. The investigation would be over soon, one way or another. She and Lewis had talked some. He wasn't pushing her into a hasty decision, he'd said. She appreciated that. Caring about Lewis had always been easy.

Joe had never been easy. As they walked into the same barren office where the first interview had taken place, she glanced at him. His expression gave away nothing of what he must be feeling. He was as closed as he'd been seven years ago.

Garrick began the discussion, saying he'd read the materials Maggie had submitted, and interviewed all

Joe's character witnesses. Then he said he and Detective Smithers had reached a decision.

Joe said, "What? You're not done already? What have you done to actually try to track down any of the witnesses to the shooting?"

Garrick ran a weary hand over his forehead. "There aren't any," he said flatly. "That's our official conclusion. We've decided. You, Detective Latham, fired on an unarmed suspect. What other conclusion is there?" His voice became emotionless, clipped. "We have no choice but to officially recommend that you be terminated from the police force."

Even though Joe told himself he should have been prepared for this, he was stunned. *Terminated. After fourteen years of late nights, of undercover assignments, of dealing with dopeheads and criminals, of counseling and protecting. Of putting his own life on the line. Terminated.* "The guy was armed." He didn't know what else to say. He started to rise. "I said the guy had a gun. I know he had a gun."

Maggie put out a hand and stayed him. But panic was a fist in Joe's chest and he couldn't remain calm. "Look, if I'm such a trigger-happy cop, how come I've never had to fire my weapon before?"

Maggie fixed her gaze on Garrick. "Detective Latham poses an interesting question, doesn't he?"

Garrick shot Joe a look, but merely shook his head regretfully.

Jesus, Joe thought, was this the end? "You've finished your investigation? I thought I had more time—''

''There's no evidence, Detective Latham.'' Smithers folded his hands. ''Unless you have something to share with us that you haven't shared?''

Maggie spoke, ''Just a minute.'' She leaned forward and put a sheaf of paper on the desk. ''Here is the city's labor contract, and here are copies of relevant parts of the Ohio Revised Code dealing with the civil service. You'll see that there are corresponding sections in both the code and the labor contract the city negotiated with the officers. These regulations allow any officer who is the subject of an investigation to have two weeks to make an additional written report.''

''You've had a lot more than two weeks,'' Smithers said.

''That doesn't count. We get fourteen days from the time we make a formal request.'' She tapped a fingernail on the report. ''Here, read it for yourself. I know it's an obscure subsection, but—'' She cut herself off and shrugged. ''I think, under the circumstances, that we'll invoke that subsection. We're going to be filing another written report, gentlemen.''

Smithers pushed the paperwork aside. ''I can't see dragging this out—''

''No, I'm sure you can't,'' Maggie replied.

Joe wanted to drag her from her chair and hug her. Somewhere, buried in the hundreds, no, thousands of government regulations, Maggie had found the one that would buy Joe time. He wanted to stand her up and spin her around. Thanks to Maggie, he was still a police officer for at least another two weeks.

Smithers said, "Oh, for God's sake."

Garrick spoke up for the first time since Maggie had put the papers on the desk. "I admit, I didn't like the conclusions I was forced to draw here. If you want more time, Detective Latham, you get more time."

Joe's body relaxed slightly. "Fine," he said.

A couple of minutes later, he and Maggie were back on the street. "Well, you were right. They sure had it in for me."

"Garrick didn't seem to. I guess he really didn't think we could come up with more."

"How did you know they were going to pull a stunt like that?"

She looked up at him, her eyes dark and serious. "I didn't. But I was trying to prepare for anything they dished out."

"Thanks."

"That's why you hired me." She cracked a small smile.

He smiled back at her. An unmistakable... something ran between them. Something undeniably physical, sexual. But something more, too. Something that said that in some way, they were in this together. The tight fist in Joe's chest started to relax a little.

She broke the moment. "I bought us some wiggle room. We could have shown them the note, but since we have reason not to trust them, I'm glad we didn't. Now we have a chance to track down Rose on our own. But time is running out, Joe.''

And just like that, the fist was back. He knew he shouldn't be thinking about touching Maggie, knew he was wrong to look at her the way he just had. After all, what did he have to offer her? He was a cop on suspension—not exactly the man of anyone's dreams.

THAT EVENING, Joe went down to the gym, determined to force himself into exhaustion. Maybe then he'd be able to sleep. But after an hour on the exercise equipment, the fist was still there.

He got back in the car, a kind of desperation pushing him tonight.

Fifteen minutes later, Maggie opened her door. ''Hello, Joe.'' She didn't sound surprised to see him. She didn't smile, but her gaze held his. The yellow light from her living room spilled all around her. It looked so warm in there. She stood aside so he could enter.

He took a step inside. He told himself he'd only come here to talk to her. Just talk. But the second he was in her house, something came over him. He pushed the door shut with a foot and took her into his arms.

He felt her initial start, her stiffening. His arms pulled her tight. Her softness touched his hardness, and she fit the way she always had—perfectly. He buried his face in her hair and hung on. She relaxed and he felt her arms around his neck, clinging to him.

He needed to kiss her like he needed to breathe. He tipped up her chin, and his mouth was on hers almost before he knew it. She moaned, and the sound sent fresh heat winging along his body. She wanted him as much as he wanted her.

He thrust his tongue in, and now she was moaning in a little, gasping rhythm and meeting those thrusts with her own tongue. Her hands ran up and down his back; his held her hips tightly against his groin. He started to move her against him.

She whispered, ''No,'' and suddenly, it was the worst word in the English language. He froze.

''No,'' she repeated. ''I can't.''

He pulled back to look at her. Her hair was down, a thick fall of brown-black. Her cheeks were bright, her lips parted.

He wanted her more than any other woman in the world.

''Just let me hold you,'' he said, and he heard the gruff note of desperation in his voice. Her eyes clouded and she opened her mouth as if to speak. He interrupted her. ''Just be my friend. I need my best friend tonight.'' Was that a lie? His body wanted her. Now. But he needed more, too, he realized. He needed her friendship. He needed her comfort.

She searched his face, her eyes wide and vulnerable. Then she nodded and laid her cheek to his chest. Her arms tightened around him, and he felt his heart increase in size until it felt as if it would break through his chest wall. She had no reason to trust him, but she had. He put his own cheek on the top of her head, and felt the smooth silk of her hair on his skin.

How long she held him, he wasn't exactly sure. He made no more attempts to clutch her to him, to press her hips to his own. He was still hard, and he knew she could feel it, just as he could feel the pointed tips of her breasts against his chest. He could tell by her shallow, rapid breathing that she was as aroused as he. But neither spoke. It was excruciating to stay still. But he didn't move a muscle, for fear that she'd pull away.

At some point, he became aware of a clock ticking in the house. For long seconds it was the only sound. Finally conscious of the time passing, he loosened his grip.

For a long moment, she didn't pull away, as if she was as reluctant as he to end their embrace. Finally, she stirred and stepped away.

"Maggie," he said. "I'm sorry." He was sorry for kissing her, when she'd made it clear she didn't want him in her life. He was sorry for complicating her life. And he was very, very sorry for the pain he'd caused her seven years ago.

She laughed a little, a couple of notes that had no humor. "No need to be sorry. I'll take care of this."

He said, "With Lewis."

"Yes."

He said, "Maggie, I know you. You plan to confess, to tell Lewis.'' She didn't say anything, but he could tell by the way her mouth tightened that she intended to do just that. He couldn't let her give up everything. ''Just let me walk out the door and I swear I'll never bother you again.''

She looked him right in the eye. ''You can't keep a promise like that.''

He knew it. And she knew it, too, for the evidence that he couldn't was still there: his aroused body. He shoved his hands in his pockets, and looked directly at her. ''You're fired,'' he said. ''I'll find myself a new lawyer.''

''YOU CAN'T DO THAT. We're near the end of an investigation here. It'd be like changing lawyers while the jury was out on a trial. It's too late for that.'' Maggie turned from him and went through the hallway. ''You might as well come in. I think we need to talk.''

She led him into the kitchen, where she busied herself with the teakettle, filling it with water and setting it on the burner, reaching overhead for cups, to a cupboard under the counter for a tray, then opening drawers. She knew she was putting off the inevitable.

He said, ''Maggie, look at me.''

She didn't. He added, ''I meant what I said in there. I won't complicate your life again.''

She slammed a spoon down on the counter. ''Quit saying that! It's too late. You've already complicated my life!''

She turned to him, and saw the concern in his face. She sighed and her flash of anger vanished. "Joe, I know you need a friend, but we have trouble being friends. Still, don't take all the blame on yourself. I've tried to stay away from you, but I can't."

Her admission hung in the air. Then she added, "It's over with Lewis."

She laid the spoon on the counter. "I realized it was over the second I went into your arms tonight." She went to the table and set out place mats. "But in a way it's not about you," she continued without looking at him. "It's about me and Lewis, and the kind of people we are. I wanted a family so much, and when Tessa and Lewis came along, and they needed me... He's a good man. He's kind, he works hard, and most of all, he loves his daughter. Any woman in the world would be thrilled if he paid attention to her. But it's not enough for me. I know that now, and it has nothing to do with you. You just managed to expose the...cracks in our relationship."

She bit her lip in an attempt to stop the tears she could feel beginning to form. She hoped he wouldn't notice.

He took a couple of steps toward her. "I don't know what to say. But..." He stopped, then took another few steps, toward where she was standing. With a gentle finger, he tipped her chin up. "Are you crying?" he asked softly.

She shook her head, even as a wayward tear trailed down her cheek.

"Aw, Maggie." He took her into his arms, but without fire this time. Instead, he held her, the way she'd held him in the hall. "I always wondered if you really loved Lewis," he said quietly.

"I thought I did." Over in the corner, the kettle started to steam. Joe took a couple of steps, still with her in his arms, and pulled the kettle from the burner.

Maggie added, "But I think maybe I was in love with the idea of being in love, of starting a family. You'd think it wouldn't be that hard to get what I've always wanted. A happy marriage, a good husband, lots of children. After all, plenty of women have a home and a family by my age. It's the norm. So why am I so different?"

"You're not different. You've been...unlucky." He knew all about her childhood. He knew she'd been in seven foster homes by the time she was eighteen.

When they'd been married, no mother and father had come to help her celebrate any of life's occasions. On birthdays, holidays, her graduation from law school, she'd had her friends, and she'd had him. She'd pretended it had been enough, but he knew how she longed for more. She'd always had this idea of a big family gathered around the table, kids playing in the backyard, meals together, fights and making up, television and Little League.

He stroked her hair and held her and simply said, "What will you do?"

"I'll tell him, of course. He'll be hurt, but I can't marry him and risk hurting him more later. I really think he'll be okay, given time. Telling Tessa's going to be the hardest part. Knowing she isn't going to be part of my family.''

"I know, sweetheart.'' He froze. The endearment had slipped out so naturally.

She didn't seem to notice. She pulled away from him fully and seemed very busy with the tea paraphernalia. "Of course, I'll still be her friend, but she was thinking she was going to get a mother out of this engagement.''

"She's sixteen. She'll be out of the house and in college in a couple of years.''

"You never outgrow your need for a mother.'' He realized she'd spoken as if she'd been sure that he wouldn't understand.

He said slowly, "I agree.'' He'd loved his mother. But his father's presence had always overshadowed his mother's. "I was only eighteen when she died. She'd always tried to be a good mother, to settle my father down when he was in one of his ugly moods.''

"You never wanted to talk about any of that.''

"I know.''

"Oh, Joe.'' She raised her hands in a gesture of frustration. "We always come back to that, don't we? To that issue of why you won't talk about things that hurt.''

Because it hurts so bad. That's why, Maggie. Because it hurts too bad.

He almost said something like, "Because there's

no point in talking about it.'' Or something equally, deliberately dismissive.

But he owed her more than that.

He opened his mouth. For a second, he had the sense that he was in terrible danger. But he said, ''I didn't talk to you about my mother because it hurt too much that I couldn't help her when my father treated her badly.'' His voice slowed. ''When we were married, I didn't talk to you about many things because they were too painful. It was easier for me to pretend that I didn't feel anything.''

A stillness fell over the kitchen. She stared at him from across the room. The clock ticked. Finally she said quietly, ''You've never said that before.''

''I know.''

She stared at him. He looked back. ''Are you saying you're ready to talk to me now?'' she asked softly.

Yes. I'm talking to you seven years too late, and even now I'm not sure I'm ready. His throat felt tight. ''I know I owe you,'' he said.

She nodded. ''I agree. You owe me. But I want to make sure of something. I want you to understand that I didn't say I was breaking up with Lewis so I could fall into bed with you.''

God, she was a direct woman. ''I don't expect that.''

Something flickered in her eyes. She didn't speak for a moment, and then she nodded, as if to herself. ''The thing is, I really wonder if the reason I can't put you out of my mind is that we haven't really finished what we started seven years ago. You kept so much of yourself to yourself. You had so many secrets.''

Secrets. Yes.

She looked him in the eye, from her position across the room.

He started to sweat.

She took a few steps toward him. ''I need to know. I've spent seven years trying to get over you, wondering what I could have done to save our marriage. I want to know why I can't seem to get on with my life.'' Her eyes were intent, and the remnants of an old hurt were in their dark, shiny depths.

She wet her lips. ''The funny thing is, I'm not sure you're the same man you were seven years ago. I think of that boy—that Kenny—who you've been doing so much for. I think about you helping at the gym for so long. I think about you putting aside your pride to come to me when you needed legal help.'' She shook her head. ''I think that maybe you've changed and we could—'' Abruptly, she stopped and pressed her lips together.

An acid bit at his gut, and he felt a bitter taste in his mouth. ''I haven't changed, Maggie.'' His voice was gruff. ''For God's sake, don't think I've changed. I was bad for you then and I'm bad for you now.''

''Tell me why. Please,'' she pleaded. ''I need to know.''

He felt a kind of chill go up his spine. He thought

of his dead son, a name that echoed in his mind, a name he'd mentioned briefly seven years ago, about the time he'd asked Maggie to marry him. A name he hadn't mentioned since.

A name she'd brought up shortly after the miscarriage. She'd been crying and she'd said, "I know you lost another child, too. I know you lost Alex."

She didn't know a damn thing, and he'd gone out of the house without saying a word. And he'd taken an undercover assignment that meant he wasn't home for three weeks. He'd come home to bitter words and divorce papers.

Joe considered her words. He didn't want her to fall in love with him again, so maybe now he could be man enough to say the words that would put her off for good. He took a deep breath, then another. Then he said, "All right."

"Really?"

He said, "It's a terrible story, and after you hear it, you'll be showing me the door for good."

She said, "Let me be the judge of that." Her mouth got all soft in the way he loved, but he knew it wouldn't make any difference after she heard what he'd done. Her mouth would never soften for him again.

CHAPTER TEN

THEY SAT in Maggie's living room. He had a sense of unreality, heightened by the fact that the room looked so normal.

Maggie was in the armchair across from him. He leaned forward, a palm resting on each knee, deceptively relaxed, the way he was when questioning a suspect.

She waited. She didn't help him, didn't ask what he had to tell her. He wondered how many witnesses had squirmed in her silence. He felt like bolting.

Instead he said, "Even though I didn't share everything with you, there was a lot you did know. You knew you were my second wife."

She nodded. "You married Joyce when you were twenty, and she was nineteen. She was pregnant."

Just the facts. "Yeah, she was pregnant, and I was the father. We were young, but that's no excuse. I'm not sure I ever loved her, but I married her because that seemed to be the right thing to do. You know how I grew up. I wanted my child to have a better family life."

Her gaze was steady on him, encouraging him.

"We shouldn't have made a child together, and we

shouldn't have gotten married. We argued constantly, right from the beginning. I worked two jobs until I got my badge. I could support us, but I didn't know how to be a husband, and she was bored with being married. Kept saying I was keeping her home, keeping her down. I didn't think I was doing that, but— It doesn't matter. I was as responsible as she was for the fact we didn't get along.''

She nodded again.

''But when Alex was born, I tried to patch things up. I really did,'' he added defensively.

''I believe you,'' she said softly. ''Just tell me.''

''You know Alex died.'' His voice cracked on the last word. He cleared his throat. She started to lean forward, to put out her hand in a gesture of sympathy, but he cut her off. ''What I've never told you is how Alex died.''

She went very still. The clock he kept hearing ticking was in the living room, a little thing on the wall, so small he couldn't believe how loud it sounded. Outside, a couple of cars went by. Then it was quiet again.

''How Alex died was...'' He stopped. There was no right way to say this, because everything about it was horribly, terribly wrong. He tried again to speak but for a moment he couldn't.

Maggie got up from her seat and came to sit beside him. She was so close he could see the tiny weave of her sweater, the places where the seams of her jeans showed white with wear. He could see the thickness

of her eyelashes, darkened by mascara, and he could
see the red softness of her lips.

There was strength in having her near, and he
grasped at that strength. "When Alex was two, Joyce
and I were arguing again. You know, I don't even
remember what we were arguing about. But it was a
hot summer day, and we were out on the lawn where
it was a little cooler. I was getting ready to go to
work. She'd been yelling, I was trying to keep my
temper. I said I was leaving, and I wanted to say
goodbye to Alex. She said he was in the house." His
voice dropped to a whisper. "She said he was in the
house."

He was forcing himself to look at Maggie, to see
the exact moment any caring, any compassion for him
would end. "So I—" His voice cracked. He tried
again. "So I was going to go into the house and say
goodbye. Joyce said, 'You're not leaving. I'm leaving.' She snatched the keys out of my hand. I was
glad to see her go. She marched over to the car—"
he was speaking faster now "—and she got in. She
turned the key and put the car in reverse and shot
down the driveway. Alex wasn't in the house. He was
playing in the driveway."

Maggie's eyes revealed her shock at what he was
saying. Her face was ghostly white. "She ran over
your son?"

He had to look away now. He whispered, "The
sound of it—the sound of it was terrible. I don't even
remember going over there. I guess I told her to call

911. Joyce says I did, but I don't remember saying that. I went over—Alex had been on his tricycle— one of those with the big, bright plastic wheels, like a peppermint candy. The tricycle was all…broken.

"I touched him. I didn't think I should pick him up, but I had to touch my son. I was trying to think what to do, but the minute I touched him… He was so still. He was too still. And then I saw that he was somehow…broken, too…"

A sob shook him, but he choked it back. Maggie moved then and took him to her. He put his cheek against the warmth of her chest and sobbed like he hadn't done since he was small. He hadn't cried when Alex died. He couldn't; it was as if every bit of liquid had been sucked from his body and he had nothing to cry with. He hadn't cried when Maggie had mis-carried and his other child was lost to him seven years ago.

But he cried this night. His son had been dead twelve years, and it was as if it had happened days ago.

Maggie rocked him like a small boy. His sobs were ragged, unchecked, rasping. His chest hurt. He whis-pered, "I didn't love Joyce, but I loved him. I loved my son."

Maggie whispered, "I know you did." He didn't have to see her face to know that she was crying, too. She stroked his hair.

She was giving him the comfort and acceptance he

craved with his whole soul. He said, "It was my fault."

Those four words. He'd said them at last, he'd taken full responsibility out loud, just as he'd always taken full responsibility in the silence of his heart.

Maggie stirred. "It was an accident."

"I would have checked on him if I hadn't been so preoccupied with pushing my own point of view, hadn't been pissed off and more interested in arguing with my wife than with checking on my son."

She lifted her head. Maggie's eyes were red, overflowing with tears. Her nose was red, too, and her lips swollen and moist. Her expression was gentle.

He didn't deserve her kindness, no matter how he might crave it. "Joyce told me it was my responsibility. That I'd started the argument. That I'd been so unreasonable that she'd simply had to get away. She said I was no kind of father. And I knew that was true, because I didn't check. But I loved Alex. I played with him every night. Just gentle stuff...."

Maggie smoothed his hair. "Maybe you should have checked where he was. But it was an accident. She was the one driving. She was the one who should have checked behind her."

Was she saying she understood? That she accepted this about him, this unforgivable breach of his duty to protect and nurture his son?

He said, "People claim that tragedy brings couples closer together. It drove me and Joyce further apart.

I was twenty-two years old, and I had no child, no wife. Only my badge.''

"Oh, Joe." Maggie touched him again.

He fought not to grab her hand and hold on tight enough to hurt.

"Listen to me." She leaned toward him. "You're a good man. Don't you realize that? You loved your son, you grieved as a father." She touched his shoulder. "Dear God, why didn't you tell me this? Why didn't you give me a chance to understand? If you wanted forgiveness, why didn't you give me a chance to forgive you?"

"I don't deserve forgiveness," he said gruffly. "That's not everything I did. Listen to me now, Maggie."

Now that he'd begun, he had to finish. "When I met you, I didn't tell you the whole story about Alex, I just told you he died. I didn't tell you the whole story because I told myself I'd put all this behind me, that I'd never forget my little boy but I could go on. That I could have a family with you. We met and we dated and I fell in love. It all went so fast. That's no excuse though. What it comes down to is, I loved you so much that I…deluded myself."

Tears misted in her eyes again. "But you didn't really want kids." She bit her lip.

"I did want kids, in a way. I like kids. I thought I could handle it. I thought we could make a go of it, be happy."

"We *were* happy. You brought me all those silly

presents.'' Her dark eyes seemed to see something far away. ''You bought me those huge fuzzy slippers. You gave me pink balloons and bubble gum for my birthday. I thought you were—well, not exactly carefree, but not—not carrying this terrible guilt around.''

''You brought out something in me I didn't even know was there. I was so happy, but I was always afraid it couldn't last. That something would happen. When you got pregnant, I was…terrified.''

He tipped her chin up so that she was forced to focus fully on him. ''Understand now? The big tough detective was terrified at the thought of being a father. He was so wrapped up in his own fear that he couldn't share his wife's happiness. What kind of husband is that? What kind of father does a man like me make?''

She just looked at him. He swallowed. ''I had my badge. I could let work suck me in, take all of me, so that I could function. So that's what I did. When you got pregnant, I just worked harder. So that I didn't have to think about what could happen again.''

She leaned back on the sofa and closed her eyes, as if the rawness in his voice was more than she could bear. ''And then something happened,'' she said softly.

''It was as if God knew I was happy. That I shouldn't be happy. And so he punished me. Punished me, and punished you because you'd hooked up with me.''

She opened her eyes. ''Joe, why didn't you tell me? We could have shared this.''

"It wasn't yours to have to share," he said simply. "I didn't watch over my son, and I married you and didn't tell you I wasn't...whole."

"So you took that undercover assignment."

"I hid from you. I didn't want you to see how I was feeling, that I was so scared. And then you lost the baby, and I came home. But I didn't want you to see that I hurt, too. That I felt responsible. It was easier not to see you, to take other assignments. It was easier not to deal with...all that. It always has been."

She touched his cheek. "I would have helped you. I loved you so much. But if you couldn't tell me then, why are you telling me now?"

He pulled back. He felt exhausted, completely, utterly drained, as though he'd been doing hard physical work. "Because you're about to break up with your fiancé. You said you couldn't get me off your mind. So, before I screw things up for you, I want you to see me as I am, so you can tell me to leave this house. So that when this case is over, you can walk away from me without a second thought." He stood. "I know what I did to you seven years ago. But this time, you get to see the real Joe Latham."

She stood up, too. She seemed sad, a little dazed. She whispered again, "I can't believe you didn't tell me."

He said, "I can't believe I just did." The odd thing was, he felt a little better for telling her. He touched her cheek and said only, "Thank you."

She put a hand over his, holding him to her. Under

his hand, she felt warm, vibrant, alive. He had the urge to take her in his arms. He didn't. Instead, he said, "I'm going now."

She walked him to the door. There, she hesitated and then said, "You're a good man, Joe. Don't ever forget it."

He wanted to believe her. He wanted to so badly that the wanting was a kind of pain in itself. But his son was dead. And even confessing that and sharing it with Maggie didn't change the facts. Alex would never get the chance to grow up. He'd never celebrate a birthday, learn to ride a bike, go to school. And Joe would never be able to clap his son on the back and shout with him when they watched a football game on television.

The loss threatened to overwhelm him, just as he'd always feared. He had to keep control. Even with Maggie. Especially with Maggie.

MAGGIE PACED. She went back and forth in her small bedroom, where a square of light from the window highlighted the middle of her high Victorian bed. Her bare feet touched a hooked rug, then the wood floor. Turning, she hit rug again, floor again.

Warm rug, cold floor.

Caring Joe.

Secretive Joe.

She hadn't known him at all.

She'd cried twice already tonight. Once in the living room, holding Joe and sharing his pain. Once later alone in bed, as full realization of what had happened to him had really sunk in.

She pulled a robe on over her nightgown and went down to the kitchen. She rooted around in the refrigerator, and pulled out a carton of vanilla yogurt. Sticking a spoon into the container, she hoped the yogurt would calm her stomach.

She wandered around the house, still in her bare feet, touching her favorite things. A silver picture frame, cool, then warming under her fingertips. The rough, feathery heads of wheat in a dried-flower bouquet. The fine, careful stitching in the old quilt that covered the back of the oak rocker. When she got to the living-room window, she looked out toward the direction of Joe's condo. Was he sleeping? Or was he looking out the window toward her? Had he shed tears again for his lost child, or was he even now burying that sadness deep inside him again?

One thing she knew: she didn't hold him responsible for Alex's death. She could picture the argument he and his wife had had, pictured the situation escalating out of control. Alex's death had been a tragic accident. She'd said that to Joe, but she knew he didn't agree.

So it didn't matter if she forgave Joe, he couldn't forgive himself. He thought he didn't deserve happiness.

She stood there, a little chilled, realizing that she'd fallen in love with her ex-husband. Again. She loved his honor, and his intellect, his values and even his overblown sense of responsibility. Nothing he'd said tonight had changed that feeling. She longed to go to him now, and hold him again, to tell him she understood and it was all right.

Maggie took the carton and spoon to the kitchen, then headed up the stairs to her bedroom.

A month ago, she'd been so sure her life was on track. That her life made sense. That she was going to be happy and content.

She was far less certain of that tonight.

THAT SUNDAY EVENING, Kenny stood in the kitchen and counted his mother's pills. There were nearly as many as there had been a week ago.

"What are you doing?"

Startled, he dropped the bottle. It rolled on the kitchen counter. "Nothing."

"You weren't getting in my nerve pills, were you?" His mom was in the doorway.

"No!"

"Good. You stay out of my pills. You stay off drugs."

He lifted his hands to ward off the lecture he felt coming on. "Whatever," he said with real belligerence.

She came into the kitchen, opened the cupboard door and took down a can of beans. Her hands were shaking.

"Hey, are you all right?"

She gave him a strained smile. "Sure. Yeah."

He wondered why she didn't take one of her pills. She seemed really rattled. He wondered why she didn't take a drink. Were they so low on money that she couldn't even buy a bottle of booze?

When he could, he headed out of the kitchen and went to his mom's bedroom. He could hear her clanking pots in the kitchen. So he went over to her dresser drawer. The dresser was old and had this crummy lock built into it. His mom had a key.

He took one of her hairpins off the dresser top and wiggled it in the lock. In a couple of seconds, he had the drawer open.

There was still some money there, not a lot.

He tried not to worry about that as he went to watch TV. But even *Cow and Chicken,* which was a really cool show for a cartoon, couldn't get him laughing tonight. He just…felt weird. Edgy, like he guessed his mom must feel on a lot of days.

He thought about Celeste. On Friday, she'd let him kiss her. He couldn't believe that, couldn't believe she liked him. He'd kissed her in the shadow of a doorway of a building near the playground. Then he'd walked her home.

Her apartment was in an even worse neighborhood than his, because it was officially Nightshade territory. You didn't hang out on the street too much there, even in daylight, and even inside, you didn't walk by a window if you could help it. There was too much shooting on the street to make that safe.

Most of the girls who lived in Celeste's block were

bad-looking, sort of hard, with black nail polish and lots of studs in their ears. Celeste wasn't like that.

Celeste was really nice. She was…sweet.

He thought how she smelled good and how she smiled at him. How good the kiss felt. He thought about touching her chest, but knew he wouldn't do that unless she wanted it, too.

She'd told him that in her neighborhood, some of the Nightshade were starting to make comments to her. Comments Kenny didn't like at all. He told her to be with him or her girlfriends all the time. At school she was pretty safe because the school didn't allow gang colors.

He'd take care of her.

Edgy again, he turned off the set.

His mom passed him on her way out the door. When he saw what she was wearing, his heart sank.

She must have seen how he was looking at her. "I'm only going out with Roger."

"It's Sunday," he said. He knew that didn't really matter. So he added, "It's early." She never went out this early, not if she was going out for…that.

"I thought I'd go early. It's, you know, safer to meet Roger when it's early."

He stood up. "What's going on?"

She bit her lip and hesitated. Then— "I saw your Joe there."

"At the bar?" Excitement gripped him. He forgot to pretend that he didn't know where she was going.

"Yes. Late one night. I saw his picture in the newspaper. Then when I saw him at the bar, I didn't recognize him at first, but then I did." It was like she was forgetting to pretend, too. "He's been back a few times, asking questions, hanging around. I'm afraid he's…trying to find me."

"Joe can help you, Mom." His heart was starting to pound.

"How?" she demanded.

"Just tell what you saw. Joe will get his badge back and he'll help you."

She gave him a sad smile. "If he had a badge, he'd just arrest me. I'm scared of the Nightshade, and I'm scared of your cop, and I'm scared of…everything." She took a step toward him. "You didn't tell, did you? You promised."

"I didn't tell." She was looking at him like maybe she didn't believe him, and he thought how when she hadn't been drinking she was pretty smart in a lot of ways. So he said again, "No." That was why he'd done the note the way he had. So he wouldn't have to lie to her.

She gave him another sad smile, and Kenny could see the relief in it. "I've got to go," she said. "Get some sleep, okay? Don't stay up too late. You've got school in the morning."

And she was gone. He sat there thinking of the weirdness of what was going on. How she was going out so early. Okay, maybe she was going out early so she wouldn't run into Joe. That part made sense. But she hadn't been drinking. He knew that. He could tell almost to the swallow how much she'd had to drink. And every other time she'd gone out, she'd had plenty.

He stood and walked to the window. He saw his mom in the street, walking, her clothes all glittery, sparking under the streetlights.

He thought about guys touching her, and he got a sick feeling in his gut. He wanted to talk to Joe about this, but what could he say? Joe, my mother is a wh—

Even in his mind he couldn't say it. Not that word. Not about his mom. For a second, he had a horrible urge to cry like a little kid.

Had that lady lawyer got his note? She must have, because Joe had been down at the bar. But now his mom was going too early for Joe to see her.

Kenny had to do something.

CHAPTER ELEVEN

THAT SAME SUNDAY evening, Maggie went to Lewis's house. Tessa was out with friends, Lewis had said when Maggie'd phoned. That was good; what she needed to say to Lewis needed to be said in private.

She rang the doorbell and put her hand in the pocket of her cotton slacks, fingering the engagement ring there. She'd taken the precaution of removing the ring at home, using soap and water to make it slide. She knew what she had to do, and she didn't want anything to go wrong, to prolong the hurt to her fiancé.

While she waited, she took in her surroundings—the red brick of the veranda floor, the solid feel of the white painted trim around the door. The four-bedroom colonial had been very much to her taste. She'd imagined filling those bedrooms with kids.

She shook off the thought. She was doing the right thing.

She had to face Lewis and tell the truth. She hadn't been honest with him—or with herself. No matter how comfortable their relationship had been, she didn't love him.

Being alone wasn't the worst thing in the world. She was used to relying on herself, after all.

Lewis opened the door. Without even waiting for him to greet her, she said, "We have to talk."

"So you said on the telephone earlier." He gave her a worried smile, and held the door for her.

She went by him through the foyer and into his study. It was a dim room with dark green walls, leather chairs, English-hunt prints on the walls. He offered her a drink; she declined. They sat together on the sofa.

She said, "Lewis—"

At the same time he said, "Maggie—"

Before she could go on, he said, "I know you've been unhappy and preoccupied. I know you're having doubts about us, and I just want to say, I've also been thinking and I know we can work this out." His lean, handsome face was sincere. "You know I love you."

She swallowed. "That's what makes it so hard. I know you care for me, and I'm going to have to hurt you. But sometimes I wonder..." She paused, because even though she'd rehearsed this conversation, actually saying the words was hard. "Do you really love me or do you love the *idea* of loving me?"

There was a long pause. Some flicker of something—guilt?—went through his gaze, and he looked away.

She said, "I think we've been a convenience for each other." She winced as she said it. She'd been planning to marry this man! Was convenience really all it had ever been about? She added, "Well, maybe convenience wasn't all of it, maybe that's the wrong word. We certainly cared about each other, but we were—we were fulfilling needs in each other."

He took her hand. "Isn't that love?" he asked quietly.

"I don't know. Maybe that's a kind of love, but I need more than that, and you deserve more than that."

He didn't respond. Instead, he was sitting frozen, her hand held loosely in his, his back straight. He didn't look at her. Finally, he said, "This is about sex, and Joe Latham."

Guilt washed over Maggie. "You said something about Joe the last time, but this is between you and me. Yes, Joe might have made me see some things—"

Lewis let out a syllable of disgust, one note that told her he wasn't as in control of himself as he appeared to be. She hurried on. "He exposed the cracks in our relationship, that's all. I like you, Lewis. I always have. But I don't love you." There. She'd said it.

"I love you," he said again.

"Do you?" she asked as gently as she could. "Don't you really mean you love my rapport with Tessa, and you love me because for the first time since Elizabeth died, you felt like leaving the house?"

"That's not true." He turned to her with a sudden desperation. He gripped her hand harder. "I'm not the kind of man who'd be with a woman because of—of convenience. I love you.''

He'd said *I love you* more times in this one conversation than he had in six months. As gently as she could, she disengaged her hand from his. ''I admire you. I think you'll be happier when you have a chance to be over me—''

''How am I supposed to get over you? Give me some credit. I'm not some teenager to be palmed off with a lot of platitudes from love songs.'' He rose and went to the desk. He picked up a silver letter opener and set it down, then made a fist and rapped it on the wooden top of the desk. His back was to her.

''I'm sorry,'' she said softly, her hands clasped in her lap. Her mind flashed to some of the good times they'd had, when they'd been getting to know each other, when she'd thought he might be the one. But she realized now that she'd decided she loved Lewis when she'd gotten to know Tessa. And that shamed her. ''I'm sorry I'm hurting you. I'm sorry I don't have the right words.''

He turned. ''Tell me what I've done wrong. I thought you were interested in my business, in cookware, I thought you liked hearing what we ought to do to put your law firm on solid ground, but I gathered you were impatient with me the other night. Because I haven't read too many books, is that it? He reads books, does he?'' His voice had risen.

''Lewis—''

"Oh, hell, Maggie, I swear, I won't talk about business all the time, I'll never talk business again—"

"Lewis, stop!"

He stopped, then said, "What in God's name am I going to tell Tessa? How am I going to tell her I blew it?" He took a couple of strides toward the window and stood looking out, his face in profile.

He looked suddenly alone, almost unbearably so. She thought of his wife's lingering death. She thought of his wonderful daughter, a daughter he loved but didn't understand.

She wished she could love him. It would be so easy. Taking the ring from her pocket, she went to him and slipped it into his palm. He made a fist over the diamond. Without looking at him, she said, "You didn't blow it," and her voice wobbled a little.

He was quiet for a minute, then he said, "You know, maybe I didn't. You have your faults, too."

She didn't want to get into an argument, so she remained silent.

He said, "Many women would be interested in what I have to offer."

"That's true. I hope you find the right woman. I really do."

"You're throwing a lot away."

She was intent now on finishing the conversation and leaving. But she had one more thing to say. One request to make. "Lewis, will you let me tell Tessa myself? You'll have plenty of time to talk to her, but I—" Her voice cracked, despite her best efforts. "I love her, Lewis. I hate that I'm not going to be her stepmother.''

He looked at her with a mixture of anger and disappointment still on his face. "Just remember whose choice that is."

"I know you're angry. But Tessa's had so much loss to deal with. I'd like to let her know I love her. Let's not let what's happening to you and me make it worse for her."

He thought, nodded. "Yes, you can tell her. It might be better that way."

She said, "Thank you. Maybe this could be an opportunity for you two to become closer. Afterward, you could talk to her—"

"She's *my* daughter. I'll decide how I'm going to handle her."

He spoke the absolute truth, she thought with a sudden stab of hurt.

He held the door for her, but he didn't walk her to her car. She heard the door slam shut behind her, and she thought, *Well, it's over.*

A few tears pricked her eyes. Maggie resolved to try hard to make Tessa understand. If she couldn't be the girl's mother, then she'd try hard to be her friend.

THE NEXT DAY Maggie sat at her desk and looked through the mail that her secretary had left there. There were motions from a big law firm in town, one that liked to dispute every point. Maggie would respond in kind; it made sense to show them that she wouldn't be intimidated. There was a report from the social worker on one of her juvenile cases. There was some paperwork appointing her to another case, in juvenile court again.

She flipped through the pile, reading rapidly. She tried to get into the groove of work, but she was distracted. She glanced at the picture on her desk. She and Lewis were seated next to each other, his hand covering hers. Sprawling on the floor at their feet, her long red hair hanging over her shoulders, her smile wide, was Tessa.

Maggie had to talk to the girl when she came in to work today.

She sighed. It was going to be rough.

At least things at the firm seemed to be improving. The stacks of mail had been growing. Today's pile was testament that she had a lot more cases than she'd had a few weeks ago. She'd got three new clients thanks to Joe. The lady who'd read the article in the newspaper, and two police officers, whose families had come in for the routine legal matters that Maggie enjoyed. Wills and estate planning, the legal work for a new house. Her partners were busy, too. Angela had picked up some criminal cases. Sharon had a new, large corporate client.

It was great to see the firm succeed. Now if she could only get the personal side of her life working.

She shook her head and forced herself to concentrate on work. There were two notes on the bottom of the stack of mail. Her secretary hadn't opened them. Maggie picked up the first and slit the envelope. She started to pull out a thank-you note when her eye fell on the second envelope.

Her heart skipped a beat. "Mrs. Hannan," it said on the front. Mrs. Blue ink. Printing. It was the same handwriting as before. She grabbed a tissue and used it to pick up the envelope. She slit it open carefully.

The lady is afraid. Go earlier.

Her hands quivering, she reread the note, once, twice, three times. She didn't know what to make of it, but one thing was clear. The writer of the note wanted to tell her something, but wasn't prepared to come out and say it.

Why? Was the person who wrote it a member of the Nightshade, in which case he'd be afraid of retaliation? But a member of the Nightshade would be an unlikely person to help Joe.

Maggie picked up the phone to call Joe, then stopped, the receiver in her hand. He was the client; he deserved to know of this latest development.

But the lady—it had to be Rose—was afraid. Of the Nightshade? Maybe. Of course, she was a prostitute, so she probably didn't care too much for cops. Was she afraid of the police? Of Joe? Maggie knew Joe had been going to the bar regularly. They didn't have too much time left, and he'd mentioned he was staking out the place late every evening. What if the "lady around the bar" had spotted him and now was staying away?

Go earlier. That was a clue, a clue that perhaps Rose was trying to avoid Joe.

Maggie worried her lower lip, then got up and looked out the window over the skyline of Plainfield. She glanced in the direction of Pierce and Goshen. Even the rooftops over there looked faded. Worn. And, she knew, dangerous.

Maggie swallowed hard as she realized that if she wanted to help Joe, there was only one thing to do. She'd have to track down Rose. And she'd have to do it alone.

She heard the outer door open and Tessa come in, calling hello. Maggie squared her shoulders. It was time to talk to Tessa.

"So, WHAT'S UP? Dad's acting weird, says you want to talk to me." Tessa stood before her. Her long hair was pulled up on top of her head, secured with a glittery plastic ring, and she wore thick mascara and just a touch of pink lip gloss. A few freckles showed through her light makeup. Her red sweater was dramatic in color but modest in design, though she wore black platform heels with big straps that made her feet seem large and clunky. She looked like a kid and an adult all at once. A child-woman.

"Yes, I needed to talk to you." Maggie had been rehearsing the words. "Let's take a walk."

"I have some cases to check on the computer for Aunt Sharon."

"You'll have time later, or tomorrow. I know

Sharon doesn't really need that brief until next week.''

"Yeah, but she hates deadlines. You know Aunt Sharon.''

"I'll clear it with her,'' Maggie promised.

A few moments later, she and Tessa were on the sidewalk. Tall buildings were all around them. Without agreeing on a destination, they walked toward the river.

Maggie said, "Tessa, I have something to tell you that makes me sad, and I don't think you're going to like it.''

They had come to the small park that overlooked the river. Maggie sat down on a bench, Tessa beside her. She took the girl's hand. It was chilled. "Whatever you think about me in the next few minutes, I want you to remember something. I love you, and I'll always love you.''

• "You better just go ahead and say what you want, Maggie. Your hand is sweaty.'' Her voice—and her eyes—revealed her anxiety.

"Your dad and I have decided to break off our engagement.''

Tessa's eyes got very round. "You're not getting married?''

"No, honey. We're not.''

"And Dad wants this?" Her voice rose on the last words, but she was still sitting down.

"He's not happy about it. It was my decision. He didn't do anything wrong.''

Tessa simply sat, her face white.

Say something, Tessa, Maggie thought. In every waking moment of Tessa's life, the girl had something to say.

Not this time. The teenager sat quietly as the cool breeze lifted strands of her hair.

Maggie drew a deep breath and continued. "I think a great deal of your father. He's a wonderful man. He's kind, and he loves you dearly, and that means a lot to me because I love you dearly, too. He's intelligent, and he works hard, and he's tried as hard as he can to make a home for you."

"So why don't you want to marry him?" There was accusation in her eyes.

"I thought that we could have a happy life, but I've decided we can't."

"Why?"

"It just isn't working out."

"Why? Don't you love him?"

Maggie had wanted to avoid having to say this part, but trust Tessa to push her. "No," she said as gently as she could. "I respect your dad, but I realized I don't love him enough to be married to him."

Tessa jumped up. "You don't love him at all if you could do this to him! Isn't that true?" Her eyes flashed fire. "You don't love him at all!"

Maggie clenched her hands in her lap. "I like him. I respect him. But you're right, I don't love him. It's not his fault, Tessa. He tried."

"Sure, he tried. He didn't break off his engagement

to you. You're the one who's screwing this up! Why can't you just marry him?''

Maggie stood, and put a hand on Tessa's forearm. ''You know that two people have to really love each other to make a marriage work.''

Tessa jerked away. ''I read in books all the time how two people get married because it makes sense, like you know, they'll keep the family estates or something like that, and then they realize how much they love each other—''

''This isn't a book, honey.'' Maggie swallowed as she saw the tears gathering in Tessa's eyes, and then start to fall on her cheeks. She reached out to hug the girl, but Tessa took a few firm steps away from her.

She tried to think of something to say, something to make this easier. She said, ''Your father and your mother loved each other so much, and I want your dad to have that with the woman he marries.''

''I want him to marry you,'' Tessa said stubbornly.

''That isn't going to happen. You're old enough to understand that you can't have everything you want. But no matter what, I still want you in my life. I still want us to be friends.''

Tessa turned away from her. ''Yeah, well, Maggie, you just said we don't always get what we want. My dad really loved you. I never thought you'd be this— this cruel.'' She flung out an arm to emphasize her words. ''Maybe you're just not good enough for my father.'' She turned and stomped up the stairs from the park to the street.

"Wait!" Maggie called. Tessa picked up her pace until she was almost running. Maggie watched as she headed back up the block to the office building, then turned in.

Maggie sat back down slowly. She'd hurt Tessa, something she'd tried so hard to avoid. She took out a tissue and wiped her own eyes. She was crying in earnest now. It was as if she'd lost another child. This time, a teenage daughter she loved dearly. Would Tessa ever forgive her? Maggie prayed that one day the two of them could be friends.

Finally, she wiped her eyes one last time, stood up, squared her shoulders and prepared to face the music. Tessa wasn't the only one Maggie had to speak to today.

She didn't have to wait long. She got back to the office to find that Tessa had cleaned out her desk and left. Her secretary shot Maggie a sympathetic glance as Maggie hurried by her. She'd not gotten much farther than the threshold of her own office when Sharon came stomping in.

Sharon pushed the door closed and stood facing Maggie, her hands on her hips. "What's this about you breaking off your engagement? How could you do it?"

Somehow Maggie found the strength to explain in words similar to the ones she'd used with Tessa. She finished with, "I realized that though he's a fine man, I just don't love him."

Sharon spoke, one note of dismissive disgust.

Maggie held out a hand in a supplicating gesture. "I wish I did, Sharon. You have no idea how much. But I don't, and it would be rotten of me to marry him when I feel like this."

"You promised to marry him. Wouldn't it have been easier to decide you didn't love the man before he put that diamond on your finger?"

"Of course it would have. But I was...confused."

"You're an awfully smart woman to be confused."

Smart had nothing to do with it, Maggie knew. The head and the heart were not connected. And she realized with a sudden insight that by ignoring her heart and listening to her head, to that voice that had said *this is perfect, this is easy,* she had hurt two people terribly.

Sharon paced. "You had everything. You should have seen Tessa. Her makeup was running. She was crying, Maggie!"

Maggie bit her lip. "I know, and I'm sorry." Her voice dropped to a whisper for a moment. "So very sorry." She stood. "Maybe you could talk to her. Maybe you could help her see—"

"I tried when her mother died. She didn't... I don't know, we couldn't...connect." Her own voice had dropped, and Maggie realized through her own misery that Sharon had been hurt, too. That at least once before, she had really tried to reach out to her niece and had been rebuffed.

"Could you try again?" Maggie asked.

"Why? So you can moon over Joe Latham without feeling guilty for abandoning her?"

Maggie winced. "No, so you and she can have something precious. Something I apparently just gave up, but that you can have, because you're family."

Sharon shook her head. She said very quietly and evenly, "I think you gave up your right to give this family advice when you took that engagement ring off your finger."

"I was just thinking of Tessa. But you're right. You usually are."

Sharon walked over to Maggie's big window and stood looking out. The silence got a little long. Finally she said, "Cliff Kincaid over at Diller, Culleng and Culleng is looking for a real estate specialist. He's been trying to get me to go to lunch and talk about joining their firm."

Maggie squeezed her eyes shut. First Tessa, now Sharon. "I don't want to lose you," she said carefully. Sharon was not one to respond to an emotional plea, but Maggie said what was in her heart anyway. "I care about you. You're my friend. We've known each other since law school, since before I ever met Lewis. Please give yourself time to think things over. You hated big-firm politics almost more than I did. Don't do anything rash."

Sharon turned to her, her eyes sad. "I just don't see how I can stay and work with you every day, Maggie. I might not say it much, but I love my brother and I love Tessa. They went through this with

Elizabeth, and I can't forgive you for hurting them again.''

''The firm won't survive if you leave,'' Maggie pointed out. ''You believed in it. You're our real estate and trust specialist. We need you.''

Sharon walked past her. ''I can't think about that now.''

''There's Angela to consider,'' Maggie said desperately. ''She didn't ask for any of this when she signed on. And she needs the money the firm brings in.''

For the first time, Sharon seemed to waver. She chewed her lip and thought. ''All right. I'll think about everything you've said and let you know. But Maggie, this is—this is hard for me.''

She was gone, shutting the door gently behind her. It was the most emotion Maggie had ever heard her friend express.

She put her head in her hands. In the space of twenty-four hours, she'd lost her fiancé, the girl she'd come to think of as her daughter, a friend, and maybe even the firm.

And worse, the one person she wanted to call, the one person she wanted to see, was Joe.

But she couldn't call him. She was afraid. Because what she wanted might not be what she needed.

And she simply couldn't stand any more heartache today.

CHAPTER TWELVE

"I COULD BEAT them up, but I'm not allowed to." Kenny's freckled face was pale and earnest. He'd hardly touched the double cheeseburger Joe had ordered for him.

"Beating people up never solves the problem," Joe said. "Let's talk about some other options you might have here."

"You sound like a counselor," Kenny said in disgust.

Joe didn't smile. He knew this was important to Kenny, though he couldn't tell—yet—how serious the threat at school was. "I *am* a counselor, with the Kids at Risk."

Kenny leaned forward. "Yeah, sure, but you're also *Joe*."

The way he said the name "Joe" sent the oddest sensation through Joe. It was a good feeling to know how much Kenny relied on him, but it scared him, too. He didn't want to blow it with this kid. "Tell me everything that's going on."

"Well, the biggest problem is Jason Sego. He's the one who's hassling Celeste."

"Why is he bothering her?"

Kenny shrugged. The crack in the lens of his glasses glinted. "I don't know, exactly. Just for stuff. Because she's pretty but she won't talk to him much. And today he brushed up against her, you know, like with his body and stuff."

Kenny's face was red but his eyes were hot with outrage. "He said something about it being because I was friends with a cop." He paused. "I don't know what to do. I'd quit the Kids at Risk, but I'm on probation and stuff, and I can't. If I went to juvenile hall, Jason could bother Celeste all he wanted and I couldn't stop it."

Joe nodded, listening. "Did he threaten her?" he asked quietly.

"It was more like hassling, you know?" Kenny pushed his plate away. "They say at school that Jason's older brother has just been taken into the Nightshade."

Joe bit back a curse. So it was serious. He knew the Nightshade were infiltrating the middle school, though a crusading principal was trying to stop the influx. There were strict policies in place. Locker searches, immediate suspensions for carrying weapons, no gang colors allowed. But kids not much older than Kenny were finding their way to the gang anyway. And even the younger siblings absorbed the violence like sponges.

"I'll call the principal," he offered. "Make sure somebody keeps an eye on Jason Sego for a while."

"The principal?" Kenny cussed, which Joe ignored. "I don't know. That might make things worse for Celeste." His finger traced a vein in the fake marble of the plastic tabletop. "Jason makes fun of her for hanging around me, because I hang with the cops. Now the principal—" He swore again. "I don't know. I told a couple of people that I only hang around the cops because I'm stuck with the Kids at Risk."

He looked up, and went pink again. "I mean, I kind of want to hang with you, you know that. But the kids can't know."

"Tell you what," Joe said. "Let me call the principal. Let me see if I think she can handle this on the q.t., okay? If she can, I'll tell her about the problems Celeste is having. If not, we'll think of something else."

Kenny beamed. There was no other word for it. His eyes lit and the corners of his mouth turned up in a smile so broad it seemed to take over his whole face. "Okay, Joe." He pulled his plate toward him and began to wolf down his hamburger.

"You know, I could of whipped his butt," Kenny boasted, picking up a French fry and dunking it in a puddle of ketchup.

Joe eyed Kenny's frail chest and arms and said, "Of course you could. But you made a good decision here. I'd say you handled this like a man."

Kenny rolled his eyes. "I'm pretty much grown up. I can take care of everything, just like my brother did." He chewed. "Which is a good thing because then my mom will get over it and everything will be okay.''

"Get over what?''

"My brother being murdered.''

The news hit Joe like a punch to the gut. "Your brother was murdered?''

"Yeah, over some girl. Three years ago. Craig was…cool, kind of like you only not so… Well, anyway, my mom—well, she changed then. She started drinking and taking pills and all.'' He focused on Joe and his eyes got suddenly wide. "She doesn't drink too much, so you don't have to have any damn social worker stopping by. I'm handling it.''

Joe nodded absently, his mind going a million miles an hour. The referral from the juvenile court had said that Kenny was delinquent, skipping school, petty theft, fighting. Nobody had ever mentioned a dead big brother.

Kenny added, "She wasn't doing that good before Craig died, but I could always handle it.''

Joe nodded again. "You're doing fine.'' He wondered if he should try to get the child welfare people out to Kenny's. But there were so many problem kids out there. He knew from his police work that social services didn't intervene unless there was a clear allegation of abuse or neglect. In this case, there wasn't one. Kenny always sounded protective of his mom.

Joe knew there was a lot that Kenny wasn't saying about his home life. For a second, he tried to picture Kenny's mother. Heck, Joe knew full well what losing a kid could do to you inside. How could he blame Kenny's mom for however she chose to deal with her grief?

But Kenny deserved more. Joe said carefully, "It's good that you love your mom and that you look out for her. But you have to decide that you want a different kind of life. A better one."

"Whatever." Kenny was looking out the window, feigning boredom, but Joe could see that he was listening. His body was still and tense.

"It's up to you."

"Yeah. Easy for you to say. You never had to be a Kid at Risk, never got called a delinquent when you were twelve years old. You never had to make sure your mom—" He cut himself off.

"Yeah, well, my old man used to hit me." There, the words were out. Joe was astonished at what he'd just said. He'd told Maggie some of what his old man had done, but he'd never begun to share the full extent of his father's abuse. Kenny was staring at him, a question in his eyes.

Joe took a deep breath and thought of Maggie. If he wanted to change, he had to share with other people. "He used to do it regularly, until I was full of fear and anger."

Another deep breath. "I had to try to do something with my life. I had to decide what kind of adult I was going to be, what kind of man, and I had to start preparing for that when I was a kid. I decided I wanted to be a cop, and that meant I had to do well in school, and I had to stay out of fights, even though I was so pissed off inside sometimes. I decided I wouldn't miss a day of school, and I didn't, even the day after my old man broke my nose.''

Kenny leaned forward. "How'd you do that? You know, like decide to stay in school and just do that? Sometimes, I don't know, I just…I just think, why not do something else. You know, like illegal. Sell some drugs, get some money. Like who gives a damn, you know?''

"I give a damn," Joe said quietly.

Kenny turned the brightest pink, and unexpectedly, his eyes teared up. Shocked, Joe said, "Hey."

Kenny coughed, a fake sound, and ducked, covering his mouth and hacking. When he straightened, he said quickly, "That cough was so deep my eyes got wet and stuff."

"Sure. I get that sometimes, too. When I cough." There was an awkward silence. Joe struggled to fill it. He said, "I have a friend. She had it tough as a kid, too, and she made it. She was in foster care, and now she's an important lawyer."

"Yeah? Really? A lawyer? She must be rich." Kenny seemed glad to change the subject, telling Joe quickly, and in some detail, what he'd buy if he were rich.

Joe understood. Things had gotten too emotional for the kid there for a minute. He understood, because it had got way too emotional for him, too. He was as glad as Kenny that the subject had been changed.

"Ready to go?" Joe asked abruptly.

"Ah, yeah, sure." Kenny almost visibly pulled himself from visions of a red Porsche and stood up.

A few minutes later, Joe offered to drive him to his door.

"You can let me off on the corner," Kenny said, right on cue. "I got some stuff to do."

Disappointed, Joe stopped the car. Kenny was still unwilling to let him see where he lived.

Well, what had he expected? Gaining Kenny's trust was going to take more than conversation and a couple of burgers.

"WHAT'S GOING ON? This place is like a morgue." Joe walked into Maggie's office a few days later, looking around in puzzlement. "Tessa's not at her desk. Where is she?"

Maggie sighed. "She quit."

Joe frowned. "She quit? Why?"

"It's complicated." She pushed back her desk chair and ran her fingers through her hair. "Oh, heck, it's not complicated at all. She quit because I broke off my engagement to her father."

Joe stopped in his tracks. His eyes followed her hand, as if looking for her ring finger.

She swiveled in her chair so that she wasn't quite facing him. It was suddenly hard to look at him. Yet in her peripheral vision, she could still see some of him—a denim-clad thigh, a taut stomach in a thermal knit shirt. More than that, she could sense him, as if his essence was somehow in the air: big, powerful, distinct. She pretended to study a pigeon that had landed on the windowsill.

He said, "I don't know what to say."

She turned to look at him fully. "You don't have to say anything. It was my decision."

Joe studied her and his body relaxed a little. He said, "I won't pretend I'm not glad." He was still looking at her intently.

Abruptly, her mind flashed to the kiss they'd shared. To the power of it, the feel of his lips on hers, his tongue in her mouth, his hard chest and legs pressed against her thighs and belly, the hard bulge of his arousal. She felt a rush of heat somewhere in the center of her body.

That embarrassed her, but she forced herself to look him in the eye. His mouth was tight, and she knew, looking into his eyes, that he was remembering that kiss, too. Suddenly nervous, she motioned to the chair next to her desk. "Have a seat."

He sat. She resisted the urge to see what the pigeon was up to now, instead keeping her eyes on Joe as if this wasn't a conversation with undercurrents. Powerful undercurrents. He said quietly, "So Tessa quit, huh? That must have been hard for you."

That sympathy, that understanding, almost undid her. Angela had been out of town for nearly a week, and Maggie had had no one to talk to about what had happened. "It was awful. She was so angry."

He said, "I'm sorry. I know you love that kid."

"Yeah." For a second, tears stung her eyes, but she blinked them away. "And on top of it, Sharon is angry and is also threatening to quit the firm."

He repeated, "I'm sorry, Maggie." Quiet and sincere. He didn't offer any platitudes, didn't say, *Have you talked to Sharon about this? Can't you convince her to stay?* He just offered…understanding.

That understanding melted something inside her. She had always loved him physically, had always wanted his kisses and his lovemaking. But she'd almost forgotten how much she'd valued his friendship, and now it seemed he was offering her some of that friendship they'd shared early in their marriage.

He asked, "Will the firm make it if she goes?"

Maggie shook her head. "The sad thing about it is that business is picking up. I got in a couple more small business clients and one that has the potential to be a big personal injury case. One of the judges told Angela he liked her work and wanted her to take more of his court appointments. But we need Sharon's clients." She hurried on, because all this was so hard to say, and she wanted to get it over with. "So, no, we won't make it without her. Actually, I've been doing some thinking. Maybe the firm was just a romantic notion, not all that practical after all—"

"Wait a minute, and just listen to me. Going off on your own was a good decision. You're a terrific attorney and you deserve to have control over what you do. You like your partners and you respect their work. It wasn't a bad decision." He paused. "I admire you for trying."

She shook her head. "Sometimes trying isn't enough. Look at us. We're both trying to solve your case, but things aren't going too well right now, are they?" She pulled a yellow legal pad toward her. "We need to talk about it, because I have to be in court in an hour."

He leaned forward. "I'm not giving up, but I've got nothing new. My source gave me the last of the arrest records a few days ago. I'd thought that was the way to track down our witness, but..." He made a chopping motion with his hand. "As it turns out, there are a couple of arrests for soliciting around the bar, but nobody who matches Rose's description. I've been down there almost every night and she hasn't been around."

Maggie pushed down a flash of guilt for not telling Joe about the note.

Maggie herself had spent the last three days going down to the bar, early every evening. She never got out of her car, and she left just about the time she figured Joe was on his way down. Once she thought she'd seen the headlights on his Jeep. On that occasion, she'd put her own car in gear and gotten out of the area in a hurry.

"We'll find Rose," she said out loud. "We've still got almost a week before we have to go in front of the I.A.D. again."

For a second, they just sat there. Finally, Joe got

to his feet. "But it doesn't look good for either one of us, does it?"

Slowly, she got to her feet, too. "No, it doesn't," she said, wondering if she sounded as discouraged as she felt. She reached for her legal file. Unexpectedly, he gripped her arm. She looked up.

He was looking down into her eyes. As their eyes made contact, her heartbeat sped up. She longed to go into his arms, feel his warmth. Just have him touch her. Reassure her that everything would be all right, when everything seemed hopeless.

He brought his hand up. It hovered in the air. He leaned forward, and she swore she saw his lips part, as if to kiss her.

He didn't kiss her. Instead, he touched her jaw. Lightly with a fingertip. He traced the fullness of her cheek, touched her lips, just one light, feathery touch that burned.

And then he was gone.

DUSK WAS FALLING earlier these days. Maggie checked her watch; it was only 7:00 p.m. and yet it was almost dark. She switched off her car radio and let the sounds of the street filter into the interior of the closed car. She closed her eyes for a second, wondering whether she was simply wasting her time. Go earlier, the note had said. So she had, but she'd yet to spot Rose.

Her life was a mess. Sharon wasn't speaking to her. Even Angela, who was back in town, had had no luck in getting Sharon to soften her stance. And Maggie had heard on the grapevine that Sharon had gone to lunch with a couple of lawyers from Diller, Culleng and Culleng.

And that wasn't all. Maggie had tried calling Tessa, but the girl had hung up on her. The second time she'd tried, she'd got Lewis. He'd been blunt. Tessa didn't want to talk to her.

Joe was going in for the final hearing by Internal Affairs in the morning. Their two weeks were up tomorrow, and Joe would be losing his badge.

And to top it all off, Maggie had fallen in love again with her ex-husband.

Her stomach was in knots as she watched out her car window, studying the patrons going in and out of the bar. She was a lawyer, not a detective. She had no business being here; for all she knew, those notes were someone's idea of a joke—

A flash of something caught her eye: the glitter from a pair of enormous hoop earrings. Red hair piled high, a leather skirt and tight top. Rose.

At last. Maggie flipped the door lock and sprang from the car. Rose was hesitating on the sidewalk outside the bar.

Then she squared her shoulders and took a couple of steps toward the door. Maggie picked up her pace. ''Hey, wait,'' she called when she was almost upon the woman.

Rose jumped and turned. When she looked at Maggie, her eyes narrowed.

"I'm the woman who paid you for the information about the shooting," Maggie explained, trying to catch her breath.

"I got nothing to say to you." Rose's tone was belligerent, but she made no move away. Instead, she looked around fearfully. "Where's Joe?"

"Not here. I came alone." Noting the other woman's skepticism, Maggie added, "I swear I came alone."

Rose took another look around and was apparently satisfied that Maggie spoke the truth. "You don't look like you're partying tonight." She looked over Maggie's jeans and cotton jacket.

Maggie looked into Rose's eyes, a little dulled from drink. "No, I'm not partying tonight."

"Maybe you aren't the partying kind."

Maggie smiled. "Maybe I'm not. Maybe I just came down here to find some things out."

"And maybe I got nothing to say to you." Quick as a wink, the belligerence was back.

"I've got another twenty bucks," Maggie said. "And I'll buy you something to eat. Have you eaten?"

She shook her head. "I can't eat before I—you know."

"Come on," Maggie said. "Twenty bucks, and all we have to do is talk. If you don't want to answer any of my questions, you don't have to. Okay? You'll still get your twenty dollars."

"I don't have to do anything? Say anything I don't

want to? And for that you'll give me twenty bucks?" Maggie nodded. "Lady, you sure are stupid."

"Stupid or not, that's the deal. Listen, you've got all night to work. When have you ever made twenty bucks so easily? Think what you'll have to do to earn that twenty bucks later."

Rose hugged herself and shuddered. In that moment, Maggie knew what she'd already suspected; Rose didn't like her "work."

Rose sighed. "I can't eat, I've got to have a couple of drinks just to make myself turn a trick. I tried not to, tried to come down here once, you know, sober, and I couldn't—I couldn't do what the guys wanted me to do. Made me sick." She shrugged, but her eyes told the story. They were sad and desperate.

"Twenty bucks for nothing but talking to me," Maggie coaxed softly.

Ten minutes later, they were seated in a diner just away from the seedy part of town. It was well lit and, Maggie judged, safe.

Rose ordered a Diet Coke. "Got to keep my figure," she joked. Her thinness was almost painful.

Maggie ordered a chicken sandwich. When the waitress had gone, she said, "I hoped you were okay. That last time when that guy pulled a knife, I was scared to death."

"Yeah, it happens. You got to pay attention."

"Listen." Maggie leaned forward. "I know that you know something about that shooting. I realized it that night. But for some reason you won't tell me. Why?''

Rose's sudden laugh rang out, so long and loud that a few people turned to stare. Finally, she looked straight at Maggie. ''You are one out-of-it woman if you don't realize why I'm scared. That guy who came after you that night, the one with the knife, he isn't the worst thing on these streets.''

''What are you afraid of?'' Maggie asked softly.

''The Nightshade,'' Rose said simply.

''You have a right to be scared—''

''So I'm sure not telling you anything,'' Rose said emphatically.

Maggie's chicken sandwich came. She pushed it across the table toward Rose. ''Here, have something to eat.''

Rose eyed it. ''I'm not hungry.'' Then she picked up the sandwich and took a bite.

Maggie said, ''In that alley that night, everyone was Nightshade, I know that much. So the person who hid the gun must be Nightshade, too—''

''Don't know anything about hiding a gun.''

''But you did see the gun,'' Maggie persisted.

Rose averted her eyes.

Yes! Maggie had always known there had been a gun. Now she could tell that Rose had seen it. Those notes hadn't been some kind of sick joke; there *was* a real live witness, who had the key to Joe's case.

Her heart pounded. She knew she had to tread carefully or Rose would bolt. ''Okay, if you don't know anything about one of the Nightshade hiding a gun, then you can't finger any of the gang members. How can you get in trouble telling the truth?''

Rose shrugged. ''With the Nightshade, you're always in trouble. They're proud of themselves. They like what they did to Joe.''

Maggie said, ''We can protect you.''

Rose coughed in derision, and put a napkin to her lips.

Maggie wondered what to say next. Rose was a mass of contradictions. A hooker who seemed so vulnerable, so approachable. Then she could turn like a spitting cat. She was a substance abuser. A caring mother.

Maybe that was the way to Rose. ''Do you want your kid to know that you didn't have the guts to do the right thing?'' Maggie asked.

Something flickered in Rose's eyes. ''My boy knows I don't do the right thing very often.''

''You have a chance to show your boy that you can do the right thing.''

''And if I'm working the street some night and a Nightshade puts a knife in my back, how 'm I going to do right by my kid?''

Maggie sighed. Drunk or sober, Rose had a point. She repeated her offer of safety, suggesting that the police put Rose and her child in a safe house until the streets settled down. The Nightshade were a youth gang. They were dangerous, but their tentacles didn't spread throughout the city. They ruled a four-block area. Get Rose off those streets and the family would be safe.

Maggie said, "There might be a permanent solution. You could get off the streets, go to school and learn something that pays well enough to take care of you and your son. Social services could help you find a place—"

"Social services!" Rose was so loud a few of the patrons turned to look again. "Social services took away my first boy once, and put him in a foster home. Took me almost two years to get him back." She stopped and picked up her glass of Coke, set it down with a thump. Her hands were shaking.

Desperately, Maggie switched tactics. "The boy they took away, that was the boy who died?"

"Yeah. Craig. He had a good job, was the best kid." With her quicksilver change of mood, Rose now looked sad again. In fact, her eyes were filled with tears.

Maggie said, "Your older son is dead, but your other boy could turn out fine if he sees you do the right thing." Rose didn't say anything, so she pressed on. "Joe is a good cop. He helps people. He's good on the streets. He never had to use his gun before that night." She leaned forward. "He's a real person with problems just like yours." She made a quick decision and said, "He had a child who died in his arms."

Rose's whole body started, a quick shudder that ran right through her.

"Joe was hurt as badly as you were. He knows

what it's like, Rose. And just like you, he's had to go on. He—well, you have your other boy, but Joe has nobody. He puts all of himself into his job.'' She needed to make Rose understand. ''So his job is what keeps him going. Keeps him getting up in the morning. He needs that job.''

Another tear slipped down Rose's cheek. ''I didn't know,'' she said softly. ''You said you lost a kid, too.''

Maggie nodded, her own throat tight. ''We can't bring our children back, but we can do the right thing. We can show other kids by example.''

There was a long, charged moment of silence. Then Rose said, ''What would I have to do?''

Hope surged in Maggie. ''All you'd have to do is tell Internal Affairs what you saw. Just that you saw a gun in Hook's hand before he got shot. Okay, what you say might end up in the newspapers, but we'd try to keep it out. You'd go to a place in a safer neighborhood. Members of the gang probably aren't big readers of newspapers. But even if the Nightshade heard about what you said or read it in the newspapers, they couldn't get to you if we had you in a safe neighborhood.''

''The police would do that for me?''

Maggie hesitated. She wasn't sure if the police would do that or not, but even if they did, it wasn't a permanent solution to Rose's problems. She'd represented enough juvenile cases to know that children's services would be the agency to help Rose.

"One way or another, you'll be protected," she said finally. "I promise you."

For a moment, she could see Rose wavering. The woman sat very still, her eyes seeing something far away. Finally she said, "No."

"Rose, we can—"

"No! I can't take that chance. No. No, no, no."

Frustrated tears welled in Maggie's eyes. She spent another couple of minutes trying to persuade Rose to talk. When Rose became angry and stood, Maggie stopped. "Okay," she said, pressing her business card into the woman's hand. "This has my work number and my home number. Think about calling me. Okay?"

. Rose shook her head, and Maggie wanted to scream. But there was nothing more she could say or do, or she'd lose whatever connection she'd made with the woman. Maggie walked back with Rose to the street corner where she'd found her. For a moment, Rose stood there. Then with a flash of glittery earrings, she took off.

Maggie watched her go, trying to see where she went. But she couldn't. As Joe said, there were plenty of hiding places. It was hopeless.

So she put her car in gear and drove away. She'd planted a seed. Would something come of that seed she'd planted? Maggie felt a sharp pinch of anxiety. She knew Rose was street smart. Maggie didn't think the woman would be back to the bar any time soon, and this bar was her only link with her witness.

Tomorrow, she'd share what she knew about Rose with both Joe and Internal Affairs. She'd try to buy some more time with the I.A.D. in the anticipation that Rose would come forward soon. But for now all she could do was wait. And hope.

THAT NIGHT, Maggie awoke with a start. She looked over at her bedside clock: 4:00 a.m. She strained to hear some sound, any reason why she'd awakened with her heart pounding. The house was quiet. There was no wind; the night was still.

Then she thought, *Joe.* She'd been thinking about him in her sleep, dreaming maybe... And there was something she'd thought of in her sleep.

Yes. She was thinking about Rose and Joe. Joe and Rose.

Rose had called him Joe. Was that in real life or in a dream?

She sat up, her heart pounding for real now. *Rose had called him Joe.* Had she, Maggie, ever said Joe's name in front of Rose? Had she done so the night the man had pulled a knife and Joe had rescued them in the alley? Had she mentioned his name the first time she'd talked to Rose? She wasn't sure, but she didn't think so.

Yet tonight, Rose had used his name as casually as she herself had.

As if Rose knew him.

CHAPTER THIRTEEN

JOE GOT THERE in fifteen minutes. He took the steps to the yellow bungalow two at a time, and Maggie opened the door as soon as his feet hit the porch steps.

"I think Rose knows you," she said. "Somehow, she knows who you are."

He stood there under the porch light, trying to make sense of her words. Roused from sleep, and seeing Maggie disheveled and pretty, was giving him problems focusing. He said, "Huh?"

"She knows you. Rose, I mean," Maggie said impatiently. Then she said, "Oh, come on in," and held open the door.

He passed by her and headed for the living room. On the telephone, she'd said only that she had something to tell him that might break the case open and he should come over right away.

Now as he passed her, he could sense her excitement.

Go slow, he told himself. His final Internal Affairs interview was at eleven this morning. He was trying to find a way to live with the fact that he was going to lose his badge. In fact, he'd had a hell of a time falling asleep before Maggie's call.

He sat on an ottoman, his knees apart, one hand on each thigh. Maggie sat across from him on the sofa. "Okay," he said, "tell me what Rose said."

"It wasn't exactly what she said." Maggie frowned. "It was just how she acted. She used your name in conversation."

He felt his own features scowling. "What were you doing having a conversation with Rose?"

She held up her hands as if to ward him off. "I know you aren't going to like this, but I've been going down to the bar in the evenings."

"Maggie, I more than don't like it. I thought I told you—"

"Do you want to hear this or not?"

He did. But he couldn't resist saying, "I never saw you at the bar."

"That's because you went too late," she said with a certain smugness. She explained that she'd received another note, urging her to go early. His gut went tight as he realized what risks she'd taken. He felt again that spurt of anger, mixed with a grudging respect. Mixed with a heady knowledge that she'd done this for him.

He cleared his throat against a tide of emotion. "Okay, you saw Rose. I don't like it, but it's done. You say she knows my name? Well she could have read it in the newspapers, or heard it on the street. For a while there, I was putting out a lot of feelers, talking to the street people."

"She could have. But it was the way she said it,

like she was used to saying your name. I don't know, it just seemed odd to me. I'm used to questioning witnesses in court. I'm used to drawing conclusions not only from what they say, but how they say it.''

Maggie bit her lip and added, ''I know you were questioning the street people. But Rose isn't part of that crowd. If she was, she would have been easy to trace. The street people would have known her. There would be a pimp around checking up on her. She doesn't come to the bar often enough to have friends. I bet she doesn't hang around any more than she has to, or talk much to anybody.''

Her voice picked up speed. ''She doesn't know your name from the street talk. She knows it from somewhere else.''

He became conscious of his heart beating faster. Maggie's logic was good. It was hard to believe, but... ''Okay, we'll go with this,'' he said slowly, thinking. ''How could she know me?''

''From your being a detective? Some crime you solved? Some domestic disturbance you've gone out on? Maybe you've questioned her before?''

He shook his head. He handled dozens of cases in a year, but he was pretty certain he'd never seen Rose before that night she'd come into the bar.

''I don't think I know her,'' he said finally.

''But she knows you. How? How?''

He shook his head again. ''We know that Rose witnessed the shooting, and we know that at least some of the time she's a hooker. Damn it, she has to be in the computer somewhere. How could she be working those streets, even sporadically, and never have been arrested?''

Maggie started to speak, but he cut her off as another possibility dawned on him. ''Oh, hell, why didn't I think of this? Can I use your phone?''

''Sure. Joe, what—''

''Maybe she's never been arrested. She isn't hooking all the time. But maybe a cop gave her a warning. I've been relying on arrest reports. But I haven't been thinking about warnings.''

Maggie stood. ''Go,'' she said. ''Use the phone, call whoever you want. We only have a few hours.''

Joe went into the kitchen and called Terry Allerton, apologizing for waking him up. He called a few other detectives he knew. She could hear his side of the conversation, but it didn't tell her much.

''What?'' she asked as soon as he came back into the living room.

''Well, I don't have anything solid, but I do have a lead. One guy I called, Duane Hyatt, had something. You remember how at first I was asking the vice cops I knew if they had anything. They offered to pass the word around, and I guess they did. I never expected too much to come of that. I thought the arrest records were the way to go. Anyway, on the phone tonight, Duane said one of the vice cops, Vince Samborn, has been on sick leave for quite some time. Vince hadn't been on the force long before he got sick, so nobody thought of him when I first began asking questions.

"Get this, Maggie. My mentioning the possibility of a warning—not an arrest—got Duane thinking. He remembered that Vince is from a small town, he wasn't used to how they ran vice in a city like Plainfield. He was inclined to give suspects several warnings before he arrested them. I don't know Vince, but Duane's going to call him first thing in the morning." He raked a hand through his hair. "Maggie, it's a long shot. I don't want you to get your hopes up."

But he couldn't stop himself from grabbing her then and dancing her around the room. He could feel her excitement, and the softness of her skin. He leaned down to press a kiss to the top of her head, a light one that he was sure she wouldn't be able to feel. But she shivered, and he realized she was as attuned to him as he was to her. The thought sent a shot of anticipation through him. Then he forced himself to get a grip. There wasn't any certainty about any of this.

So he put some distance between them, even though he longed to keep her in his arms. And from the way she was looking at him…

"All we can do is wait," he said.

The waiting was an agony. They made small talk, pretended to watch an old movie on television. The tension in the room was a live thing between them. When the phone rang at seven in the morning, they both jumped. Maggie was on her feet and racing to the phone. He followed her. She said hello, listened, said, "Just a minute," and handed the receiver to him.

What Duane said absolutely stunned him, like a punch to the gut. He hung up slowly and turned to Maggie.

"Duane got three solid names from Vince," he said. "Names of women who worked that area. One of them had red hair. He couldn't remember her last name. But the first name he remembered, because it's an unusual one. Nola. The name stuck with me, too, for the same reason. I read that name on a form, Maggie, a few months ago. Down at the Kids at Risk."

She frowned.

"Vince didn't know Nola's last name, but I do. Sheets. Nola Sheets—Kenny's mother."

"*Kenny's mother?* Your Kenny?"

"Who else could it be?" He raked a hand through his hair. "God, I can't believe it. But it makes sense. Kenny's mother might not know me, but she sure as hell knows *of* me. No wonder Kenny didn't want me to get too close. He didn't want me to know his mother is a prostitute."

For a moment they stared at each other. Maggie suddenly thought about the notes. "Joe, do you think Kenny sent the notes? There were grammar mistakes in the first note, like a kid would make. And the letters were rounded. I thought maybe it was more like a woman's handwriting. But now that I think about it, it's how a kid would write."

Joe shook his head. "But why wouldn't Kenny

have just told me?'' Hurt flickered inside him, a small flame in the middle of his excitement.

''Only one way to find out,'' Maggie noted. She checked her watch. ''If we hurry, we can catch him before he leaves for school.''

WHEN KENNY SHEETS opened the door, his jaw dropped. Then, in a recovery so rapid it startled Maggie, he said belligerently, ''So you finally came. How many notes do I gotta send?'' He held the door open wider.

Maggie stepped into the small apartment with Joe. In contrast to the filthy hallway, everything in the apartment was painfully neat. The worn furniture wasn't stained, and the carpet had been recently vacuumed.

Kenny stood almost defiantly in the middle of the room. His backpack was on the coffee table. He looked much younger than twelve.

The three of them stood there very still for a moment. Then Joe said, ''Why didn't you tell me straight out, Kenny?''

The boy shrugged. ''I promised my mom. I figured if you were really a great detective, you'd figure it out.''

Joe's face got a little red and Maggie said quickly, ''I think we'd better talk to your mom. Is she here?''

Kenny shrugged again. But in spite of the shrug, Maggie saw that his eyes were round and scared. ''She's sleeping. I'll go get her.''

A few minutes later, Rose—Nola—came out of the bedroom.

Her red hair was in disarray. Her face, bare of makeup, was pale and pretty. She took one look at Joe and burst into tears. Maggie went to her side. "Here, sit down."

She sat, dabbing at her eyes. She said, "Kenny, did you tell him?"

Kenny shook his head. "I gave him clues, though," he admitted.

"Clues? What does that mean?"

"What Kenny did or didn't do isn't important right now," Joe said. He squatted next to the terrified woman. "What's important is that you're a witness to a shooting."

Nola looked up at him, and abruptly her face crumpled. "I'm afraid."

"I know that," Joe said calmly. "I understand that. But we know you're our missing witness, we know who you are, and now it's time to tell the truth. We can help you, but only if you tell the truth."

Maggie was proud of him, of his composure, of his empathy, of his refusal to use bullying tactics. Only the rigidity of his spine showed how vitally important this information was to him.

There was a long pause. Maggie realized she was holding her breath.

"I wanted to tell after I talked to her last night," Nola whispered, pointing at Maggie. Then she focused again on Joe. "But you can't really help me. The Nightshade will come after me."

Joe said, "Listen to me. I can help you move to a place where the Nightshade won't find you. They really only hang around a small area of downtown."

She gave him a suspicious look and wiped her nose with the back of her hand. "Can you do it without social services butting in?"

Joe hesitated. Then he said, "No, they'd have to be involved."

Nola started shaking her head.

Maggie felt another spurt of pride in Joe. He'd recognized Nola's fear of social services, but he hadn't lied to her. Not even to get her testimony.

"Nola." The woman looked up as Maggie spoke. "We've discussed your boy. Is this the way you want him to think of you? Do you want him to think you're too weak and scared to do the right thing?"

Nola bit her lip, looking at Kenny. Kenny turned away, his face red.

Maggie sat down beside Nola and took her hand. "Why would social services do anything to you and Kenny? You love each other, you've made a clean home for him, and you're going to get help for your drinking, right?" She aimed for a reasonable, even tone like Joe's, though her heart was pounding.

"They wouldn't take Kenny away?" Nola's voice was doubtful.

"Not if you went for treatment and stayed out of trouble."

"I'm a..." She took one fearful, sad look at her son and said, "I'm a hooker. I didn't want my boy to know, but I guess he already does."

Kenny shifted uncomfortably and dug into the carpet with the toe of one worn sneaker.

Maggie said, "Nola, you don't want to be a prostitute. I can tell by what you say, and how you act. If you let Joe help you, you can learn some skills, get a job, and you won't have to do it."

A shudder ran through Nola. "I hate it," she whispered. "I hate it so much, it makes me...sick. Every time I'm done with it, I...throw up."

Kenny looked up. Maggie could see tears running down his cheeks. "Tell Joe what you saw, Mom. Please," he begged. "Please tell Joe, and let them do stuff for you."

Nola stood and held out her arms to her son.

Kenny went to his mother. She hugged him fiercely. She whispered, "I love you." Then over the top of his head, she looked over at Maggie, her eyes bright with tears. She said, "Okay. What do I have to do?"

Joe checked his watch. "In a few hours, I have an interview with the Internal Affairs Department. I need you to come with me and make a statement."

She hesitated. "Already you need me?"

Kenny said, "You've gotta do it, Mom."

She looked at Maggie. "You trust Joe?"

Maggie said simply, "Yes, I do."

For one moment longer she wavered. "Okay. I'll do it."

"ALL RIGHT," Joe said, grinning as he reached into a huge paper bag. "We have moo shoo pork and steamed dumplings." He put a couple of waxed cardboard containers on the counter. "Chicken chop suey and moo goo gay pan. Barbecued spareribs." An aromatic foil package joined the containers on the table.

"Stop." Maggie put out her hands to ward him off. "We'll never eat all that."

"Egg foo yong," Joe said, a twinkle in his eye. He set yet another container on the counter. "Extra gravy. Little packets of soy sauce. Fortune cookies."

She looked at the array and felt dizzy. Nothing was official yet, but Joe was cleared. Detective Garrick had said as much, and even Detective Smithers had nodded. To all intents and purposes, it was over.

At the police station after they'd left the I.A.D. office, Joe had gone out into the crowded hallway and shaken her hand, thanked her gravely. She'd looked up at him, and then he'd simply said, "Oh, Maggie," in a voice that told her what he was feeling. And then he'd grinned and offered to take her to dinner.

She'd opted for takeout instead, and now here they were in her small kitchen. It was a dangerous place to be. Because she was alone with Joe. Because they were both high from victory and relief. Because his eyes were twinkling and there was a lightness about him that she hadn't seen since the early days of their courtship.

He put another bag on the counter and extracted a bottle. "Champagne. Got a corkscrew?"

"I think so." She turned from him to rummage in the junk drawer. When she faced him again, her heart jumped.

He was holding one long-stemmed, pink rose.

"For you." He was smiling, but as she looked into his eyes, the smile faded. It was replaced by an expression of desire.

A shiver went up her spine. "Thank you." She took the flower. Then, avoiding his eyes, she stood there smelling the rose, aware that what she really wanted to do was press her nose to his chest and inhale Old Spice instead.

He put a hand on her arm. Her skin burned. "Maggie, I just want to say thank you again. That's not enough but—"

"It's enough." She tried desperately to lighten things. "That is, it's enough with that big retainer, and especially with egg foo yong with extra gravy—"

He grabbed her. He pulled her against him and put his mouth to hers. His kiss was incendiary. His lips were hot and coaxing. More than coaxing—demanding.

She met his seeking mouth with her own. She brought her hands up to his shoulders and the rose was crushed between them as he held her more fiercely. He turned, and her feet left the floor. He lifted her to the kitchen counter, pushing aside card-board containers. Packets of soy sauce hit the floor.

He was kissing her neck. She smelled Chinese five spice powder and crushed rose and now Old Spice. It was the scent that she'd longed for, and she let out an involuntary little moan.

As if he'd been waiting for the sound, he pressed more tightly against her, and she could feel his arousal between her parted legs. To keep her balance on the counter, she had to lean back a little and clutch at his upper arms. She felt warm, hard muscle beneath her fingers.

His hand reached up and cupped her breast, and she could feel her nipple harden against his palm. She was so excited her breath was coming in little pants.

It had always been this way. With this man.

A little chill went through her, because she knew how dangerous this was. But she was helpless to stem the headlong rush of her own passion.

As if he'd sensed her doubts, he looked up. His eyes were clear, dark with passion. He said, "I don't want to hurt you."

"You've changed," she whispered.

"Maybe not enough." There was raw emotion in his voice, old pain and a kind of desperation, as if he wanted so much to believe her.

That undid her. "I think you've changed. But let's take this relationship one step at a time. We don't need to make decisions now."

The relief in his eyes should have stopped her. It

didn't, because he'd just got his badge back, and they were so happy, and he'd brought her Chinese food and a rose, and it was like old times, the good old times, only better because she was convinced—

And then she was kissing him back, moving her mouth over his, and she was burning and melting all at the same time. Her hands quivered as she fumbled with the buttons on his shirt. She could tell that his were too as he worked the buttons on her silk blouse.

When he slid it down, the cool air of the kitchen washed over her bare skin, and she shivered. She parted his shirt and put her hands on his chest. It was blessedly familiar. The texture of his skin, the feel of his chest hair. The heat of his body...

"I want you," he mumbled against her mouth. "Right now."

"Yes." It was part acquiescence, part moan, part plea.

He pulled her off the counter. "Come on," he said. "We can do better than the kitchen counter. This time anyway."

Dazed, she followed him to the base of the stairs, and then led the way to her bedroom.

It was dim in there. The curtains were drawn and the cool darkness was falling.

They didn't talk; there were no words, only things to feel, places to touch, clothes to be discarded. Her skirt pooled at her feet, and she sat down on the bed to slide off her stockings and panties. When she looked up, he was naked.

Seven years hadn't changed him much. His chest was still broad, the hair there still golden. His shoulders were still so broad, his chest so muscular. And his arousal... She felt the familiar desire for him wash right through her.

He leaned in, came down gently on her, pressed her back into the old quilt. She felt the softness of cotton at her back, the hardness of his chest pressing her breasts. Oh, she remembered this, how it felt to have his body on hers, pressing her tightly, holding her to him. She remembered the scratchy roughness of his beard, the sexy, vibrant luxury of running her fingers through the layers of his hair.

He kissed her. He leaned down and touched a nipple lightly with his tongue.

She almost came off the bed. He put his hand between her legs, and she felt her own wetness coating his fingers. He stroked her and she clutched him and moaned. When he shifted and his arousal pressed between her legs, he groaned, the sound echoing in the still room.

It was a world apart, a world of sensation and celebration, of reunion and joy. Maggie grabbed at his hair and kissed him hard and whispered, ''Now.''

Through a haze, she watched as he reached down and felt for his trousers. She waited for the few seconds it took to put the condom on.

Then he thrust inside her, and she cried out. She clung to him and kissed and licked his skin. As she climaxed against him, she thought, *This is what it's like to really be home.*

IT WAS ONLY MUCH LATER, in the wee hours of the night, that she had doubts. They'd made love once more. Then they'd pulled back the quilt and the crisp sheets and crawled under the covers together. She'd fallen asleep in his arms, the way she had in the early days of their marriage. Sated and trusting.

But they'd fallen asleep very early. And now it was two in the morning and she was wide awake. Her rumbling stomach reminded her they'd eaten none of that food down in the kitchen. She thought about that pink rose he'd brought her and wondered where they'd dropped it.

She turned to look at Joe. The night was very dark; she could see little beyond the bridge of his nose. She leaned in a little closer. He lay on his back, his eyes closed, his mouth open slightly. He snored a little, and she felt a smile come and go on her lips.

It was good to have a man in her bed again. No, it was good to have Joe there, good to have the man she loved sleeping beside her.

Wasn't it? A burn of anxiety hit her again.

She slid from the bed carefully, so as not to wake him. What she needed was food, that was all.

As she pulled on a robe, she remembered their lovemaking. Now, with her desire satisfied, she remembered some things she'd registered but not thought through at the time.

The relief in Joe's eyes when she'd said, *Let's take this relationship one step at a time.*

The sleeve of her robe was inside out, and she tugged at it impatiently until she could slide her arm through.

He'd used a condom.

There would be no accidental pregnancy as a result of this night.

Her head told her he had been properly cautious, that she should thank him for thinking of protection when she had not. Oh, but her heart remembered a baby. Her heart remembered Joe saying—seven years ago, though it felt like yesterday—that he wasn't ready to have children.

She tiptoed to the door, telling herself that was seven years ago, telling herself not to read potential heartbreak in everything that passed between them from now on.

"Maggie."

She turned at the door, startled. "Oh, I'm sorry, I didn't mean to wake you."

"That's all right." He was sitting up in bed, and she could only see the shadow of his body.

"I was just going downstairs to get something to eat. We didn't have any dinner."

She thought she saw him smile. And then he said, "Don't go just yet. Don't go until I say I love you."

For a moment, her heart sang, and she wanted to rush back to bed and take him in her arms. But she said, ''I thought we agreed to take this relationship slowly this time.''

''We did. I love you.''

She said the only thing she could say, because it was the absolute truth. ''I love you, too.''

Scary as it was to hear him say those three words, it was scarier still to say them herself.

CHAPTER FOURTEEN

TESSA KNOCKED lightly on the door frame to Maggie's office. "Can I talk to you?"

Maggie started at hearing the teenager's voice. She dropped the brief she'd been reading. "Sure." She stood and motioned the girl in. Maggie hadn't seen Tessa since her breakup with Lewis nearly a month ago.

Tessa came rather hesitantly into the room.

Maggie took a step toward her. Tessa's cheeks bloomed pink and she averted her eyes. "Oh heck," Maggie said, going up to the girl and taking both her hands. "I'm so happy to see you I just don't know what to say."

"Me, neither." Tessa ducked her head.

"No shyness," Maggie warned. "I'll think I don't know you anymore."

Tessa looked at her a little askance. "Well, I'll try. It's just that it's so…"

"Awkward," Maggie supplied.

"Yeah, awkward."

"But for me, it's great."

Tessa smiled and looked her right in the eye this time. "Yeah, for me, too. I thought we ought to talk."

"Good idea." Maggie went to the office door and shut it while Tessa took one of the chairs in front of the desk. Maggie took the other one. "I'm sorry, I don't have much of anything to offer you to drink. Only coffee."

"That's all right."

"How's your dad?"

"Sad." There was a pause. "But not as sad as I thought he'd be."

"I'm glad." Maggie didn't know what else to say about that.

"He took me to a poetry reading."

"Really? That's…amazing."

Tessa cracked another smile. "No kidding. But he didn't understand a thing about it. I tried to talk to him afterward and you should have seen him struggle to pretend he got the symbolism. It was like he wanted to roll his eyes at every word I said. But he didn't."

"He's trying hard to be there for you," Maggie said gently, mentally thanking the kind man who'd been her fiancé.

"Yeah." Tessa ran her fingernail along the arm of her chair. Her nails had been airbrushed, Maggie saw. Three shades of purple, with yellow stars on the tips of her pinkies. The sight made her want to smile again.

"So, the thing is…" Tessa was casual, still rubbing at the wood of Maggie's chair, "I wondered if you got somebody else to fill in here after school. To do your intern work.''

"No, I didn't. I haven't had time and I was hoping you'd reconsider and come back."

She looked up abruptly. "Really? After all this time, and you haven't hired anybody yet? You'd want me back after I quit on you?"

"Absolutely."

"Oh, man, that is so cool."

"Does your father know you're coming back?"

"Sure. He said you'd take me back." She hesitated. "See, the thing is, I was mad at you, you know, and then I was kind of angry because I thought I should be loyal to my father. But the other day he said he realized that he didn't want to marry a woman who didn't love him. So I kind of thought, in a way you did the right thing. So I kind of said that, and my dad said well, maybe he was really trying too hard to get over my mom dying, that maybe he wasn't fair to you, either."

Maggie studied the girl. Tessa looked young and mature, all at the same time, with her perfect, dewy skin, and her jaunty ponytail, and the wise, knowing expression on her face. Maggie's heart constricted. Once, she'd wanted this girl for her daughter. But, she realized now, she was delighted to have Tessa as a friend.

Tessa added solemnly, "The only reason to marry is for true love."

Maggie's mind immediately conjured Joe. In the

three weeks since he'd been officially cleared of any wrongdoing in discharging his weapon, they'd seen each other almost every night. They'd had fun. They'd watched movies, gone out to dinner, gone for long walks, window-shopped, talked, made love. Neither had mentioned the future.

She shook her head, as if to clear it. One step at a time, she reminded herself. If she had a wish sometimes to test Joe's commitment, to do something, anything so that he'd give her the reassurance that their relationship did have some kind of future she could count on, she didn't act upon it.

Whenever she felt a pinch of anxiety, she told herself that their relationship was new, that Joe was giving her a chance to know him again, giving her a chance to really trust him. And she knew that sometimes you just had to give the people you loved time to work things out.

Tessa was a wonderful example of time helping things to work out. Maggie stood up. "Hey, come on, let's tell Angela and your Aunt Sharon that you're coming back to work here."

"Great. Maybe Angela will spring for some chocolate cupcakes from the vending machine. Like, for a celebration or something."

"Maybe so. I could always go for some chocolate."

A few minutes later, Maggie watched as Angela hugged Tessa, then gathered change and headed off to the vending machines in the basement. Sharon was smiling and talking with her niece. Sharon had told Maggie last week that she wanted to stay on, and Maggie knew Tessa's coming back—a signal of forgiveness from both the girl and Lewis—would clinch Sharon's decision.

Yes, things were going well. The firm was doing just fine. All three partners had several more cases than they'd had at this time last month. If work continued to come in so regularly, the survival of the firm was insured. Heck, by the year 2000 they'd be prospering.

Maggie poured a round of coffee for everyone as they all waited for Angela to come back with cupcakes.

The phone rang. Tessa snatched it up. "Hannan, St. John and Sawyer," she said importantly. She listened, said, "Oh sure," and handed the phone to Maggie. "It's Joe Latham."

If Tessa knew that Maggie was seeing Joe on a personal level, the girl didn't seem to mind. They'd talk about it over the weekend, Maggie decided. She told Tessa she'd take the call in her office and went in there, shutting the door.

She pressed the receiver to her ear. "Hi," she said softly.

"Hey, hi yourself. Was that Tessa's voice I heard answering the phone?"

"Sure was. She's coming back."

"That's great news."

Maggie smiled. "And how."

"By the way, did you get anything nice today?"

"You know I did. Thank you, Joe." She touched the petals on the gerbera daisies in a vase on her desk.

"You're welcome. You can thank me more properly tonight. I've got an idea of how you could thank me in the most…detailed sort of way." He mentioned something so sexy and outrageous that Maggie blushed.

"You're blushing."

"I am not! You can't see me over the phone, anyway."

"Ah, but I know you."

Warmth curled right through her. "Okay," she said recklessly. "I won't do telephone sex with you, but I'll do the real thing, exactly as you suggested. Tonight."

There was a beat of silence. Finally, Joe said, "No kidding?"

"No kidding. And you'd better not be blushing. You suggested it." When she hung up a moment later, Maggie was still smiling. She glanced at the gerbera daisies on her desk. Pink. She looked at her new crystal paperweight. From Joe. Pink again. The letter opener matched. In her purse was a perfume bottle made of hot-pink enamel.

In spite of her happiness, she felt the smallest flash of misgiving.

She was more a red woman now.

The thought made her feel ungrateful. Not ungrateful, exactly. More…worried. Concerned.

Everything was fine, she told herself. It was okay not to push Joe into making a commitment. He loved her.

She had her law firm, today she had the beginnings of a renewed relationship with Tessa. She had work she loved, friends. She had a house filled with objects she'd lovingly collected. Most importantly, she had Joe, a man she loved and who said he loved her.

Another chill went through her, exactly the feeling she'd had on the night he'd been acquitted. She had Joe. But so far, only on the terms they'd agreed to. One step at a time.

One step at a time. Okay, she recognized this as step one. He was courting her the old way. Would there ever be a step two? This time, could she really count on Joe?

She was glad to hear Angela calling her. She opened the door and pasted a smile on her face. "Okay, did anybody bring a package of cupcakes for me?"

"IT'S NOT OKAY?" Joe asked that afternoon as he and Kenny were standing in line for tickets for the first hockey game of the season. He was surprised. The social services people had put Kenny and his mother in a nice apartment building, and the last time he'd talked to the caseworker, Nola Sheets was still going to her alcohol counseling. Of course, he knew there was a high failure rate for alcoholics, and it had been less than a month since Nola decided to seek help.

"Sure, it's okay." Kenny's voice was listless.

"Hey." Joe turned to him and tipped the kid's chin up. The light glinted off the crack in the corner of his glasses. Joe had talked to the caseworker about new ones, but Kenny didn't have them yet. "Something's bugging you. Out with it."

Kenny did a kind of embarrassed shimmy and averted his eyes. "It's not Mom. It's Celeste."

Ah. "Your girlfriend."

"Well, kind of. A friend." Kenny blushed bright red. "It's just that…you know how some of the kids were kind of bothering her, like saying stuff like I was too friendly with the cops?"

"Sure." With all that had happened, Joe had forgotten about Celeste and his own phone call to the principal. He frowned. Kenny had insisted on staying at his old school until the term ended. Joe hadn't been so sure that was a good idea, but the caseworker thought that it might be better not to uproot Kenny. Of course Kenny had wanted to be near Celeste. "Are those kids still giving her grief?"

Kenny nodded. "Yeah." He hesitated. "You talked to the principal, you know? And you said the principal would watch over Celeste, but carefully. But she didn't. I mean, the hall monitors were like there so much that everybody knew. They all said I was friends with a cop, and now they say I'm friends with the principal."

Joe winced. The principal had assured him she'd be discreet, and maybe she'd tried. But he knew kids figured things out. What he couldn't tell was how serious this all was. He remembered being a kid with his first crush on a girl. He'd been all mixed up, but he'd felt pride and a sense of responsibility for her, which he gathered Kenny felt also.

So which was it, adolescent angst or was there really a problem at the school? "I could call the principal again," he mused out loud.

"No! Jeez, Joe, you want to show everybody I can come up with an armed guard or something?" Kenny squared his shoulders. "I can handle it. If all you can think to do is talk to old lady Conrad again, forget it." He took a few steps up as the line began to move. "That'd be worse than being a Kid at Risk and having to show up at the gym every day."

Joe almost smiled, relieved. If Kenny didn't want his interference, how bad could the situation at school be? Adolescent angst, he decided. He reached over and roughed up Kenny's hair. Kenny turned on him, gave him a shadow punch. They goofed around for a while like that, the restrictions of the line making the game difficult. But Joe felt warm inside.

Joe paid for the tickets. Kenny said, "Thanks, Joe." And that was something new, too, Kenny thanking him for anything.

The warm feeling lingered. And whenever he felt warm and good inside, he thought of Maggie. He was going to see her tonight when he dropped Kenny off after the game.

He bought junk food and they took their seats. But

even after the opening face-off, he was still thinking about Maggie.

Their conversation today…well, that had been some conversation. He couldn't believe she'd actually agreed to his suggestion for bedtime. Maggie in the early years had been responsive, loving, fun. But now she was apparently…adventurous. As he thought over the night to come, he felt himself start to grow hard, right in the midst of the game, with a kid sitting beside him.

He looked over at Kenny, but the boy was absorbed in watching the line changes the coach was making.

Joe couldn't stop thinking about Maggie, so he forced himself to shift his focus from the sexual. Maggie was different now. She was so self-confident. So strong. It made him want to be self-confident and strong for her, to be worthy of her.

Ah, and there was the rub. They might not talk about it, but he knew where their relationship was going. Where he wanted it to go. He loved her. She deserved a future.

She deserved a future last time, buddy, and you didn't give her one. Couldn't give her one.

He'd changed. Hadn't he?

He shifted, his gut tight with the fear that he hadn't changed enough. There was a reason both of them avoided talk of the future.

So Joe started thinking instead of what he could bring her tonight. He'd already sent flowers, and he had given her chocolate yesterday. Maybe he'd just go into some ladies' boutique and let the saleswoman tell him what Maggie ought to like. He pictured Maggie in a slinky little pink something....

Well, he was hard again, but as distractions went, it wasn't bad.

THAT NIGHT, Maggie and Joe lay sprawled together on a chaise lounge in Maggie's sunroom. Darkness had fallen, and Maggie hadn't turned on the lights, so they could see the shadows of the trees outside. Tangled branches against the sky, the halo of lights of the city giving a yellow-green glow that dimmed the stars.

Maggie pulled the quilt higher around her shoulders.

"Cold?" Joe asked quietly, tucking it around her neck.

"Not really." She smiled, replete. He shifted, and she felt his warm, naked body next to hers. The hair on his legs tickled her as he slowly rubbed his skin along hers.

She said, "This is nice,"

"Mmm," he muttered, clearly already half-asleep.

She thought about this evening. The window-shopping at the nearest mall, the peek into the collectibles store with its glittering glass cases. There had been an antiques show at the mall and they'd argued good-naturedly over whether a piece of figural pottery was whimsical—her vote—or merely weird and ugly—Joe's comment. A dinner of finger foods at a trendy bar that had an ersatz old-fashioned look. Then coming home to find he'd laid a pink satin teddy out on the sunroom chaise lounge...

"I wish we could do this all the time," she whispered.

"Sure, who wouldn't like sex twenty-four hours a day?" he muttered. "Don't know if this old body could keep up, though. The spirit is willing but the body..."

She poked him. "Yeah, right. You seemed pretty willing in body and spirit a few minutes ago. What I meant was, I wish you could be with me all the time."

He stiffened.

Ouch. She'd been physically satisfied and the sense of well-being had caused her to let down her guard. To hint at something they never spoke of: the future.

He said, "Sure, I wish that, too." He shifted. "Hey, you want to move upstairs to bed? This lounge-chair thing is pretty narrow."

Joe had been almost asleep a minute ago, and now he sounded fully awake.

Well, now she was plenty awake, too, and starting to get annoyed. "You sure don't want to talk about this, do you?"

He raked a hand through his hair. "Could I get dressed first?" he asked quietly.

A small flush heated her cheeks. "Of course." But then she added, "You know, we do need to talk about this sometime."

He blew out a long breath and retrieved his clothes

from the pile where they'd discarded them an hour before. He stood to pull on his jeans. She watched him in the dim light from outside, the quilt still pulled up to her neck. He had a broad chest designed to shelter. His long, lean legs gave him an agility that, in such a large man, made him oddly graceful. It was a body she cherished. Loved.

And if she loved him, she ought to be able to say anything, dare anything. Even find out if he thought he'd changed enough for there to be another chance for them.

Well, she'd said she wanted to talk to him. Now she should talk.

Silently, she got dressed, too, but even after they were both fully clothed, she didn't turn on the light. He finally said, "I know what you want to say."

"Do you?" She sat back down on the chaise lounge, and held out her hand to him. He took it and sat beside her. He was still, his hand resting in hers. His palm was warm, but hers suddenly felt a little cold. She said, "I love you, and we've had fun together. You brought me all those presents, and we went to that auction, and we've been talking about old movies and reading books together, and it's been wonderful. You used to be my best friend. You've become that again."

She eyed his profile. He wasn't smiling. He wasn't even really looking at her. After a second's pause, he gave her hand a small squeeze. Encouraged a little, she went on, "It reminds me of when we were going

out together before we got married, and then the first
months we were married. You swept me off my feet.''

Now a little smile played around his mouth.
"Yeah, you swept me off mine, too.''

"And now you're doing it again.''

"That was the idea.''

"All that pink. But I'm a red woman now.''

There was another pause. Then Joe said, "I'm not
sure what that means.''

"Joe, pink is more of a little-girl color, an innocent
color. I really think I've learned something in the
seven years since we split up. I might still be a romantic, but I'm not a naive one. Now I have the sense
that you're working too hard at this relationship.''
That admission hurt, so she tried for a bit of humor.
"I mean that you don't have to buy me presents more
than once a week.''

He squeezed her hand again. "I like buying you
presents.''

"That's not the point.''

"I know it. God, I know it.'' Disengaging her hand,
Joe stood up. He looked large and dark silhouetted
against the window. "I may not know about all that
pink and red stuff, but I know what you want, Maggie.'' His voice went suddenly bleak. "What you
want has never been a secret, has it?''

"I want to get married and have children,'' she
said, looking at him. "It's not a weird ambition. It's
natural and normal for a person to want a family with
the one they love.''

He started to pace. "Of course it isn't weird. It's only unnatural when you want to have children with me." There was still that aching bleakness in his tone. He got to the end of the small room, turned and paced back toward her. "Do you think there hasn't been a day that I haven't thought about it? Haven't thought, oh, tomorrow I'll ask her to marry me, and I'll tell her to hurry up and have lots of babies. And then I don't ask."

A cold feeling started within her. "It doesn't have to be tomorrow. We can take more time. But I need to know that you're thinking further than the next gift you send. I know you loved Alex." She wet her lips. "I think, because I lost our baby, I can even have a sense of your loss. But…he's gone, Joe. And no matter how you punish yourself, no matter how hard you make sure that you aren't really happy, you can't bring him back."

The room got so still. His pacing had brought him to one of her big windows, and he stood looking out. He didn't reply, didn't even move.

Watching him, so still like that, made her throat so dry it ached. Outside, a sudden wisp of breeze pushed some dry leaves against the window. Otherwise, it was quiet.

Finally, Joe said, "It was different for you, with our baby. You didn't do anything to kill him."

"Alex was a tragic accident," she said firmly. She went over to Joe and touched his hand. It was ice-cold. "We have so much going for us. We have so much in common. I admire you. I love you. But we can't have a future unless you forgive yourself.''

He turned to her, and even in the low light she saw that his gaze was haunted. ''I thought I'd forgiven myself last time, thought I could make a life for us. I wanted that for me, and I wanted that for you. You're the only woman I really ever loved, and I wanted you to have it all. Everything. And I failed you. So now, if I say it's okay now, that we can have kids, what if I...what if I can't handle it?''

''I think you've changed. And I choose to trust you. So if you tell me you've forgiven yourself, I'll believe you. I'll go on and marry you.''

He raised a frustrated fist, and lightly hit the glass of her sun porch window. ''I...don't...know. Damn it, I don't know, Maggie! How can I risk marrying you when I don't know?''

Something in her died then. If being the best cop, if helping out at the Kids at Risk for seven years, if caring about Kenny and trying so hard to make his life better, if sharing the story of Alex's death with her... If these things didn't tell him that he was capable of being a good father, then nothing she could say would convince him.

He turned to her, grabbed her shoulders and held on. ''I can't ask you to share your life with me, not when I'm scared out of my mind how I'll react the day you announce you're pregnant.''

He kissed her then, a hard and desperate kiss. There was so much tension in that mouth, so much rigidity in his neck and shoulders. She cradled his cheeks in her palms and found that his skin was damp.

She realized then that she had gambled and lost. She had told herself first not to get involved, then had told herself that they could love each other without a future. But she'd been really banking all along on the fact that he'd changed, that he could make a full emotional commitment not just to her, but to the children she hoped to make with him.

And her heart broke. It was almost as if she could feel it shattering into a million pieces, and those pieces were circulating through her body, pricking her everywhere. "You won't even try," she accused, her eyes filling with tears. "We have so much and you won't even try."

He looked at her very, very directly. "I tried seven years ago," he said softly.

She sighed, then she spoke. "I thought maybe we could just have fun together. But I can't live day to day. I'm a planner, Joe." She tried to smile at him and failed utterly. "Remember, when I was a kid, everything was always so uncertain. When I got old enough to be in charge of my life, I always made plans. I needed to think about the future.

"I love you so much. I've even thought maybe—maybe we could be happy without kids." Saying those words was hard.

"You deserve to have children."

She swallowed. "You're afraid of how you'll feel when I say I'm pregnant. But I have fears, too. I want to tell you it's okay not to have children. If for some reason you *couldn't* have kids, I could live with that. But we can have a family if you want to. And my fear is if we don't, one day I'll wake up and be so…'' Her voice dropped to a whisper, ''…angry at you.''

He took her in his arms. He held her against his chest. The soft flannel fabric of his shirt dried the tears on her face. His arms tightened, and a button pressed into her cheek. For a moment, she clung there, telling herself again that she could take Joe on his terms, that it would be better than living without him. She told herself she couldn't stand losing him a second time. But she was afraid.

He released her gently. ''I can let myself out.''

Letting him go was the hardest thing she'd ever done in her life, harder than seven years ago. Because this time she really knew he had changed, and he could be happy. They could be happy. But Joe had to know it, too.

A minute later, Maggie heard the front door slam. She pressed her forehead to the cool glass of the sunroom window, watching the night outside.

CHAPTER FIFTEEN

JOE'S LIEUTENANT gave him and Henry Muff a complicated embezzlement case, and Joe spent more than thirty hours interviewing witnesses. It was a sign of the lieutenant's faith in Joe that he was given such a high-profile case so soon after he had been exonerated. Every time he showed his badge to a witness, a part of him was reassured. He was doing good work. His life was going along on the same path he'd set it on seven years ago, the only path that worked.

Only it didn't work anymore. These days, he felt like a goddamn machine. Waking up, heading into work, going to the Kids at Risk, eating out, going for a run, any hard physical activity that would guarantee that he fell asleep fast.

He'd let Maggie down.

But he couldn't ask her to marry him, because he couldn't guarantee he'd make her happy. And now that the desperate straits that had driven him to her in the first place were over, he owed it to her to get out of her life.

He hoped things were going okay with her. In the week since they'd parted, he'd seen her going into the courthouse twice. He'd stayed in his Jeep, kept his distance.

As he did nearly every day, he headed over to the gym. He was a little worried about Kenny, who had become quiet and withdrawn. It made no sense. Things were going great for Kenny. His mother was getting help, and his probation—a probation that had gone without incident—was going to end soon.

"Hey, what's eating you?" Joe asked after he'd passed the basketball to Kenny, and the kid had dropped it and turned away.

"Nothing." Kenny shrugged and avoided his eyes.

Joe knew that Nola was making good progress in counseling. The Nightshade had never bothered with her, just as Joe had figured. As far as he could tell— and he'd checked—Nola Sheets was off the streets and well on the way to a productive life-style.

He saw Kenny head for the locker room, one of the first kids to leave the basketball court after the game. There was some roughhousing. One of the other kids reached out and tried to grab his arm to say something, but Kenny just shrugged the boy off, flipped him the bird and kept walking.

Yeah, something was wrong there. Joe picked up his pace to a jog. When he caught up with Kenny, he said, "I've got to talk to you."

Kenny made some belligerent comment that Joe knew was for the benefit of the other kids who were listening. Joe went through the locker room and told

Kenny to follow him into the small office the counselors used.

Once there, Kenny put his back to the glass door and said, "Well, okay, I mouthed off."

Joe waved aside the remark. "That's not important today. What I want to know is, what's wrong?"

"Nothing's wrong," Kenny said, looking away.

"Out with it. Something with your mom?"

"Naw."

"Something at school?"

"Why're you bugging me with all these questions?"

"Did you have an argument with Celeste?"

Kenny averted his eyes. "Can't a guy have some privacy or nothing?"

Ah, so that's how it was, Joe thought. Just an argument with his girlfriend. Joe had been off base in thinking it was anything serious. Besides, adolescents were moody. Joe picked up the basketball on the desk, and, still sitting, threw it into the wastebasket into the corner. It thunked and went round and round.

"Good shot," Kenny said.

"Thanks. Want to get a pizza?"

"No, I can't. My mom's cooking dinner and I've got to get home."

After Kenny left, Joe thought that these days, Nola Sheets probably really was cooking dinner. Despite the kid's mood, things were looking up with Kenny. It was one problem solved, anyway.

THREE DAYS LATER, he found out how wrong he had been. He picked up the ringing phone in his kitchen at eleven o'clock at night.

"Joe, this is Nola Sheets. Have you seen Kenny?"

Joe checked his watch, confirming how late it was. Concerned, he said, "I haven't seen him since he left the Kids at Risk at five. When did you see him last?"

"When he went to school this morning." Her voice rose. "Where would he be?"

A small stab of fear went through Joe. "Probably out with his friends, and he thinks it's cool to stay out late and be worrying you."

"He's never done that before. Not to me."

Joe thought of the Nightshade. He thought of how quiet Kenny had been all this week. He thought of car accidents, all the things that he knew could happen to people. He told himself Kenny was likely out having fun, but no amount of rationalization could ease the tightness in his spine. "Did you call the school?"

"No, I called you." There was a pause, and then her voice rose almost to a wail. "Kenny's all I have. I don't know what I'm going to do if he—"

"Don't even think it," Joe cut in. "I have the phone number of the principal around here somewhere. I'll call her."

He called Amelia Conrad at home. What he heard sent an even bigger stab of fear through him. Celeste Fortman was missing, too.

He called Nola, and told her what he knew. He also

told her he was putting out an APB for her son and Celeste.

"But don't they have to be missing for twenty-four hours?" Her voice was shaking.

"Not if it's kids," Joe said grimly. He did what he could to reassure Nola, then he called in a few favors, asked his fellow cops to keep a special watch out for Kenny and his girlfriend. He was getting good at asking for favors these days, he thought. Then he got into his Jeep and headed downtown, to that four-square-block area where the Nightshade ruled.

He turned the corner onto Prospect, and slowed the Jeep. He looked carefully at the shadowy doorways, the street corners, the abandoned buildings. He was looking for a kid, anybody small and skinny. He was looking for open doors. He was looking for candles in the windows, signaling that there was something going on inside.

His spine was rigid, his neck was tense as he looked around, cruising slowly. He passed a patrol car, obviously doing the same thing. He headed to where he knew some of the Nightshade hung out. No Kenny, no Celeste.

He looked for hours, both in his Jeep and on foot, until he was pretty sure Kenny wasn't here. He was wondering, had Kenny and Celeste just run away? If so, why would Kenny do that when he had Joe, and now his mom, to help him? And if they hadn't run away…

WHEN HE GOT HOME at dawn, he was physically exhausted, his nerves jangled with worry. The professional detachment required of a cop had long since left him. This was Kenny, and Joe was scared.

He was stunned to see Maggie's car in the guest parking area of his building. He climbed out of his car and sprinted over to hers. She got out slowly.

He reached her, his breath coming fast. "Maggie."

"Nola Sheets told me about Kenny. Any news?"

He shook his head. "Nothing. It's been over twelve hours. In cases like these, it's so important to find the kids in the early hours. After that, the likelihood of something—" He cut himself off.

"Oh, Joe. I'm so sorry." She paused, and then said, "I'm going to go sit with Nola in a few minutes. She really has nobody else to wait with her."

"Thank you. She'll need you." He paused. "I've been out looking for both kids. I went all over his old neighborhood, back to the gym, all through Nightshade territory, by his new apartment, by Celeste's house. Nothing. I keep going over everything he said, wondering if I've missed something."

She opened up her arms. And he went into them.

Her arms closed around him, and she held him, and he held her in a bruising grip. Her hair was in a ponytail, and he could bury his face in the softness of the bare skin of her neck. She smelled of soap and exotic perfume, of familiarity and a safe, safe haven.

"You'll find him," Maggie said fiercely. "It can't end like this. You'll find them."

He gave her a squeeze, a hard hug, as fierce as her words. "I plan to." Somehow, holding her gave him new strength. "Let's have breakfast before you go to Nola's."

He walked back into the house with her, an arm around her shoulders. They ate together, not talking much. Joe had the first sense of normality he'd had since that call at eleven o'clock last night. Hell, he had the first sense of normality he'd had since he'd walked out the door of Maggie's sunroom ten long days ago.

The day dragged. At work, he joined with several other detectives in getting the machinery going to track down missing children. He checked in with Nola and Maggie and also with Celeste's parents frequently. There was no news.

By evening, when his shift ended, he'd been up more than twenty-four hours. He knew he had to get a few hours of sleep before he hit the streets again. So he went home, bone-tired but wondering if he'd be able to fall asleep.

When he was in the shower the telephone rang. He grabbed a towel and the phone receiver.

"Joe?"

His heart slammed into his throat. "Kenny? Where are you?"

"I'm in Chicago." Kenny's voice sounded far away, little-boy scared.

Chicago? Chicago was over four hours away from Plainfield. The telephone slipped; his skin was wet.

Joe pushed the receiver harder against his ear. "Are you all right?"

"Yeah, sorta. Celeste is with me."

Joe closed his eyes for a second. Safe. Kenny was safe. Kenny was *safe*. For a moment, that was the sweetest word in the English language.

Kenny said, "We came here because the kids were hassling her, you know? She wanted to get away. She was afraid. We—I thought there might be someplace we could stay, you know? Like Celeste has a cousin in Chicago but we can't find their house. We stayed outside last night, but it was cold. Celeste cried."

Joe said, "I'm coming to get you."

"Good. I was thinking of checking into a motel, but I don't have enough money for more than one night."

Joe hardly registered how ludicrous the comment sounded—as if a twelve-year-old boy could rent a motel room. "Where are you?"

"In a park." Kenny gave him the location.

"I'm sending some cops to get you. You stay put, okay?"

"Sure. Yeah. Just—" his voice cracked. "I'm handling it, but I want you to come, Joe."

"I'm coming as fast as I can. Have you called your mom?"

"No. You're the one I thought of calling. Oh, man, Celeste's parents are going to kill her."

Not hardly, Joe thought. Celeste's mother and father had been glued to the phone, just as Nola had.

He hung up, called the Chicago cops first. He didn't want Kenny getting any ideas about taking off again.

Then he called all the people he needed to. Nola. Celeste's parents. Maggie. The local detective officially in charge of Kenny's case. He hurried to get dressed. I'm coming for you, buddy. Hold on tight.

AS IT TURNED OUT, he took both Maggie and Nola to Chicago. Celeste's parents were going in their own car.

Maggie said, "It's a good thing Kenny called you. I'm so glad he did that, Joe."

He shook his head. "This whole thing is probably my fault. I'm the one who called the principal when this first started happening with Celeste. According to Kenny, I only made things worse."

"What else could you have done?" Maggie asked in a reasonable tone. He glanced at her. Night had fallen, and the shifting lights of traffic on the expressway made her features into changing images of light and shadow.

Joe slowed for a truck in front of them. "Kenny didn't like what happened when I made that first phone call. How the principal handled it. So he didn't want my interference again." Maybe he should have anticipated something like Kenny running away, Joe thought. Especially when Kenny had been so quiet these last few days.

But then, in the tiniest corner of his brain, Joe wondered something. Just because he and Kenny had a relationship, just because he felt responsible, was he responsible for every impulsive decision of a boy who was almost a teenager? He felt his mouth tighten. Of course he was. Kenny might be half grown up, but he was still a child.

Nola said from the back seat, "Thank God he trusted you enough to call you. Thank God for that." She choked up. "If I'd been more of a mother these last years since Craig died, maybe he would have come to me."

Maggie murmured something soothing.

But Nola said, "No, Maggie. My kid was in trouble, and he called Joe. Now, that ought to hurt my feelings, and it does, but I'm just so glad my boy is all right that I can only be glad that he called Joe."

There didn't seem to be anything to say after that. In a couple of moments, Maggie reached for Joe's hand. Hers felt warm and soft.

But Nola's words stuck with him. Kenny might have run away, but he'd chosen to call Joe when he'd got in trouble. He'd called Joe because he trusted him. Joe had earned that trust by working with him, by listening to him, by helping his mother. Joe knew he'd done his best for a child he'd come to love.

Was his best good enough? Once he'd have said no way.

Once he'd been afraid to let another child—any child—truly count on him. Yet it seemed almost without his knowing it, he'd encouraged Kenny to trust him.

Once he'd been afraid to love a child, ever again. But he loved Kenny, and he'd been there for him. He'd done his best, and his best had been good enough.

He looked over at Maggie. She was looking out her window, and all he could see was the back of her head. She'd trusted him enough to get involved with him again.

Maybe all he had to do was his best.

It was the headiest thought. His hands tightened on the steering wheel as the implications sank in. He didn't have to be perfect. He only had to do his best and let other people trust him. He could forgive himself.

It was a silent epiphany, there in the car at night. But Joe felt the relief of forgiving himself all the way to his toes. An accident had killed Alex. He should have paid more attention, but, as Maggie said, it was an accident. He remembered Maggie holding him, rocking him. Giving him the forgiveness he couldn't give himself. Maggie was a strong and confident woman, an honest one, with grit and honor. And she'd forgiven him...

There was a time, long ago, when he'd tried to pray for his son. When he'd tried to communicate with Alex somehow. Until he'd gone so horribly numb. But now he found himself reaching out again.

Alex, I loved you so much. I wanted so much to see you grow up to be a man. To guide you, to play with you, to coach your ball games, to teach you right from wrong, to see you find a woman to love, and have children of your own. But I failed you and I'm sorry.

He found all of a sudden that he didn't have to struggle to find the right words. That those words were already there, dormant in his heart, until he chose to let them out.

I've found a woman of my own to love. I guess I've loved her for years. Her name's Maggie. See her over there? Even though we broke things off between us, and she had a right to be angry at me, she's here with me for the sake of a kid she doesn't even know, and for that kid's mother. That's the kind of woman she is. You'd really like her, I know you would....

He glanced over at Maggie. Now she was looking down at the map that was resting on her lap, and she said, "You need to take the next exit."

Joe had been to Chicago before, and basically, he knew where to go. He'd already spotted the sign directing him to where he needed to get off the expressway.

He took the exit, slowed, then stopped at a traffic light.

This seems an odd time to talk to you, son. But there are things I want you to know. I love Maggie and she loves me. And I want to have babies with her. A stunned sort of happiness ran through Joe as he realized that he was ready—truly ready—to be a father again. *I want to have another son, Alex. I want to have another chance. Not to forget you. Never that.*

But to forgive myself, to go on, to make a woman happy and raise good kids. Is that okay with you?

Warmth crept over him. He wasn't even really sure where it started, this warmth, except that it flowed somewhere out of the core of him, seeped into his limbs, his muscles, into every last cell of his body.

His whole body relaxed. Joe Latham forgave himself.

Maggie said, "Joe? The light's green."

He looked up. "Yeah, I see that." That warmth was singing now, flowing along his veins, sure and strong. Oblivious to Nola sitting in the back seat, he reached over and grabbed Maggie's hand. Right there at the traffic light, he said, "Maggie, I love you."

She started. He'd said it before, sincerely, but now she looked at him as if it was the first time she'd heard it. "Joe…?" she began uncertainly.

A car behind them honked. Joe grinned and said, "We've got a kid to pick up. And then we're going to talk. Really talk about the future." He put his foot on the gas pedal and headed for the police station.

WHEN THEY GOT to the station, Joe could see that Kenny had been crying. Kenny caught sight of his mother, and she held out her arms. Kenny and Nola hugged fiercely. Joe went to Kenny and put a hand on his shoulder. Off to his left, he could see Maggie comforting a girl who must be Celeste. As small and skinny as Kenny, the girl's ponytail bobbed as she anxiously explained something to Maggie.

A few minutes later, there was a hubbub as Celeste's parents arrived, and explanations and hugs were exchanged. Finally, all the parents went to sign the paperwork that would let them take their children home.

Kenny walked over to Joe. "I didn't want to say this in front of Mom, you know?" He ducked his head shyly. "The thing is, I don't know if my mom's as big of a screwup and stuff as she used to be, but I wanted to make sure somebody came. So I called you."

Joe took the kid to him, held him tight to his chest. Kenny seemed stiff and startled at first, and then his arm stole around Joe. "I'm glad you did," Joe said, hearing the gruff note of emotion in his voice. "You can call me anytime, and I'll come."

For just a second they stood there together. Then Kenny squirmed out of his embrace. "Yeah, well, everything came out all right. I wouldn't have called you except that Celeste was cold." He tried to look manly, a little disgusted, and failed miserably. In fact, Joe looked into the boy's eyes and saw the relief there. And the trust.

He gave Kenny's shoulder a final squeeze, then said, "Are you going to be okay here for a few minutes? I need to talk to Maggie."

"Sure, I'm going to be okay. Why wouldn't I be okay?"

Joe turned and asked Maggie to follow him. A few

minutes ago, he'd asked one of the uniformed officers if he could use one of the empty offices.

He took Maggie to a small office. On the window in the door was stenciled the name of a lieutenant who had presumably gone home. He closed the door. The noise from the squad room faded into a low murmur of sound.

"What's up?" Maggie asked a little suspiciously. "You've been acting strangely ever since we got off the expressway, and now here you are dragging me down empty corridors."

Joe looked her over, thinking how much he loved her. A fluorescent ceiling fixture cast a funny, bluish, virtually shadowless glow on the surroundings. Maggie hadn't put on makeup this morning. Her lips were pale. Her hair had been bunched on the back of her neck and was held by some kind of plastic ring. She wore jeans and a plain sweater, and she wasn't wearing earrings.

She had never looked more beautiful.

He said, "I love you."

She averted her eyes. "Oh, Joe—"

He reached out and clasped her chin, turning her gently to face him. "No, look at me. I want you to see that I mean what I'm going to say. I love you. I want to marry you. I want to have children."

Her eyes widened. "But you said you didn't know—"

"I know. I know, Maggie. Alex...he's gone. I can't have him back, and I can't punish myself—I can't punish you because of what happened to him. You told me that I should forgive myself. You set an example for how I should live. When you lost our baby, you let yourself be sad, and then you moved on with your life. You were ready to try again. You're courageous, and I love that about you.''

Her eyes, still on his, misted over.

''I want to be worthy of your love. I want to have the guts to live again. I want people to count on me. I'll do my best not to let them down. I want to get involved, really involved. I can't do more than that, but maybe that's enough.''

She opened her mouth, but no sound came out.

He took her into his arms. He touched his mouth to her forehead, and said, ''I could think of a million more romantic ways to do this. Roses and music, champagne and balloons. But I'm going to ask this right here. I'm going to ask you to marry me, as soon as possible. And then I want to work—'' he smiled ''—really, really hard on making a baby.''

She held him in a fierce grip, her cheek tucked against his chest. ''We don't need all those romantic trimmings. Just a few words that mean something.''

''So you're saying yes?''

Her arms tightened even further. She didn't say anything, and he had a momentary fear that he'd come to his senses too late. He let her go a fraction and tipped her chin up. ''Do you believe me?''

''Yes,'' she said softly.

''Just like that?''

"Just like that. I've believed in you for a while, Joe. You just needed to believe in yourself." She reached up and touched her lips to his in a feather-light kiss.

A kiss full of promise.

EPILOGUE

IT WAS A DIVERSE GROUP that gathered in the glittering hotel ballroom on New Year's Eve. The ballroom itself was a mixed bag, Maggie thought. Built in the 1930s, it was art deco and filled with antiques: old crystal chandeliers, curvy chrome chairs, a hodge-podge of bygone glitz. But the horns and confetti, the silly little pointed foil hats, the party favors on the table, were all true nineties funk.

Joe had planned this evening as a kind of belated wedding reception, a party for all their friends. They hadn't wanted to wait for a big wedding. So they'd married quietly a few days after going to Chicago for Kenny.

Maggie had a dress made in old lace, but she was wearing it tonight instead of at her wedding. It seemed fitting somehow—old lace, new year, the past and the future. Now she looked down the table. Joe had gathered quite a group to dance the hours away until midnight and the new millennium.

The detectives he worked with were a rowdy, noisy group of revelers near the end of the table. Closer to Maggie sat Sharon. She was dressed in navy-blue velvet, and her husband was beside her. Angela sat next to Maggie, tiny and blond, in a glittery T-shirt, her date, as she'd previously confided in Maggie, a decade younger than herself. Joe's friend Terry Allerton was there with his young wife, both looking a little out of place but very proud to be with the group of detectives and their wives.

Maggie sipped her orange juice and relaxed, perspiration on her forehead from the fast dance she'd shared with Joe. She'd have to be more careful from now on: her newly sensitive stomach was protesting again.

"Hey, Maggie," Henry Muff called from his place a way down the table. "Heard you won a big case."

Maggie smiled. Angela grinned and said, "She sure did. Maggie got an award out of that jury that's going to give us another newspaper headline. You have no idea how hitting that front page so regularly helps business."

Joe whispered in her ear, "You're the greatest. And now everybody will know how good you really are."

Maggie felt the thrill of his compliment. "I just did my best," she said. It was kind of a mantra with them. Over big things and small, they'd turn to each other and smile and say, "I did my best."

"Well, your best was a humdinger this time."

The case had been tough, and Maggie had been up a lot of late nights preparing for the trial. But she'd won. The newspaper coverage would help the firm, but Hannan, St. John and Sawyer had been running in the black for a while now. She and her partners were bringing in enough for Maggie not to have to worry anymore about the survival of the firm. It would be around into the new century.

Everything was finally working out for the people Maggie cared about. Her friendship with Tessa had survived her marriage to Joe. In fact Maggie had just had a postcard from the girl. She and her father were in the Bahamas, and Tessa had written that they were having fun.

Kenny was thriving in his new neighborhood and had made friends. He'd met all the conditions of his probation, and he no longer came to the Kids at Risk. But Joe made sure he saw the boy regularly.

Maggie had taken the reward money from Joe's retainer, and with his blessing, given it to Nola Sheets. Nola was going to school to learn to style hair, and planned to put the reward towards a down payment on a small home.

As in the way of young romance, Kenny and Celeste no longer had much interest in each other. But Maggie had followed up with Celeste, too. Celeste's principal really was interested in making the school safe. In fact, the school had recently qualified for a grant for some anti-gang measures that would help make that a reality.

Maggie took another swallow of orange juice, wondering if she should have ordered something more soothing to drink. Her stomach was still in mild rebellion. Then a waiter came by with a tray of chicken livers wrapped in bacon, and the smell sent her stomach into outright flip-flops. She quickly reached for a starchy roll and chewed slowly. Yes. That helped some.

"Are you okay?" Joe whispered in her ear.

"Better than okay. My stomach hurts, but what else is new? Did you know the doctor says nausea is a sign your hormones are really in abundance, a sign of a healthy pregnancy?"

"So you've told me…about a million times." His eyes were affectionate as he looked down at her. There was openness there, and sharing. He'd been with her every step of the way this time.

"Do you want to announce it now?" Maggie asked.

"No, we've got to wait for the stroke of midnight."

"I don't know if I'll last till the stroke of midnight." He looked momentarily concerned, so she shook her head and laughed. "I'll be okay, but only for slow dances."

When her stomach had settled, he took her up and held her and danced with her real, real slow. Tenderly. She laid her head on his shoulder. "Hey, that's Old Spice I smell."

"Some really beautiful, newly pregnant woman bought me another bottle for Christmas," he whispered back.

She inhaled and snuggled closer. "Amazingly

enough, that's the only strong smell that doesn't make me gag these days.''

''You really know how to lay on a compliment.''

She smiled against him. ''You know, there're a lot of new designer scents out there—''

''I think I'll stick with what I know.''

As he took her carefully into a turn, she thought of how strong and honorable he was, an old-fashioned male. But he was capable of change, too. She had the best of the old and the new.

And then, suddenly, it was almost midnight, and Maggie and Joe stood at the table with their friends and watched big-screen television sets to see the ball drop in Times Square. Five. Four. Three. Two. Horns blew and people shouted and kissed as the new millennium rolled in. Maggie and Joe kissed, long and hard, then blew horns along with the rest, and threw confetti and acted young and carefree and unbearably silly.

Finally, Joe brought a halt by clapping his hands and calling for quiet. He took Maggie's hand as they stood at the head of the table. ''Okay, everybody, my wife and I have an announcement to make.'' He looked proud and happy, sexy in a navy-blue suit and sparkling white shirt. ''In the new millennium, we're going to have a new baby.''

The table erupted in congratulations. Angela gave her a thumbs-up signal, tears in her eyes.

And then a guy approached with a couple of red

balloons on strings. Joe took them and handed them to Maggie. "Nowadays," he said to those near, "I'm not willing to settle, not willing to think that just getting through the day is having a life. Now I want it all. And," he added with a tender smile at Maggie, "I've got it all."

Heart of the West

*A brand-new Harlequin continuity series
begins in July 1999
with*

Husband for Hire
by
Susan Wiggs

*Beautician Twyla McCabe was Dear Abby
with a blow-dryer, listening to everyone else's
troubles. But now her well-meaning customers
have gone too far. No way was she attending
the Hell Creek High School Reunion with Rob
Carter, M.D. Who would believe a woman
who dyed hair for a living could be engaged
to such a hunk?*

Here's a preview!

CHAPTER ONE

"THIS ISN'T FOR the masquerade. This is for me."

"What's for you?"

"This."

Rob didn't move fast, but with a straightforward deliberation she found oddly thrilling. He gripped Twyla by the upper arms and pulled her to him, covering her mouth with his.

Dear God, a kiss. She couldn't remember the last time a man had kissed her. And what a kiss. It was everything a kiss should be—sweet, flavored with strawberries and wine and driven by an underlying passion that she felt surging up through him, creating an answering need in her. She rested her hands on his shoulders and let her mouth soften, open. He felt wonderful beneath her hands, his muscles firm, his skin warm, his mouth… She just wanted to drown in him, drown in the passion. If he was faking his ardor, he was damned good. When he stopped kissing her, she stepped back. Her disbelieving fingers went to her mouth, lightly touching her moist, swollen lips.

"That…wasn't in the notes," she objected weakly.

"I like to ad–lib every once in a while."

"I need to sit down." Walking backward, never taking her eyes off him, she groped behind her and found the Adirondack-style porch swing. *Get a grip,* she told herself. *It was only a kiss.*

"I think," he said mildly, "it's time you told me just why you were so reluctant to come back here for the reunion."

"And why I had to bring a fake fiancé as a shield?"

Very casually, he draped his arm along the back of the porch swing. "I'm all ears, Twyla. Why'd I have to practically hog–tie you to get you back here?"

HARLEQUIN®
SUPERROMANCE®

From July to September 1999—three special
Superromance® novels about people whose
New Millennium resolution is

By the Year 2000: CELEBRATE!

JULY 1999—*A Cop's Good Name* by Linda Markowiak
Joe Latham's only hope of saving his badge and his reputation is
to persuade lawyer Maggie Hannan to take his case. Only Maggie—
his ex-wife—knows him well enough to believe him.

AUGUST 1999—*Mr. Miracle* by Carolyn McSparren
Scotsman Jamey McLachlan's come to Tennessee to keep the
promise he made to his stepfather. But Victoria Jamerson stands
between him and his goal, and hurting Vic is the last thing he wants
to do.

SEPTEMBER 1999—*Talk to Me* by Jan Freed
To save her grandmother's business, Kara Taylor has to co-host a
TV show with her ex about the differing points of view between men
and women. A topic Kara and Travis know plenty about.

By the end of the year,
everyone will have something to celebrate!

HARLEQUIN®
Makes any time special ™

HARLEQUIN®
SUPERROMANCE®

Join us in celebrating Harlequin's 50th Anniversary!

The LYON LEGACY is a very
special book containing *three* brand-new stories by
three popular Superromance® authors, Peg Sutherland,
Roz Denny Fox and Ruth Jean Dale—all in one volume!

*In July 1999, follow the fortunes of the powerful
Lyon family of New Orleans. Share the lives, loves,
feuds and triumphs of three generations...
culminating in a 50th anniversary celebration
of the family business!*

**The Lyon Legacy continues with three more
brand-new, full-length books:**

August 1999—**FAMILY SECRETS** by Ruth Jean Dale
September 1999—**FAMILY FORTUNE** by Roz Denny Fox
October 1999—**FAMILY REUNION** by Peg Sutherland

Available wherever Harlequin books are sold.

HARLEQUIN®
Makes any time special ™

Harlequin is proud to introduce:

HEART OF THE WEST

...Where Every Man Has His Price!

Lost Springs Ranch was famous for turning young
mavericks into good men. Word that the ranch was in
financial trouble sent a herd of loyal bachelors
stampeding back to Wyoming to put themselves on the
auction block.

This is a brand-new 12-book continuity,
which includes some of Harlequin's
most talented authors.

Don't miss the first book,
Husband for Hire by Susan Wiggs.
It will be at your favorite retail outlet in July 1999.

HARLEQUIN®

Makes any time special ™